MINOS
BOOK
ONE
HEART

NINO'S
BOOK
ONE HEART

J.D. KEENE

Published by JDKeene Publishing

www.jdkeene.com

ISBN: 978-1-7330881-2-1

Cover Design by Dawn Gardner / dawngardnerdgee@gmail.com

Interior formatting: Mark Thomas / Coverness.com

To my parents, Andrew, and Marjorie Keene,

who are always with me.

And as always, to my wife Katie who is a constant source

of wisdom and encouragement.

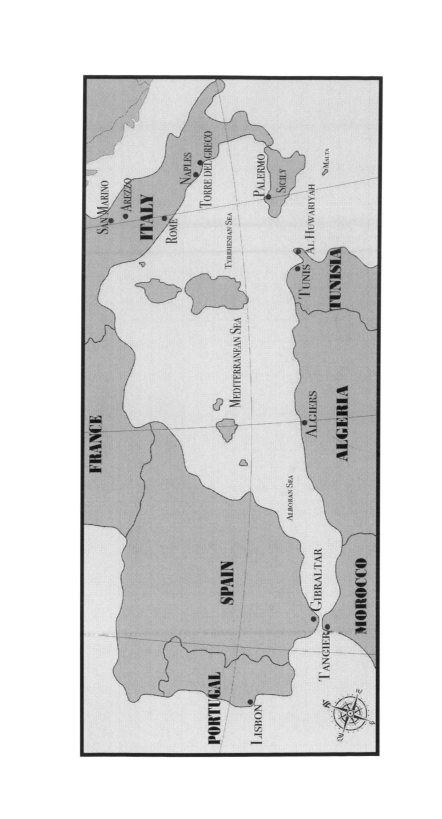

CAST OF CHARACTERS

DiVincenzo Family

Alfonso, *Capo di tutti capi* (Godfather) of Sicily

Salvador, Alfonso's son, New York City crime boss

Maria, Salvador's wife

Angelo, eldest son

Nino, youngest son

Roseman Family

Solomon, father, owner of the Roseman Cameo Company

Beulah, wife

Manuel, eldest son

Olivia, Manuel's wife

Camillo, youngest son

Hannah, Camillo's wife

Leone Family

Bruno, grandfather, and patriarch of the Leone citrus dynasty

Lorenzo, Bruno's son

Aldo, Lorenzo's son

Isabella, Lorenzo's daughter

Other Characters

Mr. Giovanni, pharmacist, owner of Giovanni's Drugstore

Fredo Romano, employee (lieutenant) of Salvador DiVincenzo

Monsignor Nunzio, the Church of Our Lady of Mercy

Father Russo, the Abbey of Santa Maria

Father Doyle, Saint Michael's Home for Orphaned Boys

Omar, employee (lieutenant) of Alfonso DiVincenzo

Vito Bianchi, student at the University of Rome

Rosa Zerilli, Vito's girlfriend

Cecilia Zerilli, Rosa's mother

Father De Carlo, the Basilica of San Marino

Lilia, orphan

Zita Stein, elderly Jewish refugee

1934

CHAPTER 1

H e sat in the back of the classroom because that's what his father had instructed him to do. His older brother, Angelo, who attended a different school, did the same.

"Watch your back, and never let anyone behind you," their father would say.

They obeyed because the consequences of doing otherwise were severe.

Even though he was in his second year at Saint Francis Preparatory School for boys, he barely knew any of the other students. They kept their distance from him, and he knew why.

"We're sorry, Nino, but our parents told us to stay away from you," they would say.

This led to a lonely existence for the fourteen-year-old Nino DiVincenzo, who was also self-conscious of his small size.

The details of his father's companies were unknown to Nino — that was intentional. There were many men who worked for him. Some of them came by the apartment once per week and dropped off large sums of cash.

Frequently out all night, Nino's father would come home

and sleep for a few hours, then leave again for several days. During his long absences, Nino's mother would sometimes sit and stare out the window. On rare occasions, she would get angry and swear in Italian.

"Salvador DiVincenzo, *sei un maiale e anche le tue puttane sono maiali,*" she would say. *You are a pig and your whores are pigs, too.*

Why she switched to Italian when swearing, Nino never knew. By order of their father, she had taught her sons to speak Italian as well as any Sicilian. After her outbursts, she would pray the Rosary and apologize to Nino and Angelo for her coarse language.

After being dismissed from his final class of the day, Nino grabbed his books, pulled his flat cap over his thick, black hair, and sprinted down the stairs. Once free of the building, he slowed his pace to a walk. The early September air had an unusual chill, but Nino's blue blazer, which displayed his school's red emblem, kept him warm.

His family lived in Hoffman Towers, one of the most prestigious apartment buildings in the Bronx. Although it was out of the way, Nino would take East 188th Street home. He liked to stop at Giovanni's Drugstore. Mr. Giovanni was kind to Nino. He was kind to everyone, always addressing each of his customers by name. He was popular with the local children because he handed out free candy and had been doing so for two generations of neighborhood kids.

"Good afternoon, Nino. How was school today?" Mr. Giovanni said as a bell over the door rang when Nino entered.

Mr. Giovanni had a thick Italian accent he'd never been able to shake, even after three decades in America.

"It was fine, Mr. Giovanni."

Wearing his white pharmacist coat, Mr. Giovanni turned to the icebox behind the counter.

"Do you want the vanilla or do I mix the strawberries in your ice cream today?"

"I'll stick with vanilla," Nino said as he set his books and cap on the soda fountain counter and climbed up on the stool.

Mr. Giovanni said, "I have seen no Angelo, how is your brother?"

"His school suspended him two weeks ago for fighting. They won't let him return until next year. Papa isn't happy and is making him work loading trucks at the docks."

"Work is good for a young man. It will help him grow up."

"That's what Papa says, too."

As Mr. Giovanni turned to set the porcelain bowl on the counter, it slipped from his hand. When it hit the wooden floor, it shattered, splattering ice cream in all directions.

"*Sarò dannato, Mamma mia,*" Mr. Giovanni said. "I'm so sorry, Nino. After I clean this up, I will make you more."

"I'll help you, Mr. Giovanni. I'll go get a bucket and a mop from the storage room. I know where they are. You keep them next to the big sink near the toilet."

"Thank you, Nino. While you do that, I'll make you another ice cream."

Nino jumped down from the stool and stepped behind the curtain separating the front of the store and the storage room. He made his way to the rear and placed the bucket in the deep sink. While he was filling it, he heard the bell at the front door.

Another customer, Nino thought.

He shut off the water and heard what sounded like pleading from Mr. Giovanni. He was begging for something.

"Please, please, I will pay you I promise," Mr. Giovanni said from the other side of the curtain. "Business has been slow. I don't have the money right now. Please, give me more time."

"I don't want excuses," said the other man in a deep, gruff tone. "I have given you plenty of time. Too many in this neighborhood have fallen behind on their payments. I need to make an example of someone and today is your unlucky day."

"No, no please, I beg you," shouted Mr. Giovanni before his words turned into a series of gurgles and gasps.

Nino left the bucket in the sink and ducked behind a row of shelves, caution in each step. Crashing and banging echoed throughout the building. It sounded as though everything was being knocked over and thrown about the store.

When the clanging stopped, Nino crawled toward the front on his hands and knees. The store was quiet now. He pulled the curtain back just enough to see past it. He saw Mr. Giovanni lying on the floor behind the counter. His blood flowed like a small river before mixing with the melting ice cream.

Bent at the waist and standing over Mr. Giovanni's body, a large man wiped a bloody knife on the white coat of the corpse. Nino couldn't see his face. He wore a wide-brimmed hat and a trench coat. Nino let loose of the curtain and ran to the back door. The swaying cloth drew the man's attention toward the storage room entrance. When Nino arrived at the door, his hope of escape vanished when he found the rear exit locked.

I'm trapped.

Moving swiftly for a man his size, the pursuer was at Nino in an instant.

Nino turned and saw the massive killer glaring at him. Evil reflected in his eyes. He held the knife in his right hand. The remnants of Mr. Giovanni's blood clung to the blade that was as long as Nino's forearm.

I've seen him. He works for Papa. He has been to our apartment.

Nino stood with his back pressed against the door. His stomach tightened. His mind raced as he fought the urge to vomit.

The man paused and tilted his head to the side, squinted his eyes, and stared at Nino as though he was studying him.

He recognizes me. He knows who I am. He knows where I live. He will kill me.

Without saying a word, the man slipped the knife in a pouch sewn into the inside of his trench coat. He then turned and casually walked to the front of the store. The hard leather soles of his shoes scraped over the floor. Nino heard the bell at the entrance ring as the man exited Mr. Giovanni's drugstore.

*

The apartment occupied the entire seventh floor of Hoffman Towers. The doors of the elevator opened in front of two large oak doors that led into a foyer of marble floors, walls accented with cherry wood, and a gold chandelier imported from South America.

With the live-in maid out of town visiting family, Maria DiVincenzo was in the apartment by herself. She stood at a cast-iron stove preparing dinner.

One of the large double doors of their apartment swung open, then slammed.

"Mama! Mama! Where are you?"

"I'm here, Nino. I'm in the kitchen. What's wrong?"

As he approached her, he wiped the tears from his cheeks.

"Mr. Giovanni has been killed. I was there. I saw it. Mr.

Giovanni is lying on the floor of his drugstore. He is behind the counter. I saw the man who killed him, and he saw me. He is one of the men who works for Papa. We need to tell him. Papa needs to tell the police."

Maria knelt next to her son. "Are you sure, Nino? Are you sure this is what you saw?"

"Yes, Mama." The words spewed out of him like a firehose. "I was in the back room of the drugstore filling a bucket with water. First, I heard Mr. Giovanni talking to the man. Then, I heard Mr. Giovanni begging for his life. After that, I looked through the curtain and saw Mr. Giovanni on the floor. Blood was flowing out of him. That big man who works for Papa was standing over him. I tried to get away, but the back door was locked. He had me trapped in the storage room. I thought he would kill me, too, but then when he looked at my face, he just stood there. Then he turned and left the store. He has been here before. He knows where I live. He will come after me."

She embraced him. "No, Nino. He will never come here again, I promise. I will speak to your father, he'll make certain of that."

He pushed her away. "I don't understand. How can Papa do that? I walk to school by myself. If the man wants to kill me, how can Papa stop him? We need to call the police."

She grabbed his hands and looked into his eyes. "Listen to me, Nino. Everything will be fine. Your father will take care of this. Now, let me ask you something, and this is important: Was there anyone else there? Did anyone see you leave Mr. Giovanni's drugstore?"

"Nobody else was in the store. When I ran out, I passed a

few people on the sidewalk. Some of them looked at me, but I just kept running until I got home."

"Did you know any of those people? Would they know you if they saw you again?"

Nino paused and said nothing while he stared into his mother's eyes.

Why was she not concerned about Mr. Giovanni?

Pulling away from her grip a second time, his voice crackled with emotion. "I don't understand, Mama. Why are you asking me these questions? Why aren't we going to the police station to tell them what happened?"

Maria noticed the look of confusion in her son's eyes. "Nino, we need to wait for your father to come home before we do anything. He will know what to do. But in the meantime, you mustn't tell anyone what you saw. Not your teachers. Not your classmates at school. No one. Do you understand, Nino? Will you promise me you will tell only me?"

Nino stood speechless as he weighed his mother's response to the bloodshed he had witnessed. Confused, he turned, ran into his bedroom, and slammed the door.

CHICAGO, IL
THE ROSEMAN CAMEO SHOP

As Hannah Roseman stepped onto the bus, the eyes of other passengers locked on to her as if she were an actress stepping on stage. They studied her every movement, watching as she paid the fare. While they gazed at her, she brushed her long sandy-blond hair from her face, her brown eyes searching the rows for an open seat. The experience of being gawked at was neither unusual nor significant for Hannah. It's simply how it was. It had always been that way. Several men stood, offering their seats to her. She refused their generosity, yet thanked them, as she made her way to the rear. Halfway down, a little girl in an aisle seat dropped her doll. Hannah bent down and retrieved it. "Here you are, sweetheart."

"Thank you, ma'am."

"You're welcome. Your doll is very pretty, just like you."

The little girl looked up at her and smiled.

Upon finding an open seat, Hannah removed one of her white gloves and brushed dirt from the wooden surface. She didn't want to soil her new blue skirt and matching waistcoat. After sitting, she took several deep breaths. Motion sickness overcame her even though the bus had barely left the curb. She was in the twelfth week of her second pregnancy, having lost her first child shortly after conceiving.

Following her exit from the bus at the corner of Michigan Avenue and Lakeshore Drive, she walked half a block to the Roseman Cameo Shop.

"Good morning, Clara," Hannah said, entering the showroom.

"Good morning, Mrs. Roseman. I trust your doctor's visit went well."

"Dr. Jacobs said the baby appears to be healthy."

"I say my prayers for you, Camillo, and the baby. I know you will make wonderful parents."

"You are very kind."

"When is Camillo due back from Italy?"

"Not for two more weeks. I wish it were sooner. I miss him terribly."

"I was wondering if you could help me with something, Mrs. Roseman?"

"What's that?"

"At Camillo's request, I sent several cameos to a customer in Kansas City. Yesterday, we received a telegram from the man, and he said he never received them. He demands an immediate refund. What should I do?"

"I'm awfully sorry, but I can't help you. The customer will need to remain patient until Camillo returns. I don't get involved in his business affairs."

The door opened and two elderly women walked in. As Clara waited on them, Hannah made her way to the door. "I'm going home to rest, Clara. I'll bring you lunch today since you're here by yourself. Do you like navy bean soup? I just prepared it yesterday."

"That sounds delightful, Mrs. Roseman. You're always so very thoughtful. Thank you."

"I'm happy to do it."

After Hannah left, one of the customers said, "That young woman was strikingly beautiful. Is she the owner of the store?"

"Her husband is. He comes from a wealthy Italian family. They own other stores in Italy. He is there now on business."

MANHATTAN, NY
THE MEATPACKING DISTRICT

Fourteen men wearing fedoras and three-piece suits in varying shades of dark paced the floor of the warehouse. They smoked cigarettes and discussed the murder of Giovanni the druggist.

Fredo Romano stared at his watch in thirty second intervals

as he stood in the back waiting for Salvador DiVincenzo to arrive. It was early Friday evening, and he was late. He was always late. Although never verbalized, each of the men standing in the dank, dusty building knew the purpose of his delay. It was a statement of power. A tactic Salvador had learned from his father—Alfonso DiVincenzo, the *Capo di tutti capi* of Sicily. Salvador's lieutenants were to be there at 6:00 p.m., but Salvador arrived when he arrived. Usually around 6:20 p.m., but often later—much later when he was pissed off, and Fredo Romano's last glance at his wrist read 7:06 p.m.

The purpose of their meetings was to review their individual business dealings. Salvador's lieutenants ran brothels, drug distribution rings, and illegal distilleries. Others, like Fredo Romano, controlled various forms of racketeering. Most commonly, extorting money from local businesses for protection against vandals and other ruffians.

"He's here," shouted one of the men peeking through a scratch in the painted glass.

Two men ran over and grabbed the handles of the bulky carriage doors and pulled. With headlights shining in their eyes, the assembly of thugs watched the Cadillac V-16 452 Fleetwood roll in. Dim, overhead lights in the warehouse reflected on the polished black paint. The rumble of the engine reverberated off the brick walls as the men stepped to either side, the vehicle dividing them like Moses parting the Red Sea.

After bringing the vehicle to a stop, the driver exited before opening the door for his boss.

"Good evening, Mr. DiVincenzo," the group shouted in unison as the Don stepped out of the limousine.

Without responding, he strutted to the back office with a

forty-dollar cigar hanging from his mouth. He was pudgy, yet sharp. He dressed to the nines in dark, pinstriped suits that cost most men a four-month wage. He exuded confidence.

"Fredo Romano, in the office. Now!" Salvador DiVincenzo shouted. "DeFazio and Moretti, I want you in there, too."

With their eyes locked on Fredo, the other men made a path for him so he could trail behind Salvador. DeFazio and Moretti, both as large as Fredo, brought up the rear as they entered the office.

"Close the door, Moretti, and have a seat, Romano," Salvador said.

Fredo sat down behind a desk covered with old newspapers and coffee cups that held more mold than a high school science project.

Standing in the middle of the office, Salvador said, "What the hell happened, Romano? I never told you to cut nobody."

"I'm sorry, Mr. DiVincenzo. I lost my head. The druggist was the fourth person of the day I went to collect from who said they didn't have no money. I had to make an example of someone."

Salvador removed the cigar from his mouth and walked toward Fredo, "You make an example of someone by busting up their place or breaking their fingers. You don't slice nobody unless I tell you to slice them. You are one dumb shit, Romano. This will stack heat on me like I was rolling in a coal furnace."

Salvador paced back and forth in the office, taking a quick puff of his cigar. He then walked back toward Romano. "I hope you were at least smart enough to make certain nobody saw you. Were there any witnesses, Romano? Did anyone see you leave that store?"

Fredo leaned forward thinking he might be ill. He twisted the wedding ring on his finger, wondering if he would ever see his wife and children again. Beads of sweat rolled down his forehead. Lying would only make it worse. He sat in the chair speechless.

Breaking the silence, Salvador said, "The fact that you ain't sayin' nothin' tells me you don't have good news. How many saw you, Romano? Did you recognize any of them? If you know them, tell me now so I can send DeFazio and Moretti to shut them up."

Knowing he could no longer stay silent, Fredo blurted out, "It was Nino, Mr. DiVincenzo. Your son, Nino."

Salvador paused and said nothing. Holding the cigar in his hand, he tilted his head to the side, stared at Romano, then at the other two men in the room. He flicked his cigar on the floor and slammed his forearm on the desk before swinging it across the top, sending the newspapers and coffee cups against the wall.

Moving his face inches from Fredo's, Salvador said, "My son Nino was there? You killed a man while my son watched you do it?"

"No, no, no, Mr. DiVincenzo. Let me explain. It wasn't like that. It wasn't like that at all. Nino was in the back room. I didn't know he was there. He must have heard the noise and peeked around the curtain and saw me standing over the dead guy. At first, I didn't know it was him. He ran to the back of the storage room, and I went after him. I was going to take him out, but when I got there, I saw it was Nino. So, I turned and left the store."

Salvador stood up straight and stared down at Romano.

"When did all of this happen?"

"This afternoon, about three thirty."

Salvador turned and opened the office door then said to DeFazio and Moretti, "Don't let this fat shit out of your sight. I would tell you to take him out back and shoot him, but somebody is going to the electric chair for this, and it sure as hell ain't going to be me."

BRONX, NY
HOFFMAN TOWERS

"I'm home, Mama," Angelo shouted while crossing the foyer of their apartment. His work boots left a trail of dirt across the marble floor.

"Take your shoes off at the door," Maria yelled from the master bedroom. "And leave your brother alone. Say nothing to him until your father comes home."

Angelo and Nino shared one of the three bedrooms in the apartment. The live-in maid, Elsa, stayed in another, and Salvador and Maria occupied the master suite.

Angelo grabbed the doorknob of the bedroom, but it wouldn't turn.

"Unlock the door, Nino. What are you doing in there, playing with yourself again? Come on, open up. I need to change my clothes and wash up before dinner."

"Go away, Angelo," Nino shouted.

Angelo beat on the door. "I don't have time for this. Open up."

Nino unlocked the door and let his brother enter their bedroom.

"What the hell is wrong with you, Nino?"

Saying nothing to Angelo, Nino crossed the room and sat in a wooden chair in the corner. His face was red, and he stared at the floor. He was trembling.

Angelo said, "Talk to me, little brother. I have never seen you like this. I know something is wrong because Mama told me not to talk to you until Papa gets home."

Nino remained silent. Angelo crossed the room and sat on Nino's bed.

"Nino, it's me, Angelo. I know I treat you like crap, but you know I have always been there for you when you needed me. And you look like you need me now. What's going on?"

"I saw Mr. Giovanni get murdered today."

"Oh, shit. Is that what happened? I heard the cops were hanging out at his store, but nobody knew why. So, you are telling me somebody whacked Mr. Giovanni and you saw them do it? Did the guy see you?"

"Yes."

"What did he do?"

"He did nothing. He just stared at me. I thought he was going to kill me, then he turned and walked away."

"Have you ever seen him before?"

"It was that really big guy who works for Papa. The one who comes here sometimes and gives him money."

"Fredo Romano, Nino? Was it Fredo Romano?"

"I don't know his name."

"What happened? What did you see?"

Nino explained every detail to Angelo, including their mother's indifference toward Mr. Giovanni's fate.

"Just like Mama told you, you can't tell nobody what you

saw. Do you understand that?"

"No, I don't understand. Mr. Giovanni was a nice man. He was my friend, and I'll tell the police."

Angelo said, "For someone who is so smart, you sure can be a moron sometimes."

"Don't talk to me like that."

"It's time someone opens your eyes to what goes on around here and it will be me right here, right now. If I don't, you will screw everything up for all of us—our whole family."

"What are you talking about?"

"Wake up, Nino. Have you ever wondered why we live in a big ass apartment on the seventh floor of this building? You go to a private school with the wealthiest kids in New York City, but everyone else around you is standing in soup lines or begging for food. Have you ever asked yourself those questions?"

"I just figured it's because Papa owns all of his companies. That's what Mama says."

"And what the hell do you think those companies do?"

"I don't know, Angelo. You work for Papa, you tell me."

"Okay, brace yourself, little brother. I'll start with the best part. My favorite. Do you know what a whore is?"

"I think it is a woman who has sex for money."

"That's right. And when the whores here in the Bronx have sex for money, who do you think keeps the money?"

"I don't know. I guess they do."

"No, Nino, they don't. All the whore gets is a chance to not get the crap beat out of her by one of Papa's men. The person who gets the money is Papa. Papa owns all the whores in the Bronx."

"That's a lie. I don't believe it."

"Believe it, Nino. I have seen it myself. And that's just the beginning.

Nino stood up to leave the room, but Angelo grabbed his arm.

"Sit down. There's a lot more for you to know, and you need to know all of it. I'm telling you because if you go to the police and tell them about what you saw, Papa may go to the electric chair."

"You're wrong. Papa didn't kill Mr. Giovanni, that man did. I saw him."

"But don't you see, Nino? That man works for Papa. Papa ordered that man to go see Mr. Giovanni. That man's job is to collect money from the businesses in the Bronx."

"Collect money for what?"

"Collect money to keep Papa from busting up their stores and beating them up."

Nino bowed his head and wept.

"Get control of yourself, little brother. You'll learn to accept the family business. Just like Mama and I have. Papa has big plans for both of us, especially you. I've heard Papa tell Mama many times that since you are the smart one, he is sending you to law school when you get older. That's why you are going to that expensive prep school. Papa has many lawyers who work for him. You will be in charge of all of them. He says, 'I need someone I can trust, and there's nobody you can trust like family.'"

Nino stood and stepped toward the door.

"I don't believe any of this, Angelo. You are making it all up. But if what you say is true, I'll never work for Papa."

*

The Cadillac Fleetwood came to a stop in front of Hoffman Towers. The sun had set, and there was a chill in the air. Salvador DiVincenzo didn't wait for the driver to open his door before sprinting through the light drizzle and up the six steps to the entrance. Ignoring the doorman's nod, he opened the door of the lobby to see Deputy Inspector Murphy of the 43rd Precinct.

"What the hell are you doing here, Murphy?"

"Good evening, Mr. DiVincenzo. I am here because I have a message for you. It's important. Is there someplace we can speak in private?"

Salvador looked at the doorman. "If anyone comes by to see me or my family—I don't care who it is—we ain't home, you got it?"

"Yes sir, Mr. DiVincenzo."

Salvador reached for the elevator button and said to Inspector Murphy, "Come up to the apartment."

On the elevator, Salvador said, "Are you stupid? You and me together don't look good."

"I'm sorry, Mr. DiVincenzo, but what I have to say to you is urgent."

Exiting the elevator, the two men entered the foyer of the apartment. Salvador shouted, "Maria, I'm home. I have a guest. We will be in my den. Don't disturb us."

They entered the office and Salvador closed the French doors behind them before walking around the oak desk.

Salvador sat in his leather chair. "Would you like a cigar? They are Cubans."

"No, Mr. DiVincenzo. I'm fine. Thank you."

"Have a seat, Murphy, and tell me, is this about that druggist?"

"Yes, Mr. DiVincenzo."

"What the hell am I up against? What does the brass down at the station know?"

"It ain't good, sir. Everyone suspects you were behind the murder of the druggist."

"Of course they do. Every time someone gets whacked, I am the number one suspect. But I tell you, Murphy, I ain't got nothin' to do with it. My lawyers will clear me. They always do."

"That may be the case, Mr. DiVincenzo, but there's a twist to this story."

Placing his cigar in an ash tray, Salvador leaned forward and put both elbows on the desk. "What the hell are you talking about? What is this twist that has you all worked up?"

"When our boys at the scene showed up, there was a cap and schoolbooks on the counter of the drugstore."

Salvador picked up the cigar and puffed while leaning back in his chair. "Why is this of interest to me?"

Leaning forward toward Salvador, Murphy said, "There was a name in the hat. The name was Nino DiVincenzo."

Salvador stared back at Murphy, "How can you fix this for me?"

"I'm sorry Mr. DiVincenzo. Had I been the first on the scene, I would have walked out of there with Nino's stuff. But by the time I arrived, it was too late. All the other cops who were there are clean. I was the only one on your payroll."

"What happens now?"

"The good thing is I'm here is to bring Nino down to the

station for questioning. Two other guys were supposed to come with me, but they were called away to a mugging. Since it's just you and me, we can talk to Nino and come up with a story."

Salvador paused and looked up at the ceiling. "I know nobody else was there when it happened. Nino was the only witness."

Murphy said, "I won't ask you how you know that."

"Don't."

Salvador rose from the chair. "Stay here, I'll get Nino."

Opening one of the double doors, Salvador yelled through the apartment, "Nino, come here now!"

Maria crossed the foyer from the kitchen. "What is it Salvador? What is so urgent?"

"Go find Nino, Maria, and bring him here to my den, now!"

Maria turned and made her way down the hallway before knocking on the boy's bedroom.

"Come in," Angelo said.

"Where is Nino? Your father wants to speak to him."

"I don't know, Mama. I thought he was with you. He left here about an hour ago, and he was really upset."

Maria turned and walked through the apartment, checking each room and shouting, "Nino, your father needs to see you."

Salvador approached Maria. "Well, where the hell is he?"

"He's not here. He must have snuck out of the apartment. I told him to stay in his room until you got home."

"Where the hell could he have gone?"

Angelo stepped out of his bedroom. "He said he was going to go to the police, but I thought I'd talked him out of it."

*

The drizzle intensified to a downpour as Nino crossed 188th

Street and stepped onto the sidewalk of Marion Avenue. He'd left the apartment without his jacket, and the chilly rain drenched his white shirt and blue pants. Vandals had broken several streetlights, and Nino could barely see the sidewalk.

His mind raced.

I can't stay quiet. I must confess what I know. None of this makes any sense. All along, Mama has known of Papa's evil businesses.

Since the time Nino was an infant, he had witnessed his mother volunteer for every Catholic charity she could squeeze into her schedule. She worked in soup kitchens preparing meals. In the winter, she passed out blankets to the poor. The Gospels were what she'd used to teach Nino to read. Twice each week, they attended Mass.

How can Mama accept that Papa hurts so many people?

Drenched and shivering, Nino hugged himself, trying to stay warm. When he arrived, he sprinted up the stairs and huddled against the door, attempting to avoid the downpour.

Bam, bam, bam.

Nino pounded several times before the back door of The Church of Our Lady of Mercy opened.

"Nino, what are you doing standing out in this cold rain at this time of night? Get in here and let me get you a blanket. Where is your mother?"

"She is at home, Monsignor."

Msgr. Nunzio led Nino to a leather chair.

"Wait here, Nino, I will get you that blanket."

After Msgr. Nunzio left the room, although Nino sat shivering, he felt safe. Like Mr. Giovanni, Msgr. Nunzio was one of his only friends.

With the exception of the lamp on the monsignor's desk, the room was dark and smelled of a musty mixture of leather and pipe tobacco.

Recessed into the walls were oak bookshelves from floor to ceiling. There wasn't a single open space for any more books, and Msgr. Nunzio had several stacked high on his desk.

Msgr. Nunzio returned with a blanket. "Here you are, Nino. Put this around yourself."

"Thank you, Monsignor."

Walking around his desk, Msgr. Nunzio sat and reached for a pipe to stuff it with tobacco.

"So, tell me, Nino. What is troubling you so much that you came to see me in this frigid rain?"

"I know something. Something really bad, and I don't know what to do."

"I see," Msgr. Nunzio said. "Have you done something bad or do you just know about something bad?"

"No sir, I haven't done anything bad. Well, at least not as bad as the reason I am here."

Removing his pipe from his mouth, Msgr. Nunzio said, "Nino as I have always told you, what you tell me in this office will never leave here unless you give me permission to tell someone else. Do you understand that?"

"Yes sir."

"Okay, so what is it that is so bad?"

Nino remained silent as he grabbed the edges of the blanket and pulled them tight around his shivering body. He stared at a circular rug in front of the desk.

"Nino, this is me you are talking to. We are friends. You know you can trust me."

Nino took a deep breath before speaking. "I saw Mr. Giovanni get murdered."

Msgr. Nunzio, stunned by what he had just heard, restrained his reaction. He sat back in his chair and looked up at the ceiling while taking two puffs from his pipe, maintaining a look of calm for Nino's benefit.

"I see. And do the police know what you saw?"

"No sir. I can't tell the police. If I do, my Papa may get in trouble. My brother Angelo said if I tell, my Papa may go to the electric chair."

Looking at Nino, who still stared at the floor in front of him, Msgr. Nunzio continued to puff on his pipe. Although he had been a priest for thirty-two years and had counseled many people on many topics relating to their spiritual journey, what Nino presented to him was uncharted territory. He knew he must be measured with his words.

"Are you certain your father was involved in the death of Mr. Giovanni? Is there any way you could be mistaken?"

Nino explained every detail of the day's events. Everything from what he witnessed in the drugstore to his disappointment with his mother's reaction to his conversation with Angelo.

He then bowed his head and wept. "I'm scared, Monsignor. I'm scared because I don't know what to do."

Msgr. Nunzio stood, walked around his desk and sat in the vacant leather chair next to Nino. He handed him a handkerchief and said, "You have been placed in a difficult moral dilemma, Nino. A moral dilemma that no boy your age should find himself in."

Looking up, Nino asked, "What should I do?"

He stared at Nino, wishing he had an answer, but he himself was uncertain.

"For now, my son, listen to your mother. Your mother has a good heart. A heart that loves God and loves you. I'm sure she has prayed for guidance. We must trust that God will guide her, and she will direct you accordingly."

Nino said, "So, I shouldn't go to the police? But what about, Mr. Giovanni? What if the man who killed him kills someone else?"

"I said *for now* listen to your mother. However, that doesn't mean that sometime soon God won't direct your heart to do otherwise. Do you understand, Nino?"

"I'm confused. How will I know if God wants me to tell the police?"

"He may never tell you. His wish may be for you to remain silent about what you saw. And if that's his desire, remain silent with a peaceful heart. You and I will continue to pray for Mr. Giovanni's soul, and God will embrace him. As for you, Nino, God understands the position you are in. It isn't your fault. Do not live with guilt over what you know or what your father has done. What your father does is no reflection on you."

Nino sat speechless, then used the blanket to wipe his nose.

Msgr. Nunzio rubbed the top of Nino's head, and said, "It sounds like the rain has stopped. I know you only live a few blocks away, but it is dark. How about I call your mother to pick you up?"

"If it is all the same to you, Monsignor, I would like to walk home. I still have a lot of thinking to do."

"Okay, Nino. But promise me you will go right home. No more stops."

"Okay."

As Nino stood to leave, he said, "Thank you for talking to me, Msgr. Nunzio."

"Of course. You are an exceptional young man, Nino DiVincenzo, and I am proud to call you my friend."

*

As Nino made his way along Marion Avenue, he knew he was in trouble. Yet his disillusionment with his family dwarfed his fear of his father. His world had transformed over the last few hours. Exhausted, he wanted to go to bed.

Squealing brakes behind him jolted him out of his reflections. He turned to see two policemen advancing from their patrol car. Both appeared tall by Nino's standards—one thin and one husky. The thin one had an Irish accent. He did the talking.

"It's rather late for ya to be out here by yourself. Where do ya live, lad?"

"On Hoffman Street, sir."

"Where on Hoffman Street?"

"In Hoffman Towers."

"What's ya name, lad?"

"Nino DiVincenzo."

"And ya fatha—would he be Salvador DiVincenzo?"

Nino took a step back. He didn't want to answer, although he sensed they knew who his father was.

"Why do you want to know that?"

"I'm sure he is worried about ya. Ya shouldn't be out this late. How about we take ya to the police station and we will contact ya fatha to come get ya."

"I'm almost home. Can't I just walk the rest of the way?"

"No, lad. There are a lot of bad things that happen on these streets in the dark. Come with us. Ya fatha can come get ya at the police station."

Nino considered running away.

The larger policeman stepped forward and grabbed Nino by his arm then pulled him to the squad car. "Come on, young man, off we go. We have some questions for you."

*

They had said nothing to Nino since arriving at the 43rd Precinct.

When is Papa going to get here? Nino sat alone on a wooden chair next to O'Hara's desk.

I will be in so much trouble when he gets here.

Officer O'Hara approached the desk and sat. "Have you eaten, Nino? Are you hungry?"

Nino was starving. He hadn't had food since lunch.

"No sir. I'm not hungry."

"Are you sure? We have a little kitchen in the back, and Officer Baily just made spaghetti and meatballs. You should eat, lad."

"No. Sir, I just want to go home. When will my Papa get here?"

"We have sent for him. He will be here soon."

After a pause, O'Hara reached into his desk drawer, pulled out Nino's books and cap, then laid them on the desk.

"You wouldn't know who these belong to do you, Nino?"

Nino sat silent. His heart began to race as he stared at his belongings on the desk. The trauma and breakneck pace of the day had caused him to forget he had left them on the drugstore counter.

"Do you know something about these items, Nino? You look like you will be sick."

"No sir, I don't know who those things belong to."

O'Hara picked up the hat, turned it inside out and showed Nino his name written on the inside. "Well that's strange. There must be another lad running around the Bronx with your name because it is written right here, Nino DiVincenzo. Do you know of another young lad in the Bronx with your name?"

Nino remained silent.

O'Hara leaned forward and slammed his fist on the desk. "Stop lying to me, Nino. You can get in big trouble for lying to the police."

Nino began to weep.

"I want to speak to my Papa."

"Why, Nino?" O'Hara shouted. "Does your Papa know who killed Mr. Giovanni? Did he do it himself, or did he pay one of his thugs to do it for him? Maybe it was you, Nino. Were you the murderer? Did you kill Mr. Giovanni? We usually don't send boys your age to the electric chair, but in this case, the judge will probably make an exception."

Nino became agitated. With his heart pounding, his face turned red, and he shook his head from side to side. Without thinking, the words flowed. "No, I didn't kill Mr. Giovanni. Mr. Giovanni was my friend. And my Papa didn't kill Mr. Giovanni. It was Fredo Romano. Fredo Romano killed Mr. Giovanni. He stabbed him with a long knife. He was going to kill me, too. He had me trapped in the back room, then he looked at my face and turned around and left the store."

After Nino confessed what he had seen, he felt relieved. The guilt had left him like a deflated balloon.

"So, you were there, Nino. You saw everything?"

Still trembling, Nino said, "No, I didn't actually see it. I was in the back room. I heard them talking. I heard Mr. Giovanni begging for his life. Then I heard Mr. Giovanni making sounds like … like … he was choking or something. I peeked through the curtain, and Fredo Romano was standing over Mr. Giovanni wiping the blood from his knife on Mr. Giovanni's white coat. You've got to believe me."

"I believe you, Nino. I know you wouldn't kill Mr. Giovanni," O'Hara said as he crossed his arms and leaned back in his chair.

"Nino, I'm going to ask you a few more questions, and I want you to think long and hard before you answer. Take your time before you speak. Will you do that?"

"Yes sir."

"Okay, lad, you believe Fredo Romano was going to kill you until he saw your face, is that correct?"

"Yes sir."

"Why do you think he changed his mind when he saw you? What would have made him do that?"

"I don't know, sir. Maybe he saw I was just a kid and didn't want to kill a kid."

"Maybe that's what he thought. Or maybe he had seen you before. Maybe he knew you were the son of Salvador DiVincenzo. Do you think that could be why he didn't kill you?"

"I don't know."

"Yes you do. You know exactly why he didn't kill you, don't you?"

"No sir."

O'Hara once again leaned forward in his chair, this time

lifting out of his seat. His face was inches from Nino's. He raised his voice and said, "Fredo Romano works for your Papa, doesn't he? Fredo Romano didn't kill you because he knew if he did, your Papa would kill him, isn't that right, Nino?"

Nino tucked his chin into his chest. His tears flowed uncontrollably. "I want to go home. Where is my Papa?"

O'Hara sat back in his chair and took a deep breath as another officer entered the room. "The boy's father is here, and he has two lawyers with him. He's pissed off and is demanding to see his son."

*

Nino and Angelo sat in their room with their door shut, listening to their parents argue.

"He is no longer my son," Salvador DiVincenzo shouted as he paced in the foyer of their apartment, his leather shoes clicking on the marble floor.

"You don't mean that," Maria shouted back at him. "He is just a boy. The police coerced him into giving up Fredo's name."

"All of this time, I thought he was so brilliant. Yet, he was too stupid not to betray his own father—his own family, Maria. You included."

"Calm down, Salvador. Nino can hear you."

Taking a step toward his son's bedroom, he raised his voice. "Good. I want him to hear me. I want Angelo to hear me, too. You never, ever betray your own family. Never!"

"He didn't betray you, Salvador. Your lawyers will get you out of this."

Storming back to the center of the foyer, he paced angrily. "Maybe they will and maybe they won't. The cops have already hauled Fredo's fat ass in. Fredo is a weak man. He's already spilled his guts, I'm sure of it. He has probably already fingered me. I should have killed that bastard the moment he told me what happened."

Salvador took several puffs before removing his cigar, "You know what my solution for Nino is, Maria? You know where he is going to go? He is going to go live with my father in Sicily. He will make a man out of Nino, just like he did for me."

"No, Salvador. I will not allow that."

"It will do the boy some good, Maria. It will only be for a year or two. Maybe three. Hell, he may even learn to love it. We have been too soft on him. He needs to go live in Sicily where he can learn to be a man, just like I did. His grandfather will toughen him up. He will teach him loyalty to the family."

"Salvador DiVincenzo, I have put up with a lot from you over the years. Your whores, your drinking, your staying away for days, but you will not send Nino away to Sicily. If you do, you will send me with him."

Salvador turned and walked toward his den before stopping at the door. "That's fine, Maria. If you want to live in Sicily with Nino that is your choice. It is only one extra ticket on an ocean liner. I'm sure my father would love to meet you."

CHAPTER 2

H e never drove the same road two days in a row. A shotgun lay across his lap and holstered to his belt was a Berretta handgun. Armed with machine guns, his two most trusted gunmen, brothers Pasquale and Eduardo Butto, sat in the bed of the pickup truck. Their destination was the Abbey of Santa Maria on top of the Monti Sicani mountain range.

On the bench seat next to Lorenzo Leone, his ten-year-old daughter, Isabella, sat straight up, her neck straining to peek over the dashboard.

Lorenzo said, "Isabella, your grandpapà will pick you up from school today. Your brother and I are traveling to Palermo to pick up supplies for the farm, and we won't be home for two days."

"Papà, I don't understand why I can't go to Palermo with you and Aldo."

"Because you need to be in school studying with Father Russo and the nuns. You need to learn your Gospels and your music. Remember how proud your mamma was when you began violin lessons? You need to keep studying as your mamma wished."

"I know, Papà. That is what you always say."

When Isabella was six years old, her mother died from what the doctors in Palermo referred to as a mysterious illness. They had encouraged Lorenzo to take his wife, Eva, to a specialist in Rome. While Isabella held her hand on the train from southern Italy, her mother took her last breath just north of Naples.

"When you return from Palermo, will you have my cameo necklace—the blue one with Mamma's image on it?"

"If it has arrived. It's carved by hand. Beautiful art takes time. You must learn to be patient."

"And will it have a silver chain?"

"Yes, Isabella, we have discussed all of this many times."

"I know, but I am so excited. Once you bring it home, I can wear it around my neck and Mamma will be with me always."

"Your mamma is with you always anyway. You know that."

"But the moment I put on my cameo she will be next to my heart."

The Abbey of Santa Maria, where Isabella attended school, rested on the steepest side of the mountain range. The south side of the structure overlooked the valley—owned by Lorenzo's family, who had cultivated it for centuries. Lorenzo was the ninth generation Leone to run the lucrative citrus farm. Isabella and her brother Aldo would be the tenth.

Four days per week, Lorenzo dropped ten-year-old Isabella off with Fr. Russo and the nuns at the monastery within the abbey walls.

When they arrived, the only gate in the eight-meter-high wall was open. Fr. Russo didn't believe in closing it, "The abbey is always open for anyone in need," he would say.

Besides the school, there were three buildings used for living quarters, as well as a chapel and an infirmary. The tallest building was the chapel, and the other buildings were smaller, single-story stucco structures.

Lorenzo parked the pickup outside of the gate. He did so out of respect for Fr. Russo, who preferred to keep firearms outside the walls.

Lorenzo laid his shotgun and Berretta on the seat, and he and Isabella exited the front cab.

"Eduardo, you will stay here all day. Guard the entrance of the abbey and walk the perimeter each hour. Today, the children will venture on foot down the mountain to the waterfall. Follow them but keep your distance. You know how Fr. Russo feels about having guns around. But whatever you do, don't let Isabella out of your sight. When Isabella's grandfather picks her up this afternoon, ride back to the farm with them."

"*Si, Signor* Leone."

Eduardo put his arm through the leather strap of the machine gun and grabbed his knapsack of food. He then walked up an incline and positioned himself under a tree, and behind a row of bushes to conceal himself.

"Pasquale you can get in the front cab for the ride back to the farm with me," Lorenzo said.

Isabella adored Pasquale. He always played with her, made her laugh, and loved her as if she were his little sister.

After he leapt from the rear truck bed, Isabella embraced him and gave him a kiss on his cheek. "Pasquale, will you help me with my homework tonight?"

"Oh no, *Signorina* Isabella, you are much too smart for me.

But maybe you can teach me what you learn today?"

"I will teach you the Gospels."

"Si, I need to learn the Gospels. We will learn them together."

Isabella turned then said, "*Addio,* Pasquale."

She then ran through the entranceway, Lorenzo following behind her.

As they entered, a dozen children played in the courtyard. Some resided in a small orphanage nearby, others were from various villages scattered throughout the mountain.

Cloaked in a full-length brown robe tied around his thick middle, Fr. Russo stepped out of an arched entranceway in front of the chapel.

Isabella approached him.

Fr. Russo said, "Good morning, Isabella. Are you ready to learn wonderful things today?"

After they embraced, Isabella said, "Yes, Father, I am excited for school today. Today is the day we eat lunch at the waterfall."

"That's right. You remembered."

From the opposite side of the courtyard, little voices shouted, "Isabella, come play with us."

"I'm coming," Isabella said as she ran in the direction the other children, her long black hair flowing behind her.

Lorenzo was taller than the average man, and his muscular frame was intimidating even though he had just celebrated his fiftieth birthday. His son Aldo, now seventeen, resembled him. Their Greek and Arab heritage reflected in their appearance.

Approaching Lorenzo, Fr. Russo reached into a pocket under his robe and said, "Before I forget, Lorenzo, this is the list of supplies we need. If you could bring these items back from Palermo, the children would be most grateful."

"Yes, of course. I will be happy to, Father."

"You have been so kind to us, Lorenzo. If it were not for you, we could never survive."

"Father, as I have told you many times, God has blessed the Leone family. For centuries we have had some of the most fertile land in Sicily. He didn't bless us to be greedy with his gifts. Anything we can do for you and your mission is our obligation."

Fr. Russo embraced Lorenzo. "Bless you, Lorenzo, we pray that you have a safe journey down the mountain."

Lorenzo said, "Father, there is something I need to speak with you about."

Pointing to a wooden bench under an olive tree, Fr. Russo said, "May we have a seat? Before my morning prayers, I had been on my feet in the kitchen helping Sister Anna prepare breakfast for the children."

After sitting, Lorenzo removed the flat wool cap he wore on his head and tucked it inside his dark vest.

"Father, this is a difficult, but necessary conversation for me to have with you. As you know, Alfonso DiVincenzo has been strong-arming the local farmers in central Sicily for many years. He has coerced many of them to sell their land to him at prices well below market value. Most of those same farmers now work for him at wages that keep them in poverty. Fortunately, my family and I are wealthy enough to have been able to hire armed guards to protect our property. We have withstood his intimidation."

Lorenzo paused and looked down at the ground. "Lately, DiVincenzo has been increasing the pressure. He's determined to break us. What he fails to realize is that we will never cave—

ever. It has taken several generations of Leone sweat to build *Bellissima Valle*. We refuse to let it fall into DiVincenzo's hands."

"When you say 'increasing the pressure' ... How do you mean?"

Lorenzo raised his head and looked Fr. Russo in the eye. "Last month, two acres of grapefruit trees were burned to the ground in the dark of night. DiVincenzo's men have shot at my workers—they hit one in the leg. After that, several of the others stopped showing up for work. In recent weeks, I have had to hire more men to guard my orchards. I'm afraid I will soon have more gunmen on my payroll than field workers. If that continues, my expenses will be too high, and one or two bad growing seasons will break us. So far, our harvest has been bountiful this season. But what about next year? What if next year we have a bad year? What if we have two bad years in a row? It has happened before. We are due for a dry season."

"And the *polizia* have been no help?"

Lorenzo laughed and shook his head. "No. A decade ago, Mussolini sent Cesare Mori to crack down on *La Cosa Nostra*, and many of them are still in prison, but Capo DiVincenzo is different. Half of the polizia fear him, and the other half are on his payroll. The same is true for the judges in Palermo. I'm afraid we are on our own."

"Have you approached me to seek my counsel or do you just need a friend to share this with?"

"Neither, Father. I approached you because I am concerned about Isabella."

"Isabella? I don't understand."

"Before Mussolini and Mori cracked down on the *Mafioso*, their violence was unprecedented in other parts of Sicily.

Their vengeance was fierce and at times—" Lorenzo paused and looked toward Isabella who was playing in the courtyard. "Sometimes they would kidnap the children of those they were trying to intimidate. Sometimes, if their demands weren't met, they would do worse. Because of this, Father, I am asking your permission to leave Eduardo here to guard the abbey while Isabella is here. He's armed. He will stay outside the walls and patrol the perimeter. Neither you, nor the children will know he is here."

Fr. Russo hesitated then said, "I trust Eduardo, that is not the question. But you know my feelings about guns. No good comes from them. My fear is that having an armed guard here, even if he is outside of the walls of Santa Maria, will only bring trouble."

"I understand your concern, Father. I don't want you to feel as though you are putting the other children at risk. Whatever decision you make, I will respect and our friendship will remain. However, I am afraid that I cannot leave Isabella here if you refuse my request."

"I haven't refused your request, Lorenzo. I was merely thinking out loud and sharing my concerns. For today, I will say yes. Eduardo can stay. I will spend the remainder of the day praying for guidance. The next time we meet, I will have a firm answer for you."

"Thank you for your consideration, Father. That is all I can ask."

"Of course, my son."

"There is one last thing, Father."

"What is that, Lorenzo?"

"You know the history of my family well. We have owned

and farmed Bellissima Valle since the time of the Spanish rule. Dozens of nations have invaded Sicily, and my family has fought and survived them all. And I am here to tell you, Father, that myself—along with Isabella's grandfather and brother— will fight Capo DiVincenzo just as hard. We will fight to the death if we must."

"I pray it doesn't come to that," Fr. Russo said.

"But if it does, I need to know that if something happens and there is no one left to care for Isabella that she will always have a home here at Santa Maria. Can you promise me that, Father? Will you put my mind to rest?"

"Yes, Lorenzo. That decision is much easier than allowing a gunman on the property. It requires no prayer. I love Isabella as if she were my child. And the nuns and I would care for her as such. But you are talking crazy. The feud between you and Capo DiVincenzo can't be that bad, can it?"

Without answering, Lorenzo stood and placed his hat on his head, pulling it tight to protect his eyes from the rising sun. "Isabella's grandpapà will pick her up from school. I will return from Palermo in two days with your supplies."

THE ISLAND OF SICILY
PALERMO, ITALY
THE ROSEMAN CAMEO SHOP

"Do you think it has arrived, Papà?" Aldo said as Lorenzo parked the truck in front of Piazza Fonderia 23.

"I don't know. But since we are here in Palermo, we will check," Lorenzo said.

The shop wasn't large but, like the main Roseman Cameo

Factory in Torre del Greco, the Palermo location displayed some of the most stunning pieces of ornate jewelry in the world.

"Good afternoon, Manuel," Lorenzo said as he and Aldo entered the shop. "How is Olivia?"

"Olivia is fine. She is in Torre del Greco this week helping Mamma in the showroom of the factory."

"How are your parents? It has been too long since I have seen them."

"Papà is fine, but Mamma has been ill. That is why she needs Olivia's help."

"Tell them the Leone family sends our best."

"I will," Manuel said. "But on to the reason you are here. I have good news for you."

"So, it is here?" Lorenzo said. "Isabella will be so pleased."

"My younger brother Camillo just arrived with it yesterday. You remember Camillo, don't you Lorenzo?"

"Of course, is he still living in Chicago?"

"Yes," Manuel said. "He is visiting for a few weeks. Wait here, I'll go get him."

While they waited, Aldo studied the display cases.

"Look at these beautiful cameos, Papà."

"They are exquisite aren't they, Aldo? The Roseman family has been making cameos for two generations. They are true artisans."

The most common image was that of a beautiful woman, yet others were of flowers or doves. Some were blue, some were made from the cornelian shell. But most on display were crafted from the sardonyx shell—common along the Italian coast.

As Manuel and Camillo entered the showroom, Camillo reached out his hand to Lorenzo. "It is so good to see you again,

Lorenzo. I believe it has been eight years. That's when I moved to Chicago."

"Has it been that long?"

Camillo was four years younger than Manuel, who was thirty-three. Both men were slight in stature.

Lorenzo said, "Do you remember my son?"

"Is this Aldo?" Camillo asked. "You were just a small boy when I saw you last."

"He isn't a small boy anymore," Lorenzo said. "He is seventeen now."

Camillo reached into his pocket and pulled out a small case revealing a blue cameo necklace with a brushed silver chain. "Look what I have here."

"It looks just like her. It looks just like my beautiful Eva," Lorenzo said, patting his heart. "How do you do it?" he asked as he turned and handed the cameo to Aldo.

Manuel said, "There are no finer craftsmen in the world than those who work for the Roseman Cameo Company. My father, Solomon, is a natural craftsman. He has taught both Camillo and me, and we in turn have handpicked the finest artisans in all of Italy to work for us. It takes many years of experience to hand carve a piece such as yours."

"Did you carve this image of Eva, Camillo?" Lorenzo asked.

"No. I am good, but not this good. Our papà made your piece. When my ship arrived in Naples from America, I went to Terre del Greco first. Papà was in the polishing phase when I arrived. He instructed me to wait for him to finish so I could bring it down with me. When Papà found out you had commissioned us to make Eva's image, he insisted on doing the work himself."

"It is even more beautiful knowing it was made with your Papà's hands. Tell Solomon I am grateful. Most of all, Isabella will be grateful. It is my gift to her. She misses her mother so. She still weeps for her, as we all do."

"We were honored to do it, my friend," Manuel said.

Lorenzo said to Camillo, "Did you take the train down from Torre del Greco or did you bring one of the boats?"

"Papà had me bring one of the company boats."

Lorenzo said, "I want to bring you a few cases of limoncello to take back for your family. Do you have room?"

"For your limoncello, I will make room. My family will be most grateful, I know."

Lorenzo said, "There is a ship arriving in Palermo from Britain on Thursday. They will be in the market for produce. We will be here with two truckloads of chinotto oranges. Will you still be here?"

"I don't return until Friday," Camillo said.

"What time are you departing? We will meet you at the dock."

"It is an eleven-hour voyage. I need to leave at sunup."

"We will be at the dock at sunup, then."

Aldo said to Camillo, "What is it like in America? Have you met any movie stars?"

Manuel laughed. "Met any? He is married to one."

"Married to one?" Aldo said with excitement, "Is it Greta Garbo or Vivien Leigh?"

Camillo laughed. "Manuel exaggerates. She isn't a movie star. Although she used to scrape a few dollars together performing in small theaters here and there. She was performing in *Show Boat* when I met her. I went to see the play one night, and I couldn't take my eyes off her. I went there night after night, just to see her. The night of the last performance, I finally worked up the courage to ask her to dinner. We were married in a small ceremony here in Italy a few months later."

Manuel said, "Their wedding was in Torre del Greco. Then, they honeymooned on the Island of Capri. Papà went all out for his baby boy's ceremony."

"That was only because Mamma was afraid I would elope in Chicago," Camillo said. "They were buying me off."

Camillo reached into his breast pocket and pulled out a leather pouch containing several large American bills intermingled with Italian lire. He pulled out a photo, laid it on the glass countertop, and slid it to Aldo. "That is my Hannah."

"*Oh mio*, she is beautiful," Aldo said.

"Si, she is. She is a wonderful girl, too, though a real fireball. She isn't afraid to speak her mind and takes nothing off anyone. Especially me. She is still in Chicago. She is carrying our first child, and the doctor believed the trip would be risky for the baby."

The front door of the shop opened, and a large man entered. His tattered clothes appeared as though they hadn't been washed in weeks. He was about forty, tall with wide shoulders, and thick around the middle. He carried a Berretta handgun holstered to his belt, as did Lorenzo and Aldo, who watched him enter. Manuel kept his weapons concealed in hidden compartments throughout the shop.

Manuel said, "Omar, you aren't welcome here. I am asking you to leave."

Omar said, "You know I am here to help you. To protect you from bad people. I thought I made that clear during my last visit."

"We don't need your help. We can protect ourselves."

"You would be much better protected if you paid my boss a stipend."

"Tell old man DiVincenzo we have no interest in his extortion," Manuel said.

"I have passed your message to him before. It didn't make him happy."

"I don't care what makes him happy or unhappy. Now get out of my shop," Manuel said before pulling a shotgun from behind the counter.

While resting his hand on his holstered Berretta, Lorenzo turned toward Omar and stared him down

"Who are you?" Omar asked, as he stood eye to eye with Lorenzo.

"I am someone else who makes Mr. DiVincenzo unhappy. And I don't care either. Tell your boss he needs to stop strong-arming the citizens of Sicily."

"And who may I say is telling him such a thing?"

"Lorenzo Leone. He knows me well."

"Oh yes, he has spoken of you often. You are the one with the beautiful citrus farm up in the Monti Sicanis. He greatly admires your property. That is not good for you. Not good at all," Omar said as he made his way to the door.

As he reached for the doorknob, Omar looked at Manuel and said, "Your time is running out, my little Jew friend. I suggest you reconsider soon."

Enraged, Camillo stepped between Omar and the door. He stood shorter than the large man yet refused to be intimidated. Omar's breath was a mixture of rotten teeth and stale tobacco.

"You listen to me, you fat son of a bitch," Camillo said. "I don't know who you are, and I don't know who your boss is, but you are messing with the wrong 'little Jew' family."

Omar used his forearm to shove Camillo out of the way, knocking him to the ground. Camillo leaped to his feet, drew his fist back, and punched Omar in the groin, causing him to hunch over and drop to the ground.

Omar reached for his Berretta before thinking better of it. Manuel pointed a shotgun at his head while Lorenzo and Aldo pulled their weapons on him.

Camillo stood over him. His fist out in front, ready to go at it again if the big man wished to fight.

Omar, panting hard, grabbed his hat that lay next to him and stood, "I'm outnumbered, it would appear."

As he exited, Omar stared Camillo down before spitting on the floor in front of him.

THE ISLAND OF SICILY
MONTI SICANI MOUNTAIN RANGE
BELLISSIMA VALLE

Located on the southern face of the mountain range, Bellissima Valle had changed little over the past century. Tradition could be found in the soil of their citrus dynasty, and the Leone family had passed their growing process down for generations. Even their recipe for limoncello was so ancient, nobody in the family knew who the original creator was.

Flanked on both sides by lemon trees, the main entrance was a lengthy dirt road that originated on the hilltop. Visitors would often take their time traveling the road in order to enjoy the citrus smell that hung heavy in the air.

At the base of the mountain range, the center of the compound was comprised of a vast dirt courtyard. Around the perimeter stood the main house—a two-story stucco—and a series of barns and sheds where they kept their horses and vehicles. On the direct opposite side of the courtyard from the main house were two wooden bunkhouses. These were temporary homes for seasonal field hands and armed guards during the harvest. Others lived in the tiny villages in the mountain range and arrived on foot or on the back of mules.

As their truck entered the courtyard, Lorenzo said to Aldo, "Do you see those four men on the west hillside?"

"Yes, I see them," Aldo said. "They are Capo DiVincenzo's men. They were there the day we left for Palermo, and three days before that."

Lorenzo replied, "They aren't just his men. The fat one on the white horse is Alfonso DiVincenzo himself."

When their truck stopped, Lorenzo's father, Bruno—grandpapa to Aldo and Isabella—stood in the center of the courtyard. Like his son and grandson, Bruno was tall, but thick around the belly from his own pasta and rich spaghetti sauce that he loved to make from scratch.

After exiting the front cab, Lorenzo and Aldo approached Bruno, who pointed up the hill.

"Do you see them, Lorenzo?"

"Don't point, Papà. That's what they want—to get us worked up. To intimidate us."

Bruno said, "But they are on our land. I say we shoot them. If we put an end to that fat bastard, we will do all of Sicily a favor."

"It will also get us thrown into prison with DiVincenzo's other *Mafioso*, and they would kill us out of revenge. So no,

Papà, we will not shoot them. Not unless we have to."

Looking at Aldo, Lorenzo said, "Go get Eduardo, Pasquale, and a group of field hands. Start loading two trucks with chinotto oranges. We have a long journey back to Palermo tomorrow."

"Okay, Papà," Aldo said.

As Lorenzo and Bruno turned to walk toward the house, Isabella ran out, the screen door slamming behind her.

"Do you have it, Papà? Do you have Mamma's cameo?"

As she neared Lorenzo, he knelt and embraced her. "Oh, it is so good to see you, Isabella. I missed you."

"I missed you too, Papà. Do you not have it?"

"Hmm," Lorenzo said as he stood and patted his pockets. First his trousers, then his chest, before reaching inside his vest. "Well what is this? Do you think this might be what you are looking for, Isabella?"

He removed the box, knelt, and opened it in front of her. Isabella gently grabbed it from his hands and caressed her mother's image.

"Mamma," she said as she kissed it. "It is beautiful, Papà. Thank you for getting it for me."

"Of course, my sweet. Your mamma loves you. She will always be with you."

"Yes, I know. Will you help me put it on?"

Isabella turned around and lifted her long black hair above her neck so Lorenzo could fasten the clasp.

When Isabella turned back around, the cameo rested at her waistline.

"I think the chain is too long, Papà. I want her near my heart."

"When we return from Palermo, I will shorten the chain for you. Will that be okay, my darling?"

"Yes, Papà. I'm just glad I have it."

After leaning forward and kissing Lorenzo on his cheek, she turned and ran back into the house.

As Lorenzo stood, Bruno looked up into the hill and said, "They are coming our way."

They watched as the four horsemen, armed with rifles and handguns, galloped down the hill.

When they arrived in the courtyard, Lorenzo said, "What brings you to Bellissima Valle, Alfonso? I thought the last time we spoke I made it clear that we have no interest in selling."

Alfonso DiVincenzo was a stout man. No taller than average height, he had a husky build with a thick chest and shoulders and a belly to match. The DiVincenzo and Leone families had a long history of conflict. When they were boys, Bruno and Alfonso were rivals and had gotten into more fisticuffs than they could remember. They'd passed the tradition on to Lorenzo and Salvador, although Salvador had moved to the Bronx in New York City two decades earlier.

Alfonso said, "Many men over the years have told me they wouldn't sell their property. Now, most of them are employed by me, working the very land they once clung to so desperately. There are only a few holdouts left. You are the most prominent. Bellissima Valle is the most beautiful and fertile land in all of central Sicily. It is only right that I possess it."

Lorenzo said, "You flatter us with your longing for Bellissima Valle, Alfonso, but it will never be yours. Now get the hell out of here."

"That is no way to speak to a guest, Lorenzo. Didn't your father teach you better manners?"

Bruno moved his hand to the Beretta holstered to his side. When he did, the three men with Alfonso raised their rifles and pointed them at Bruno.

Alfonso raised his hand and said to them, "There will be none of that, boys. We are guests on their property. It wouldn't be right to shoot them here."

From the barn, Aldo, Eduardo, and Pasquale ran toward the small group before stopping behind Alfonso and his men. All three wielded machine guns.

The usually quiet Aldo said to the men on horseback, "Drop your weapons."

Alfonso turned his horse to face his rival's grandson. "No, Aldo, we will not be dropping our weapons, and you will not shoot us because you are a coward just like your father and grandfather."

Bruno and Lorenzo pulled their Berettas from their holsters and surrounded Alfonso and his men. Alfonso stared at the three machine guns and two handguns now pointing at him.

Laughing, Alfonso placated them. "Okay, gentlemen. There is no need for violence. We will depart. For now."

As he turned his horse toward the western hills, he tipped his hat and said, "Until our next meeting."

He then spurred his horse, and the four men rode away.

THE ISLAND OF SICILY
PALERMO, ITALY
PORT OF PALERMO

Solomon Roseman had named all four of his boats after shells he used for carving cameos, and the *Sardonyx*, a forty-five-meter motor yacht, was the vessel Camillo preferred. It was the boat he and Manuel learned to sail on, and there was a comfort level on the *Sardonyx* he didn't feel on the others.

Lorenzo led the way, followed by Aldo. They each carried a case of limoncello as they approached Camillo who stood in the center of the pier.

"The seas are rough today. It looks like a difficult voyage back to Torre del Greco," Lorenzo said.

Camillo turned and said, "Good morning, gentlemen."

Lorenzo said, "We bring gifts. Tell Solomon it is our thanks for personally crafting Eva's image on Isabella's cameo."

"The famous Leone limoncello. Papa will be pleased."

"It was good to see you again, Camillo. Let it not be another eight years before you return. And bring Hannah and the baby with you next time. We would love to meet your family."

"I would like that. I'm sure they will be with me when I return next year."

"We look forward to it."

"Okay, my friend. I must leave now," Camillo said.

"Tell Solomon that Isabella cherishes her cameo."

"I shall," Camillo said before glancing at Aldo. "Keep your papà safe, Aldo."

"We'll keep each other safe."

After helping Camillo load his supplies and the two cases

of limoncello aboard the *Sardonyx*, Lorenzo and Aldo returned to their trucks, parked at the end of the pier. They climbed into the vehicles, Aldo in the second and Lorenzo in the lead.

They watched as Camillo untied the mooring lines, threw them onto the boat, then boarded himself.

Lorenzo waved at Camillo, who returned the gesture.

As Lorenzo and Aldo drove away from the pier, they heard an explosion that reverberated through the air. Stopping, they leaped from their trucks and stared down the pier to see a floating ball of fire.

The *Sardonyx* was ablaze.

CHAPTER 3

BRONX, NEW YORK
THE CHURCH OF OUR LADY OF MERCY

"**W**hy are we here, Mama?"

"Because I need to speak to Msgr. Nunzio about something."

"About me, Mama? About Papa?"

"About a lot of things, Nino."

"Am I going to move to Sicily to live with Grandpapa DiVincenzo?"

"No, Nino. You are not moving to Sicily. I won't allow it."

"But what if Papa says I have to?"

"I let your father dictate just about everything that goes on in our home. But as for you and where you live, he will not make that decision. He will not send you to Sicily. I promise you."

Msgr. Nunzio turned the corner toward Nino and Maria, smiling when he saw them, and said, "Well, good morning. This is a pleasant surprise. What brings me the pleasure of your company?"

Maria said, "Monsignor, I know you are busy. But would you have a moment to speak with me privately?"

"Maria, you know I will always make time for you and Nino. Please come in," Msgr. Nunzio said as he opened his door and gestured toward the office.

Maria said, "Nino, you stay here. The things I need to discuss with Msgr. Nunzio are between us for now."

"But if you are going to talk about me, why can't I go in, too?"

"I know you are upset. But I'm asking you to do as I tell you and stay out here. We won't be long."

"How long is long?"

"Nino, have a seat," Maria said.

Msgr. Nunzio said, "Nino, wait here. I know you like to look at my atlas. Let me get it. You can look through it and travel the world while I speak to your mother."

"Okay, I'll do that."

Msgr. Nunzio entered his office and returned with the atlas, handing it to Nino before he and Maria closed the door behind them.

Maria sat in the same leather chair Nino had sat in many times, and Msgr. Nunzio sat in the chair next her.

"Maria, you look distraught. What is it? How may I help you?"

Unaware that Nino had discussed Mr. Giovanni's murder with Msgr. Nunzio, Maria said, "Monsignor, much has happened in the past few weeks. I can't get into all of it other than to say that Salvador might be in trouble—serious trouble—and it involves Nino. Salvador is very unhappy with Nino right now."

"It all sounds rather complicated. Share with me what you feel comfortable sharing, and I will counsel you in any way that I can."

"Monsignor, a crime was committed, and it involved one of Salvador's men. The police found out that Nino was a witness, and they interrogated him. Salvador believes that Nino told them more than he should have. He feels betrayed by Nino and is furious. He's so angry that he has threatened to send Nino to Sicily to live with his father, Nino's grandfather. I don't know if I have the power to stop it."

"Let some more time pass. Surely, Salvador will calm down and come to his senses."

"You don't know Salvador DiVincenzo. He has no respect for me or my concerns. To keep Nino from moving to Sicily, I may need to run away with him. To hide Nino from his own father."

"Where would you go?"

"I don't know. My father has been dead for many years and my mother is ill. Salvador is paying for her care and has told me that if I ever leave him, he will stop. If I run away with Nino, what would become of my mother? And I have no way of supporting Nino and myself."

"I see your dilemma," Msgr. Nunzio said as he stood and paced his office, rubbing his chin and looking down as he walked.

Stopping to turn back to Maria, he queried, "What if I had an alternative for Nino where he wouldn't have to leave the country or even the state of New York?"

"I don't understand. What do you mean?"

"It sounds like Salvador just wants Nino out of the house as a means of punishment for his perceived wrongdoing. If Nino moved to someplace other than your apartment, would that satisfy Salvador?"

"Where would he go?"

"Maria, do you recall a fundraiser you helped me with four years ago? It was for Saint Michael's Home for Orphaned Boys in Syracuse."

"Yes, I remember. We raised money to help them build a new wing for their school."

"That's right."

"Aren't those boys distressed? Haven't they been in trouble with the police?"

"Some have had their troubles, yes, but most of the residents are good boys who have been orphaned. We live in troubled economic times. Many of the boys who live there were dropped off by their parents because they were just an extra mouth to feed."

"You mean their parents abandoned them."

"Sometimes a parent loves their child so much, they entrust them to others because that's what is best for the child."

"Oh Monsignor, Syracuse is so far away, and the thought of Nino living on his own upsets me. He's only fourteen."

"It's only nine hours away by train. You could visit him whenever you wished. And he wouldn't be alone, there are dozens of priests and nuns who would care for and provide guidance for Nino. I know the headmaster of the school well. We attended seminary in Rome together. His name is Father Doyle, and the New York archdiocese handpicked him to run Saint Michael's. They have a wonderful school, and Nino would be immersed in the faith as well as science, literature, and the arts. And unlike Saint Francis Preparatory School, the boys at Saint Michael's have no knowledge of Salvador's reputation. They won't fear Nino because his last name is DiVincenzo. He will finally have a chance to build friendships with other boys. I believe this might be the best solution for Nino."

"But Nino's papa"—Maria looked down and wept, then continued—"Salvador's mind is set on sending Nino to Sicily to live with his grandfather. If Salvador insists, I don't see how I can stop him."

"I understand the challenges you face. Yet, you must find a way to do what is best for Nino and yourself. You must convince Salvador that this is the best solution for all."

CHICAGO, IL
THE ROSEMAN APARTMENT

"I need to speak to Doctor Jacobs. It is urgent," Hannah said as she sat on her sofa with the telephone receiver to her ear.

The pain she felt was intense. It had started in her abdomen the previous evening and now radiated throughout her stomach and lower back.

"What is it, Mrs. Roseman?" Dr. Jacobs said after being handed the telephone.

"Something is wrong. I have immense pain in my stomach and lower back. I can't possibly make it to your office. Can you come to my apartment? And hurry please."

"I'm on my way. Lay on your back and rest as much as possible until I arrive. It will take a while to get there."

Moments after Hannah returned the telephone receiver to its cradle, she heard a knock on her apartment door. She slowly raised herself up and made her way across the room.

She opened the door to find a Western Union telegram carrier.

He handed her an envelope and said, "Can you sign here, ma'am?"

After closing the door, she made her way back to the sofa. The telegram was from Camillo's brother, Manuel.

Why is Manuel sending me a telegram? Has something happened to Camillo?

CHAPTER 4

Manuel leaned against the alley wall. The saloon's open door cast light onto the dirt parking area, which was otherwise pitch black. A steady flow of customers and prostitutes came and went. He saw Omar's car parked next to the woods. Manuel made his way across the dirt street and approached Omar's Fiat. The drunks congregating around the front of the building were too intoxicated to perceive him as anything other than another patron. He stepped around Omar's car and positioned himself between the vehicle and the woods. He opened the front passenger door and felt under the seat where he found a Berretta, then leaned forward and repeated his search under the driver's seat, finding a revolver. He removed both weapons and tossed them into the woods. Manuel then stepped into the forest, leaves and sticks crunching under his boots. A faint smell of decaying vegetation emanated in the air. Manuel had a Berretta holstered on his belt and a six-inch dagger tucked into his boot.

An hour passed. And then another.

Finally, Omar stepped out of the front door of the saloon. He had a woman under his right arm and a bottle in his left hand. He stumbled as he made his way to the Fiat.

Manuel pulled out a bandana, tied it around his face, then removed the dagger from his boot.

Omar lost his balance and released his arm from the prostitute as he fell against his car. Silently, Manuel stepped out of the woods, covered Omar's mouth with his left hand and plunged the dagger into his throat. The woman became frantic, yelping and screaming repeatedly. Manuel released Omar's lifeless body, and it dropped to the ground like a sack of potatoes. Manuel watched the woman sprint back to the entrance of the saloon, screaming at the other patrons before he escaped into the woods.

The Island of Sicily
Palermo, Italy
The Roseman Cameo Shop

Olivia Roseman locked the cash from that day's sales in the safe of the cameo shop as her husband balanced the ledger.

"How much longer will it be, Manuel? I'm ready to go home."

"Me too, Olivia. This can wait until morning."

Manuel closed the ledger, slid it into his desk drawer, and followed his wife to the front of the shop. He watched as Olivia stopped abruptly, stifled a gasp, took a breath, and stared at three men standing at the counter.

Alfonso DiVincenzo stood in front of two men. Their extraordinary size left little room between the front display case and the door. Dressed in a suit and fedora, Alfonso stared back at Manuel as a cigar hung from his mouth. The two men behind him appeared to be field workers and flaunted long metal rods in their hands. Each wore a Berretta holstered to his belt.

Manuel said to his wife, "Go back into the office, and exit through the back door. I will handle this."

"No, Manuel. I won't leave you here alone."

"Do as I tell you, Olivia."

"I won't leave you."

"You are angering me. I can handle this better on my own."

Ignoring her husband's comments, she asked, "Is one of them this Omar you were telling me about? The one you think killed Camillo."

"No. I don't know who they are. Leave now. I won't tell you again."

"I am your wife, and I am not leaving your side."

Addressing the three men, Manuel said, "We are closed. How did you get in here?"

"You need a better lock, Roseman," Alfonso said.

"What do you want?"

"I want to know who killed Omar."

"I don't know what you are talking about."

"I believe you do. It is only logical. Nobody plays the game of revenge better than me. I send my man Omar to collect the money you owe me. He gets into a scuffle with your brother. Your brother gets baked when his boat explodes, then Omar has a knife plunged into his throat. It all makes perfect sense."

"Are you Alfonso DiVincenzo?" Manuel asked.

"I am."

Manuel said, "I know nothing of Omar's death."

Alfonso laughed, "I don't believe you killed my man

yourself. You're nothing but a puny little Jew. Jews aren't murderers. Jews use their filthy Jew money to hire other people to kill their enemies."

Manuel said, "Like you paid Omar to kill my brother?"

"You are rather mouthy considering the position you currently find yourself in."

Manuel had weapons hidden under each counter. He could get to any of them instantly—he had rehearsed this scenario—but Olivia would be caught in the crossfire.

"Are you going to kill us?" Olivia asked.

Alfonso shrugged his shoulders. "I currently have it under consideration, signora. The problem is, I'm not in the mood. It would be a shame to end the life of such a beautiful woman. But my biggest hesitation is that one day I'm going to buy the entire Roseman cameo dynasty from your papà, Solomon. One of my men has already killed one of his sons. Killing his second son and his lovely daughter-in-law would make him a stubborn negotiator, don't you think? Besides, Omar wasn't of much value to me anyway."

"So, what do you want?" Manuel said.

Alfonso flicked his cigar onto the rug Manuel was standing on.

"You might want to put that out, I don't want my cigar to burn the shop down."

Manuel used his shoe to extinguish the smoldering embers.

Alfonso said, "This is my suggestion, Roseman. You go home and have a nice pleasant dinner with your wife, and my boys and I will stay behind and remodel your shop for you. When you arrive in the morning, you won't recognize the place."

"Get out," Manuel said.

Alfonso leaned back and laughed, then nodded toward his men. They raised the metal rods over their heads and brought them down on the glass display case in front of them. Manuel stepped in front of Olivia to shield her from the flying glass. As he put his hands over his face, his left hand and ear were slashed by debris.

After the two thugs brought several more blows down on the front display case, they made their way to the other sections of the shop. Manuel and Olivia stepped to the back of the office to avoid the flying glass and the large metal rods.

As Olivia sat on the floor in the corner of the office, Manuel peered into the showroom and watched the two men smash everything in sight. Alfonso looked on in amusement. The event was over in a few minutes, but the damage was catastrophic.

"Help yourselves to whatever you want boys," Alfonso told his two musclemen.

Manuel watched as they bent over and picked up dozens of loose cameos off the floor and inserted them into their pockets.

"My mamma will love these," one of the men said.

As Manuel looked on, he thought about the thousands of hours his family and their skilled craftsmen had put into carving the delicate pieces of art.

He swallowed hard as he struggled with his own anger and humiliation for not fighting back while Olivia sat cowering in the corner, terrified for their lives.

Manuel stepped out of the office and into the shop. Broken glass crunched under his feet as the two big men continue to help themselves to their treasure.

Alfonso approached Manuel until he was inches from his face.

"Don't mess with me, Roseman. And tell your papà that your family hasn't seen the last of me. My reach expands far past Sicily. I have connections everywhere, including in the highest reaches of the Italian government. I even have connections within the walls of the Vatican. How do you think I have survived even after Mussolini killed or imprisoned most of the other Sicilian *Mafioso*?"

Manuel swallowed hard, yet stared directly into Alfonso's eyes, trying to hide his fear.

Alfonso pulled another cigar from his jacket pocket, bit down on it and patted his pockets.

"I appear to be out of matches, Roseman. Do you have one?"

"Take your smelly pigs and get out of my shop," Manuel said.

Alfonso stepped away from Manuel and turned to the two men behind him.

"Did you hear what he called you, gentlemen? He called you smelly pigs."

The man closest to Manuel raised the metal rod and brought it down on Manuel, who blocked it with his forearm. He dropped to his knees in agony.

The rod was raised one more time, but Alfonso said, "No more! We don't want him dead. We need him alive to tell his papà who is in charge."

Manuel rolled on the broken glass, while holding his arm. He watched the three men as they exited the shop.

Olivia stepped out of the office and dropped to her knees next to her husband.

Manuel grimaced in pain. He never took his eyes from Alfonso and his men. With one swoop, the man who'd beat

Manuel raised the bar one last time and swung it through the window. Manuel threw his body across Olivia to protect her from the shattered plate glass window which seconds earlier had displayed the Roseman name.

*

Lorenzo counted the cash payment he'd received from the British fruit brokers at the Palermo docks.

He then turned to Aldo and Eduardo. "Before we return to Bellissima Valle, we must refuel and find a café for lunch. But first, I want to visit with Manuel and Olivia. Follow me to their shop."

"We'll be right behind you," Aldo said as he and Eduardo climbed into the second truck.

The Roseman Cameo Shop was three blocks from the docks. The proximity to the portside ocean liners was good for business, as tourists would pass by after disembarking their ships.

As Lorenzo turned onto Piazza Fonderia, he saw Solomon standing in front of the store sweeping up shards of glass and debris.

They parked their trucks across the street. Lorenzo approached the store with Aldo and Eduardo trailing behind.

"Solomon, what happened? Where are Manuel and Olivia?"

"He and Olivia are at the doctor. DiVincenzo paid them a visit yesterday. He busted up the store, and one of his men beat Manuel. Both he and Olivia have cuts from the flying glass."

"Was there someone by the name of Omar with him?"

"Whoever this Omar is you speak of, he is dead. Manuel said the reason DiVincenzo busted up the store was out of revenge for Omar's death."

"Who would have killed him?"

"Does it really matter? I'm just glad he's dead."

"How long before you reopen?"

"Not long," Solomon said. "I have more product being shipped down next week. We just need to get the store cleaned up as soon as possible."

Lorenzo said to Aldo and Eduardo, "Let's give Solomon a hand."

CHAPTER 5

Nino peered out of the window as the train approached Syracuse. His stomach was tight. He would miss seeing Fr. Nunzio every week. He would even miss Angelo, despite the fact that his brother picked on him incessantly. Most of all, he would miss his mother—his best friend.

During the trip from the Bronx, Maria had only spoken to Nino of his new home in a positive tone. Though relieved that Salvador had agreed that sending Nino to Sicily was not his best idea, she had her doubts that Saint Michael's would be good for Nino.

"You will like it, Nino. Unlike Saint Francis Preparatory School, none of these boys have heard of your father or anything about our family. They won't fear being your friend because of our last name. It will give you a chance to gain friends. That's what you have wanted."

"But I don't want to move away. Can't you tell Papa to let me stay?"

"We have been through this. It is best that you stay away from your papa for a while. At least until he can get out of trouble over Mr. Giovanni's death."

"I did bad, didn't I, Mama?"

"No, you didn't do bad. The policeman asked you a few questions, and you answered them. That is all that happened. Don't you worry about your papa. Nothing will happen to him. Fredo will be the one punished for what happened to Mr. Giovanni. Not your papa. His lawyers will get him out of it."

"Will Papa still want me to become a lawyer when I get older so I can work for him?"

"Don't think about that. That is still a long way off. You just focus on your new school and all the friends you will make."

The scenery transformed from open country to an urban setting. Houses appeared, along with a few small shanties. Cars and horse-drawn carriages were more frequent.

As the brakes were applied, their train car jerked, and they began to decelerate.

"I'm scared, Mama."

"Don't be. You know what Msgr. Nunzio said to you. Sometimes God has us do things we don't want to do, but those things change our lives forever, so we can do what is best for him. You must trust that God wants you to be here."

With the train whistle blowing, Nino watched as the crowded platform came into view. There were men in suits holding attaché cases, standing next to women and children in rags, and working men in coveralls. A priest stood in the back of the crowd.

"That must be Fr. Doyle. He is the one Msgr. Nunzio said would meet us."

"No, I don't believe it is. Fr. Doyle went to seminary in Rome with Msgr. Nunzio. That priest on the platform is too young to be Fr. Doyle."

After the train came to a stop, they pulled Nino's suitcase from the overhead compartment. Maria grabbed Nino's hand, and they exited the car. Once on the platform, they approached the priest they had seen from a distance.

"Hello," Maria said. "Are you here to pick up Nino DiVincenzo?"

"Yes, I am. My name is Fr. Walters." Looking down he said, "And you must be Nino. It is so good to have you with us. I know you will like your new home."

"I will try, Father," Nino said as his lower lip quivered with the realization his mother would soon be leaving him behind when she boarded the train back to the Bronx.

Father Walters addressed Maria. "Will you be returning to the city right away, or do you have time to come see your son's new home?"

"I want to see where he will be living."

"I will bring you back here after your visit."

Maria looked at Nino. "We still have some time together."

Father Walters said, "Let me grab your bag, Nino. Follow me, I will take you to the car."

*

The 1929 Ford Model A drove up a narrow path. A large, three-story building came into view. Behind the main building were smaller buildings. One of which was also brick, but most were one-story, wooden outbuildings. Twelve acres held the entire complex, four of which comprised the front yard where dozens of boys were playing.

"Here is your new home, Nino," Father Walters said. "What do you think?"

Nino remained silent, but Maria spoke up. "It's a large

building, Padre. How many boys live here?"

"We have one hundred and twenty-seven. Nino, you will make the one hundred and twenty-eighth."

The car came to a stop in front of a broad, twenty-six-step stairway that led to a double door entrance. There were several boys sitting on the steps. Some were doing homework, others were talking. Sitting off to the side by himself was another boy. His skin was dark and appeared to be the only child in view who wasn't Caucasian.

Fr. Walters carried Nino's bag, and Maria grabbed Nino's hand as they climbed the stairs.

Halfway up, Fr. Walters stopped and introduced Nino to the boys. They were suspicious because Nino appeared to have something they didn't—a mother. Her dress and pearls were something they had only seen sketched in a Sears, Roebuck catalog.

"Boys, this is Nino DiVincenzo. Say hello," Fr. Walters said.

"Hello, Nino," the boys replied in unison.

"Do you want to play baseball?" one of them said.

Nino grinned and looked up at his mother.

Maria nodded her head in approval. "Run off and have fun, Nino. I will meet with Fr. Doyle and come find you before I leave."

Leave?

That word stabbed Nino. It was a jolt. A quick reminder that his Mama would no longer be part of his everyday life. He had a lump in his throat.

Sensing his hesitance, she said, "Everything will be fine, Nino."

Nino said to the boys, "I'll play."

"Okay. Follow us to the courtyard."

Maria smiled as Nino ran off with the other boys.

"He appears to be adjusting quickly," Fr. Walters said.

"I'm pleased to see that," Maria said.

"Come with me, Mrs. DiVincenzo. I will introduce you to Fr. Doyle, and he will explain what life is like here for the boys."

As they turned to climb the stairs, Maria glanced over at the dark-skinned boy. He appeared to be Nino's age.

After entering the building, Maria said to Fr. Walters, "That Negro boy. He looks so lonely. Does he live here, too?"

"That's Clarence. His mother died and his father dropped him off. He said he was going to North Carolina to find his sister—the boy's aunt. Once he found her, he would come back and get him. That was two years ago when the boy was eleven."

"Are there other Negro boys here?" Maria asked.

"Clarence is the only one."

"Does he eat and sleep with the other boys?"

Abruptly stopping in the hallway, Fr. Walters turned to Maria. "Yes, Mrs. DiVincenzo, he does. Fr. Doyle doesn't believe in separating God's children because of the color He made them."

"But that just isn't normal, Father. I mean it isn't normal to have a Negro living with white children."

As they continued their walk through the hall, Fr. Walters said, "As you just witnessed, Mrs. DiVincenzo, the problem sorts itself out. Clarence stays to himself, and the other boys don't bother him. He occasionally gets into a dustup, but we keep that under control."

"So, he is an outcast here?" Maria asked.

"We try not to look at it like that."

"Aren't there homes for colored boys where he could go live? Wouldn't he be happier there?"

"Fr. Doyle has visited the Negro orphanage. He said it's not fit for animals. Their school only has three or four books per classroom, it has little heat in the winter, the food is limited, and many of the children appear to be malnourished. Even though the diocese wants Clarence sent there, Fr. Doyle refuses. He says that if God wanted him there, that's where his father would have dropped him off."

Upon entering the office, Fr. Walters said, "Fr. Doyle, this is Maria DiVincenzo. Nino's mother."

Fr. Doyle had short gray hair and, like Msgr. Nunzio, was thick around the middle.

After removing his glasses and laying them on the document he was reading, Fr. Doyle stood and stepped around from behind his desk, "Good afternoon, Mrs. DiVincenzo. It is a pleasure to meet you. And where is Nino? I would like to meet him."

Fr. Walters spoke up, "He was intercepted by some of the boys who invited him to play in the courtyard."

"Well, that most certainly is a good sign, isn't it?" Fr. Doyle said as he looked at Maria.

"I will leave you two alone," Fr. Walters said before exiting and closing the door behind him.

Once they were seated, Fr. Doyle said, "I'm sure you are experiencing a significant amount of apprehension, Mrs. DiVincenzo. However, let me assure you, Nino will be fine here. Msgr. Nunzio speaks highly of him. 'Nino is an exceptional young man, both in intelligence and character,' I believe were the words he used. You apparently have done a magnificent job raising him."

"Please, call me Maria. And thank you for the kind words. Msgr. Nunzio has been a tremendous help during these trying times. He said he will travel here occasionally to visit with Nino, at least until he gets settled in."

"He told me that. It will be good for Nino to see a familiar face."

Maria sat silently for a moment before she began to weep. "I will miss my Nino so. I believe I need him more than he needs me."

Fr. Doyle reached in his desk drawer for a handkerchief before handing it to her. "You are welcome here anytime, too, Maria. Our quarters are not fancy, but I'm sure the nuns would welcome you in their dormitory if you ever wished to come and spend a few days with Nino."

"That would be wonderful. And don't let this dress and my jewelry deceive you. I don't need fancy things. I grew up the daughter of poor Italian immigrants. I think I would feel right at home here. If I stayed for a few days, you might not get rid of me," Maria said as her tears turned into a grin.

While using the handkerchief to wipe her eyes, she added, "This is one of the most difficult days of my life. I feel ill. But I have tried to stay strong for Nino, even though I feel as if I am abandoning my precious child."

Fr. Doyle leaned back in his chair, gripping the ends of the armrests. "No Maria, you are not abandoning Nino. Your husband has presented you with an impossible situation, and you are doing what is best for your family, especially Nino. I know I am speaking out of turn, so forgive me, but I believe your husband is a scoundrel. Any father who would remove his child from his own home for telling the truth to the police is not fit to have a child."

"Salvador loves his boys, both Nino and Angelo, in his own way."

"My point is, if Nino is as wonderful as Msgr. Nunzio says he is, it is clearly because of you, and you alone." Rising from his chair, he said, "Let me give you a tour. I'll show you Nino's dorm room, then the dining hall, and of course, the school itself. Follow me please."

*

Upon completion of the visit, Fr. Doyle escorted Maria to the front of the building where they exited the same double doors she had first entered.

While standing on the top step, Maria scanned the dozens of boys in the courtyard, and said to Fr. Doyle, "Let me say goodbye to Nino. This will be heartbreaking for me."

Initially, she couldn't spot him. Then she heard the unmistakable sound of Nino's laughter. She glanced to her left and halfway down the stairs, there was Nino. He was sitting with Clarence. They were both smiling.

1937

CHAPTER 6

"Nino, you grow taller every time I see you. You are maturing into an impressive young man."

"Thank you, Msgr. Nunzio. My mother has had to bring me a new set of clothes every few months because I outgrow them. Sometimes I wear the hand-me-downs from the older boys here at the school, and I give mine to the younger boys in the grades behind me. It's the shoes that are the problem. Nobody wants to wear someone else's worn-out shoes."

"Don't let that stop you. Just keep growing."

"I will, Monsignor."

"Let's step into the office, Nino. I want you to fill me in on how things have been going."

Nino had been meeting with Msgr. Nunzio regularly since arriving at Saint Michael's three years earlier. At first, Maria visited every week, yet over time, her visits became less frequent as Nino adjusted to his surroundings. Angelo had visited once—long enough to complain that there weren't any girls around—and his father hadn't seen or spoken to Nino since the day he left the family apartment for the last time.

"Have a seat, Nino," Msgr. Nunzio said.

Nino sat in the same wooden chair he always sat in for their visits. The firm surface was uncomfortable and it wobbled because the left front leg was shorter than the others. Visiting priests used the sparse office to spend time with the boys from their local parishes. The room offered the bare necessities: a scratched wooden desk with a ripped cloth chair for Msgr. Nunzio, an empty filing cabinet, and Nino's wooden chair. The room smelled of mold, and the windows had cobwebs.

"So, how is life treating you, Nino? Fr. Doyle says you continue to be at the top of your class. You are excelling in Latin, he tells me."

"I love Latin. It is the root of all of the Romance languages."

"He says you spend several hours each week tutoring some of the boys who are failing, and your efforts are paying off with many of them."

"I like to learn. I have a thirst for knowledge, and I hate to see others struggle when I know I can help them."

"I am proud of you, Nino. And I know your mother is, too."

Nervously shifting in his chair, Nino said, "Monsignor, I was hoping you could help me. I don't like asking for money, but I need some."

Tilting his head to the side, the monsignor said, "Oh, and what do you need this money for?"

"On Saturdays, I gather a group of boys together and we travel into the city to help at one of the local soup kitchens. They are short on supplies. They operate in a little shack, their stove seldom works, and we always run out of food before everyone is fed. Mama has sent me money, but she can only do so much with the allowance Papa gives her. I was hoping you could arrange for the diocese to contribute. Anything would help."

Msgr. Nunzio laughed. "That is the money you hesitated to ask me for? You need it to help a soup kitchen? Nino, your kind heart never ceases to surprise me. To answer your question, yes, I believe I could persuade the diocese to contribute a little something to your cause."

"Thank you, Monsignor, I knew I could count on you."

Sitting up in his chair, Nino said, "There is something else I would like to discuss with you."

"And what might that be?"

"Since entering Saint Michael's, I have changed. When I first arrived, I was homesick and scared. I had a lot of regret for disappointing my papa. Yet, over time, all of that passed. I feel at peace. I feel at peace because every day I feel like I am growing closer to God. I feel like He is talking to me. Like He is always by my side."

"That is wonderful, Nino. It is a precious thing when a young man opens his heart to the Holy Spirit. I remember when that began to happen for me."

"It is more than just that, Monsignor. I feel like God is calling me. I feel like He is calling me to help others, just as you have helped me and the other members of your parish."

"And what direction is God leading you? How does He want you to serve others?"

"I believe He wants me to become a priest. I want to become a priest like you and Fr. Doyle. I have always received pleasure from helping other people. God tends to direct me to those who are less fortunate. Once I find them, a determination to help them overcomes me. When I can do so, my heart becomes filled with happiness. It is as though God is telling me, 'Well done, Nino. I am proud of you.' Monsignor, that is why I don't just *want* to become a priest, but I feel I *need* to become a priest. Nothing has ever been made clearer to me."

"As I have told you many times, Nino. You are truly an exceptional young man. I feel comfortable telling you that because it never goes to your head. You always remain humble."

"Thank you, Monsignor, but aren't all servants of God humble?"

Msgr. Nunzio grinned. "In theory yes, but—"

The monsignor shook his head and stopped himself before setting off into a diatribe.

"This is an incredible decision for a young man of seventeen. It is not to be taken lightly. There are many sacrifices that one must make to become a priest. Have you thought all of them through?"

"I know that there are things I must do. There are many years of study for one thing."

"Yes, there is that. You will need to get a four-year degree, followed by seminary school. I can certainly help you with all of that. I have connections at the highest levels of the Catholic Church—even the Vatican. But it isn't your education that I am referring to. You have always been a brilliant student, and the academics won't be a challenge for you. What I am referring to, Nino, is your family life. Becoming a priest means sacrificing the opportunity to have a wife and children. Have you thought that through, Nino?"

"Yes, Monsignor, I have. I don't discard those things lightly.

But I don't think that a family would leave me as fulfilled as serving God directly through the Church."

The room fell silent. Nino watched as Msgr. Nunzio leaned back in his chair and folded his arms across his chest, never taking his eyes from Nino. That look was familiar. It was a look of premeditation. The priest was both precise and frugal with his words, particularly when those words had significant consequences.

"Okay, Nino. Here is what we will do. You have another year before you graduate and are ready to move on to the next step of your life. We will revisit this in two months when I return. Between now and then, I want you to be deep in prayer, asking for God's guidance. I will do the same. If, when I return, you are still of this mindset, I will write to my connections in Rome. Fr. Doyle and I both received our entire education in the ancient city. First our undergraduate studies, then our seminary education. There would be no better way to begin your career than by immersing yourself deep in the location of the genesis of Catholicism. It would be an experience like no other. The New York diocese even has a scholarship program. You would be a perfect candidate."

A grin appeared on Nino's face, "The thought of living and studying in Rome excites me. I wish I could leave today."

"In due time, my son. It will arrive before you know it."

*

Nino watched the heavy snowfall as he gingerly made his way down the icy steps.

"Mama!" he yelled before arriving at the taxi and greeting her with a kiss.

"Oh, Nino, my darling. It is so good to see you," Maria said before she paid the taxi driver.

Nino picked up her two large bags.

"You always bring enough clothes for a month, even though you only stay a few days."

"You would think I would learn by now. Your papa expects me to always look my best in public. After a few days of rooming with the nuns, I become rather humbled and wish I had something more unrefined to wear."

"Do you own anything unrefined?"

Maria laughed. "No, I guess I don't. Your papa wouldn't tolerate that."

Nino said, "This wind is bitter cold. Let's get inside. I'm anxious to share some news with you. We'll take your bags to the nun's quarters, then we can go to the library. I have a favorite spot in the corner where I study. It is quiet and near the fireplace."

The library was the showcase of an otherwise unimpressive Saint Michael's. Fr. Doyle believed that education was the way out of poverty, and much of the donation money received by the school went to buying books and making the library an inviting sanctuary for the boys.

Nino's corner, as it came to be known by the younger students he tutored, had two high-back chairs and a round desk, which was tucked into a bay window. A few feet away was a fireplace Maria took comfort from as she watched the white blanket of snow fall pristinely outside.

"This is a lovely little corner of the world, Nino. I see why you like to immerse yourself in your studies."

"Mama, I am so glad you came. I have such wonderful news,

and Msgr. Nunzio just finalized the arrangements for me this week."

"Arrangements for what?"

"I have been giving my life a lot of thought. I don't think that Papa will ever want to see me again. He is a prideful man who believes I betrayed him, and I have accepted that."

Before Nino could continue, Maria interrupted him. "That's not true. Your father loves you."

Nino asked, "Since I moved away three years ago, and you have been coming here to visit me, has he ever once asked about me? Does he ever inquire about how I am doing?"

Maria looked down. A moment of stillness lingered.

"Whenever I tell him about you, he never tells me to stop."

"That's different. What I mean is, has he ever referred to me in a conversation. Have you heard him even speak my name since I moved away?"

"I won't lie to you. Your father hasn't spoken your name since you walked out of the apartment for the last time."

Nino placed his hand on hers. "It's okay, Mama. That is what I suspected, and I am fine with that. I have moved on from Papa. Having that information is more confirmation that my decisions are correct."

"What decisions do you mean?"

"There are two. Let me explain. In just a few months, I will graduate from Saint Michael's. After that, I will be moving to Rome. I am going there to study to become a priest. I have many years of study and I don't want to waste any time, so I have enrolled in the summer session."

"You are leaving me? You are moving to Rome?"

Maria pulled a handkerchief from a small cloth purse and patted her eyes.

"It won't be forever, Mama. It's just to study. It will only be a few years. Then I'll come back to New York. I promise."

"Nino, I am so proud of you. You are such a loving young man, and you have always been so kind, and you love God with all your heart. It doesn't surprise me that you feel called to become a priest. But it takes many years. Why must you travel to Rome for your studies? Why can't you study here in America? In New York, so I can continue to see you."

"Because Msgr. Nunzio and Fr. Doyle have both told me that there is something special about studying in Rome. Monsignor has even arranged for me to receive a scholarship. I love you, Mama, and yes, I will miss you, too, but I feel that this is what I must do."

"But what about children? I was looking forward to having grandchildren. Are you going to deny me that?"

"Angelo can provide you with grandchildren. You won't miss out on that experience."

"Angelo chases more whores than your papa. He may have already provided me with a grandchild but is afraid to tell me he has produced a bastard. I wouldn't be surprised if your father has a few himself. That's why I have been counting on you. Angelo and your father live in their own world that I am not part of. You are my world, Nino. I will miss you so," Maria said as she wept uncontrollably.

Nino knelt beside his mother and embraced her.

"We will see each other, Mama. I will come home for Christmas, and you can come visit me in Rome. You have relatives in Italy. I'm sure they would love to see you."

"They know nothing of me. They have no desire to see

someone they know nothing about. Besides, there is much turmoil in Europe right now. Have you read the papers? I overheard two women in the dress shop recently. They said their families are scared. Many are moving to America to escape the rise of fascism."

"Much of that is hearsay. It is not good to listen to gossip. If those things are true, the little bit I have read said that it is simply German politics. That's not Italy. And much of my time in Rome will be spent at the Vatican, which is its own country entirely. I will be safe, Mama. And you will be, too, when you come visit."

Nino stood and returned to his chair.

Maria said, "You said there are two things you wanted to tell me. I hope the second isn't as heartbreaking as the first."

"Mama, when I was young, I had no friends my own age because my last name was DiVincenzo. Adults would stop talking to me and walk away once they found out who my papa was. The last name DiVincenzo has only brought pain for me—it has been a curse. And I haven't been the son of Salvador DiVincenzo since the day he made me leave his home. My only father is God. My two greatest loves in this world are God and you, Mama. You were the one who taught me about my Father in heaven. You showed me his love each day with your actions. During my darkest moments when I was the loneliest, you became my friend—my absolute best friend in the world. I will always be grateful to you. Because of that, I am taking your family's last name. I am legally changing my name from Nino DiVincenzo to Nino Servidei—your maiden name. I'm doing so first to honor you, but also to honor God."

Nino grabbed a notebook and pencil from the desk and began to write.

"You see, Mama, in Latin, the word *servei* means servant. The word *Dei* refers to God. So, I believe that centuries ago, when one of your ancestors first began referring to themselves as Servidei, they were announcing to the world that they were a servant of God. That is how I want to live my life. I want to live my life by serving God. It only makes sense that I take your maiden name so I can honor you and God at the same time. From this day forward, nobody I meet will ever know my last name was once DiVincenzo."

Maria said, "I don't know what to say. Your papa will not be pleased, and—"

"I don't care what Papa thinks. I doubt he will even care. In his mind, I don't exist."

"That's not true. I have your picture on my dresser. I catch him looking at it sometimes. When I walk in the room, he looks the other way hoping I don't notice, but I do. He thinks of you, Nino. I know he does."

There was a pause.

"Nino, I am so glad we have each other. My love for you has no bounds, and the fact that you are honoring me by taking my family's last name fills my heart with joy. I only wish you could have met my papa. He died so young. He would have loved you so."

"At least I met Grandma Servidei before she died."

Standing, Nino presented his arm to his mother and said, "I'm hungry. Let us go see what kind of slop the boys in the kitchen crew cooked up today."

Maria stood, put her arm through Nino's, and they made their way out of the library.

1938

CHAPTER 7

BRONX, NEW YORK
FORDHAM TRAIN STATION

"Nino's train is late, Mama," Angelo said. "I can't stay here all day. Papa is expecting me. We have a meeting with the dockworkers."

Maria said, "You haven't seen your brother in over three years. Just wait."

"Papa didn't want me to come. Now I will be late because we are waiting here for Nino. I'll catch hell."

"If you wish to go, then go. Take the car. I will find my way back home. I'll take a bus or a taxi. Just stop your complaining."

"That's a good idea, Mama. Tell Nino I'm sorry I couldn't stay. Let him know Papa was expecting me. He'll understand."

Angelo gave his mother a kiss on her cheek, then ran through the train station to the waiting car. Maria watched him leave in disgust, disturbed that Angelo had morphed into the same selfish rogue his father had always been. She redirected her attention past the dozens of people on the platform. She studied the empty track over the horizon, awaiting Nino's arrival.

"There it is!" shouted a voice behind her.

Maria watched as the train expelled black smoke into the

89

air. Her excitement increased as the distance between the train and the platform diminished. Steam spewed from under the train as its brakes were applied, and the locomotive decelerated before coming to a halt next to the platform.

After it stopped, Maria shuffled from side to side, stealing glimpses through the crowd in an attempt to find Nino exiting one of the railroad cars.

When she saw him, he wasn't alone. A young girl about his age was with him, and he was carrying her bags, as well as his lone suitcase.

As they approached, Nino set the bags down and embraced and kissed his mother.

"Mama, I would like to introduce you to Katie Keene. We met on the train. She is coming to New York from St. Louis, where she has been away at school. Speaking to her on the train made the ride go by quickly."

"How do you do, Katie. I'm Maria."

"It is nice to meet you, ma'am," Katie said as she bowed her head.

Nino asked Katie, "Do you see your father?"

"There he is. He is looking for me," she said before shouting and waving. "I'm over here, Papa."

After he arrived, Katie said, "Papa I want you to meet this nice boy I met on the train. His name is Nino Servidei. He is going to Rome to study to be a priest. And this is his mother, Maria."

The man tipped his hat and said, "Good afternoon, Mrs. Servidei. Thank you, Nino, for keeping Katie company on the train. If she had to travel with a handsome young man, I'm glad that handsome young man aspires to be a priest."

Katie slapped his arm and said, "Oh Papa, you are embarrassing me."

"We need to go, Katie. Linda, Wanda, and your mama are home preparing dinner for you. And Michael just got home from college."

Katie stepped away with her father, but looking back she said, "I enjoyed talking to you, Nino. Thank you for sitting with me. Good luck in Rome. I hope everything works out splendidly."

"Thank you, Katie," Nino said as he waved goodbye. He watched her disappear into the crowd and was saddened he would never see her again.

Maria grabbed his hand. "Katie is a pretty girl. What did you two talk about?"

"She talked about school. She is studying to be a teacher."

"It is so good to see you, Nino. You are finally taller than I am."

"It appears I am, Mama. I will never be a large man, but at least I am now taller than the average girl I meet, even though I haven't met too many."

"You look very handsome."

"I'm sorry that my new name caused Katie's papa to refer to you as Mrs. Servidei. That must have felt odd for you."

"It actually sounded rather pleasant. That was my last name for many years."

Nino picked up his bag, and they strolled down the platform.

"Nino, it breaks my heart to tell you this, but you must find someplace other than our apartment to stay. Your papa—"

Nino interrupted her. "Msgr. Nunzio has already found a place for me to live until I leave for Rome."

CHAPTER 8

She was breathtaking. Each of her movements was more alluring than the last.

She wore a gray wool waistcoat and matching skirt that draped just above her ankles. He was uncertain of the length of her sandy-blond hair as she had much of it under a sizable hat, the brim of which blocked her face when she turned her head away. What he could glimpse of it was as stunning as the rest of her. Nino couldn't see her eyes, for he looked away when she glanced in his direction. She rested on her steamer trunk, causing the hem of her skirt to rise halfway up her shin, exposing black lace stockings. With her left hand, which was absent a diamond ring, she guided a red-lipstick-stained cigarette to her mouth. The only jewelry he noticed was a white pearl necklace and a broach pinned to her jacket—possibly a cameo, but it was difficult to see from a distance. He guessed that she was a decade older than his eighteen years—more, perhaps.

Had he seen her before? In a magazine or motion picture? Nino had only watched two films recently—*All Quiet on the Western Front* and *King Kong*—and she was even more beautiful than its star Fay Wray.

Is she traveling alone or waiting for someone?

After the steam whistle on the SS *Vulcania* blew, Nino returned his focus to his immediate surroundings. He had been waiting nearly an hour, the woman even longer. He adjusted his tie and brushed from his black suit the hints of coal dust which had spewed from the ocean liner he was about to board.

As the departure time neared, the number of dockworkers speeding around passengers multiplied, a sense of urgency ignited them. As hundreds of awaiting passengers pulled their boarding passes from their coats and bags, Nino noticed most of them were embracing and kissing their loved ones. Yet the woman remained alone, seated on her trunk, smoking her second cigarette.

He turned and looked toward the dock entrance.

Where is Mama? I can't leave without saying goodbye. It may be years before I see her again.

Nino saw them in the distance. They were standing on tiptoe, scanning the crowd.

Nino jumped up and down, waving, and hoping the woman he had been admiring wouldn't notice his unsophisticated and juvenile behavior.

"There he is," Maria shouted.

Angelo astonished Nino by wearing a pinstripe suit, however it was no surprise to see his mama dressed every bit as sharp as the beautiful woman on the dock he had been worshipping from afar.

"We are sorry we are late, Nino. I wanted Angelo here, too, and at the last moment, your father made him make a delivery to a warehouse this morning."

"That's okay. You are here now," Nino said as they embraced, and he kissed her cheek.

Reaching out to shake Nino's hand, Angelo said, "Mama said you changed your last name to her parents name—Servidei. What the hell, Nino? That takes a lot of balls to slap Papa around."

"Your papa doesn't know yet, Nino," Maria said. "I haven't told him about your name change, and Angelo knows better than to tell him."

"I don't care if he knows," Nino said. "I want him to know."

"You shouldn't resent your father so much that you want to hurt him like that."

"That's not the only reason I did it, Mama. I explained that before."

Angelo said, "So, this is it, little brother. You're off to Rome to become a priest."

"It will be a long time before I'm a man of the cloth. I have many years of study."

"Don't come home until you can wear that white collar thing around your neck. I want to show you off as my brother, the man who works directly for God."

"It's called a Roman collar," Nino said.

"Whatever it's called, it will look good wrapped around that puny neck of yours."

"I think you meant that as a complement, so that's how I'll take it."

The steam whistle, which had blown twice since Maria and Angelo arrived at the dock, blew a third time.

"I guess this is goodbye for now," Nino said while embracing his mother. Her tears moistened the shoulder of his jacket.

Nino reached to shake Angelo's hand. Angelo grabbed it and pulled Nino tight, whispering in his ear so their mother couldn't hear, "Look, little brother. We haven't been together much over the past few years, but I think I know you well enough to know that you are probably still a virgin. Promise me that before you get to Rome and sign away your sex life, you find yourself a girl and give it a go."

As Angelo slipped a few dollars into Nino's jacket pocket, he whispered, "Go to a whorehouse in Naples before you hop on the train to Rome. The experience may change your mind about all of that priest bullshit you have in your head."

Nino pulled away as they both laughed.

Nino said, "Angelo, you haven't changed a bit."

"I never will, little brother. I am our papa's son, and you are our mama's."

Maria, while wiping her tears, said, "What on earth are you two talking about?"

"Angelo is just being Angelo."

Nino gave his mother one last kiss and embrace before grabbing his suitcase and turning toward the gangway.

Maria raised her voice so Nino could hear her over the crowd, "Wait, Nino. I almost forgot."

Nino paused and Maria approached him, reaching into her purse to pull out a cloth bag with a string. It was lavender, and small enough to hold in the palm of her hand.

"I want you to have my rosary."

"But Mama, this belonged to your mother. You cherish this."

"I cherish you more, Nino. It will protect you and keep you safe."

"Thank you, Mama. I will always have it with me. It will remind me of you."

Reaching back into her purse, she said, "You will need this, too."

She gave him an envelope stuffed with cash—large bills.

"There is a lot of money in here. I know Papa didn't give this to you so you could just turn around and hand it to me."

"Yes he did. He just doesn't know it. When you get on the ship, promise me you will use part of it to upgrade your cabin. It is too long of a voyage to be stuck in steerage the entire time. Exchange what remains for Italian lire. Be careful. Don't let them cheat you."

"I won't."

"Write to me. I want to know all about your new life. Let me know if you need more money. I'll wire it to you."

"Thank you for always looking out for me, Mama."

As Nino turned toward the ship, he looked for the woman. She had moved on.

It's time to focus on God.

Nino made his way past several pallets of steamer trunks waiting in the queue for the crane to hoist them onto the SS *Vulcania*. The mass of passengers stood at the end of the gangway leading up to the ocean liner. They formed a bottleneck, causing him to stop. With his heavy suitcase in his hand and Mama's envelope in his breast pocket, he glanced up at the massive vessel that would carry him across the Atlantic Ocean. Then he saw her.

She had already boarded and was standing on the main deck. Both of her hands rested on the railing as she looked out over the crowd. The only thing separating her from Nino was the water between the ship and the dock.

Is she staring at me? That can't be. Something else must have caught her attention.

*

As his mother suggested, Nino used some of the money she had given him to upgrade from steerage to third class. When he entered his cabin, it smelled of fresh paint. The bulkheads appeared to have recently received a fresh coat of white. He laid his suitcase on the lower bunk, removed his Bible, and laid it on the wooden desk in the corner.

The door opened, and in walked an older gentleman of considerable girth. His suit was soiled with dirt, his collar moist from perspiration. He emitted an odor matched only by the fresh coat of paint. With him he carried a suitcase twice the size of Nino's.

"Young man, I'm pleased to make your acquaintance. My name is J. Howard Kruger. Please call me Howard. I hate to make a request upon our first encounter, but would it trouble you to give me the bottom bunk? As you can see by my size, climbing into the top bunk may be unpleasant for both of us."

"My name is Nino Servidei. I will happily sleep in the top bunk. Let me move my suitcase out of your way."

Mr. Kruger said, "Do you know where the lavatory is? It has been a long day. I traveled by train from Albany. I just arrived in time to board. I want to unpack, get cleaned up, and crawl into bed."

"The lavatory is down the passageway and to the left."

"Are you traveling alone, Nino?"

"Yes."

"You are fortunate. I am with my pretentious brother and

his wife. He's in oil and has made it big. I'm supposed to join them as their guest in the first-class dining hall this evening. That is another reason why I'm just going to go to bed."

"Won't they miss you if you don't show up?"

"I'll explain it to them in the morning."

The cabin had just enough room for Nino to step around Mr. Kruger. As Nino grabbed the doorknob to exit, Mr. Kruger said, "What are your plans for dinner?"

"I was on my way to find out where the third-class dining room was."

"How would you like to eat dinner in the first-class dining hall this evening? As my brother's guest, of course."

"He won't mind?"

"He may, but I doubt it. It will give him the opportunity to tell someone new about how successful he is."

"I don't have a dinner jacket."

"Neither do I. I've never owned one. They strangle me. You are dressed fine."

After reaching into his breast pocket, Mr. Kruger pulled out a formal invitation. "Here, take this. Enjoy yourself. The food in first class is exquisite."

*

Nino had gone to the lavatory, washed his face, dusted off his suit, and straightened his tie, yet as he entered the dining hall, he felt underdressed. With few exceptions, every man wore a dinner jacket and each woman a formal gown.

He stood at the entrance and scanned the room. Although opulent, it was no more impressive than his boyhood apartment in Hoffman Towers.

"May I help you?" asked the chief steward.

Nino reached into his jacket pocket. "I have an invitation."

After glancing at the card, the man said, "Follow me please."

Nino trailed behind him as they weaved between the tables and toward their destination in the corner. Occupying two of the four seats were a broad-shouldered gray-haired woman and a gentleman with the same size and facial features as his cabin mate, J. Howard Kruger.

"You will be dining here, sir," the chief steward said as he rested his hand on the back of one of the two remaining open chairs.

The tablecloth was white, and the center had a small vase holding paper flowers.

His seat faced the bulkhead, his back was to the other tables.

The large man stood. "My name is Augustus Kruger, and this is my wife, Beatrice."

"It is my pleasure to meet you both," Nino said.

"We were curious as to who our fourth dinner companion would be. My brother will be arriving shortly."

"Mr. Kruger, your brother is my cabinmate. He felt the need to rest and has provided me with the invitation you arranged for him. I hope it is satisfactory for me to dine with you this evening."

Beatrice Kruger shook her head. "Your brother is incorrigible, Augustus. Why does he always do these things?"

Nino said, "If you prefer, I can dine in the third-class dining room."

"We won't hear of it," Mr. Kruger said. "You are welcome to join us. Please have a seat."

After Nino sat, Mr. Kruger said, "What takes you to Italy, Nino? Will you be staying in Naples?"

"No sir. I am headed to Rome to study."

"What will you be studying?"

"First, I will study philosophy at the University of Rome. Then, my plan is to enter the seminary at the *Pontificio Collegio Etiopico* at the Vatican. I hope to one day be a priest."

"Oh, my! A priest," Mrs. Kruger said while shaking her head and cupping her hands over her face.

"Does that unsettle you?" Nino asked.

"Please forgive my wife. She comes from an extensive line of Protestant blood. Catholics and Protestants have a history of tension."

"I know of the history," Nino said. "After three hundred years, I am hopeful we can get past that?"

"I'm sure we can," Mr. Kruger said, while grimacing at his wife.

"Are you from New York, Nino?"

"I grew up in the Bronx."

"We are from Oklahoma," Mr. Kruger said. "Our train arrived two days ago."

Mrs. Kruger said, "We haven't seen Howard in almost a year, yet he shunned our dinner invitation."

"*Buona serata,*" their waiter announced, arriving tableside. "My name is Umberto. It will be my pleasure to serve you this evening."

Addressing Nino, "Will your companion be arriving, sir?"

"I'm traveling alone. I'm uncertain who this person is."

"That is fine. I will bring you coffee unless you would prefer something else."

Augustus Kruger said, "My wife would like a glass of red wine, and I will have a scotch. Make it your finest."

"Of course, sir." The waiter addressed Nino, "And you, sir?"

"I would like a glass of cool water."

"Of course."

Mrs. Kruger said, "I don't know who our other dinner companion is, but it is rather rude to be late."

"Maybe they won't be joining us," Nino said.

Augustus Kruger was an executive with an independent oil refining company in Oklahoma. Their largest client was Texaco. Mr. Kruger made it a point to tell Nino that he had closed that deal himself. As Mr. Kruger went on to discuss other deals he had made, Nino found himself regretting accepting Howard's invitation. Nino struggled to keep his eyes open when he heard Mr. Kruger say, "Had it not been for me, the entire company would have —"

Mr. Kruger stopped mid-sentence while looking over Nino's shoulder. Mrs. Kruger noticed her husband's sudden distraction and turned her head, too. She appeared perturbed.

Nino followed their lead, twisting in his chair so he could see what caught their eye. It was her. The woman on the dock. She was wearing a long blue gown that embraced the contour of her slim figure. Like Mr. Kruger's wife, her white gloves extended to her elbows. Unlike on the dock, she wore no hat and her long, sandy-blond hair rested on her shoulders. It was a stark contrast to her brilliant red lipstick.

After glancing at her card, the chief steward led her toward their table.

Nino watched as she followed, weaving around tables while other men in the room attempted to disguise their glances — most failed — leaving their own wives as perturbed as Mrs. Kruger. The woman was ravishing, even more so than earlier in the day.

When they approached, Nino rose first, then Mr. Kruger. Mrs. Kruger remained seated. The steward held her chair while she sat. The table was silent. They watched her unfold the linen napkin and place it across her lap.

Mr. Kruger spoke first, "Good evening, madam, I'm Mr. Augustus Kruger, and this is my wife, Beatrice.

"How do you do. I'm Hannah Roseman," she said with a nod.

She then turned to Nino, who hadn't taken his eyes off her since she entered the room. He stared at her with a childlike enchantment.

"Good evening, I'm Hannah Roseman."

"Ah, good evening, um, I'm Nino DiVin—I'm Nino Servidei."

"It is a pleasure to meet you, Mr. Servidei," Hannah said with a playful grin.

Her voice is like velvet, Nino thought, before saying, "It is a pleasure to meet you, too."

As she turned her head to speak to the Krugers, Nino realized she found his nervousness amusing. Even as she spoke to the Krugers, she continued to glance at him, alternating between grins and giggles. As far as Nino was concerned, the Krugers were no longer at the table. It was only he and Hannah Roseman. He heard her ask them questions yet had no interest in their response.

Hannah pushed the hair away from her face, exposing her left ear and a cameo earring. It matched the broach pinned to her gown.

Even her ear is beautiful.

Hannah, still looking toward the Krugers, had a puzzled look on her face. Nino turned to see Mrs. Kruger whispering to her husband who glanced at Hannah then to Nino.

The conversation stopped and they smirked at her.

Mrs. Kruger said, "Are you traveling unaccompanied, Miss Roseman?"

"I often travel alone. My husband is deceased. If I don't travel alone, I would never travel."

"Isn't it a little unheard of for a young lady so ... attractive to travel by herself?" asked Mrs. Kruger.

"I appreciate the compliment, madam, but why should my appearance have anything to do with my travel plans? If I wish to be someplace, I simply go."

"Forgive my wife, madam. She can be rather outspoken."

Mrs. Kruger said, "Augustus, you need not apologize on my behalf. I just believe that it is entirely inappropriate for a young lady to make a voyage across the ocean by herself."

"And how else might I travel, madam?" Hannah asked.

"With a man at your side, of course. If not your husband, then your father or your brother ... or somebody."

Hannah chuckled and looked to Nino. "Mr. Servidei, to satisfy Mrs. Kruger's eighteenth-century view of oppressive female travel etiquette, will you please accompany me for the remainder of our voyage?"

Nino's eyes darted between his three tablemates, unaware of what to say.

Nino turned red, looked to Hannah, and mumbled, "Um, yes, of course. Ah, I would be delighted."

Mrs. Kruger glanced at them both and clenched her teeth, then turned her nose to the ceiling and appeared to be fighting the urge to say something.

Nino squirmed in his chair.

When is the waiter going to come and take our order?

After a period of uncomfortable silence, Mr. Kruger said to Hannah, "The papers have reported that Europe is not a welcoming place for Jews these days. Are you concerned?"

"I am well aware of the atmosphere in Europe, sir. My deceased husband's family lives in Italy. I am traveling to stay with them for a while, maybe permanently."

Mrs. Kruger asked with a sneer, "And what have they been telling you?"

"About what, Mrs. Kruger? About the torment of European Jews? I hate to disappoint you, madam, but Jews are surviving fine in Italy. My late husband's family owns a business, and it has never done better."

"My wife wasn't taking delight in your potential misfortune."

"No, of course not," Hannah said with a direct stare at Mrs. Kruger.

Nino, now hiding behind his menu, said, "What will everyone be having for dinner?"

Mrs. Kruger peered across the table at Hannah. "I'll be having pork. And you, Miss Roseman? Will you be having the pork?"

Hannah dropped her menu and stared directly into the eyes of Mrs. Kruger. "No, I will not. As I'm sure you are aware, Jews don't eat pork. And besides, my observation has been that women who eat pork tend to be rather unhealthy looking. Thick around the middle some might say. Take yourself for example."

"Oh, my word. Augustus, tell the chief steward that we would like a different table."

"I'll do no such thing, Beatrice. You need to sit here and

behave yourself and stop antagonizing Miss Roseman. You are making a scene."

"You *know* I can make a scene and this isn't one yet. But unless you get us moved to a different table, I will make a scene that no one in here will soon forget. I refuse to sit at the same table with a boy studying to become a Catholic priest while he escorts a Jewess hussy several years his senior."

"At least we know what your true feelings are, don't we, Mrs. Kruger?" Hannah said.

Nino said, "Mr. Kruger, I think it would be best if Miss Roseman and I found a different table."

"No, Mr. Servidei. We aren't going anywhere," Hannah said.

"Augustus!" Mrs. Kruger said.

Mr. Kruger threw his napkin on the table and stood. "Oh, all right, Beatrice. Sometimes your blue-blooded Protestant vanity is too prideful for your own good." Looking to Hannah then Nino, he said, "If you'll excuse me," and left the table.

The table remained silent as Nino, Hannah, and Mrs. Kruger sat uncomfortably for several minutes. Mrs. Kruger stared daggers at her two tablemates, then broke the tension by rising from her seat, pivoting, and crossing the dining room with her nose in the air. Mr. Kruger watched her approach him with a look of disgust.

Hannah said, "Please forgive me, Mr. Servidei. I'm usually not impolite like that. I don't know what came over me."

"Don't apologize. She was disrespectful toward you, Miss Roseman."

"She was disrespectful toward you, too, but you didn't respond as reprehensibly as I did. And please, call me Hannah."

"And I would prefer if you called me Nino."

The waiter approached with their drinks.

He set Mrs. Kruger's wine at her place setting, followed by Mr. Kruger's scotch, and then gave Nino his water.

Looking to Hannah, the waiter asked, "What may I bring you to drink, signora?"

Hannah pointed at Mr. Kruger's drink. "What was he having?"

"He ordered a Scotch whisky."

"Just give me his drink. He won't be returning."

The waiter looked to Nino.

"The lady is correct. They will not be returning."

Hannah asked, "Would you also like a scotch, Nino, or do you just want to share this one with me?"

"I think I will stick with water for now."

Addressing the waiter, Hannah said, "At least give him the lady's glass of wine, will you?"

The waiter picked up Mrs. Kruger's wine glass and placed it in front of Nino before stepping away from their table.

Hannah said, "I'm so glad that silly prohibition ended. It was dreadful having to drink in hiding. Don't you agree, Nino?"

"I was too young to—" Nino cut himself off, not wanting to emphasize his youth. "I meant to say, I didn't start drinking wine until recently. And then, only at communion."

"Oh, that's right. When Mrs. Kruger stormed off, she said something about you studying to be a priest. Where are you attending school?"

"In Rome."

"Have you begun your studies yet?"

"No. I won't start until next month."

"So, you aren't officially a man of the cloth, as they say."

"No."

"As Mrs. Kruger made abundantly clear, I am a Jew. I know little of the Catholic faith. However, one thing I'm perplexed by is the vow of celibacy. Is that really mandatory or just a suggestion?"

Nino grinned at Hannah's naivete. "No, it's mandatory."

"So, you're telling me once you become a priest you can't, you know, be with a woman?"

"No."

"Never, ever?"

"Never, ever," replied Nino.

"How dreadful," Hannah said as she reached into her handbag and removed a gold-plated cigarette case.

Nino took a sip of wine.

"How old are you, Nino?" Hannah asked, offering him a cigarette.

"I'm eighteen," Nino said, waving away the cigarette case.

"You are so young. Why would you want to become a priest and give up everything? The Catholic Church will constrain you for your entire life. No wife and no children. Do you really want to live a life with no children, Nino? That would mean that one day when you are gone, there will be no part of you remaining on this earth."

"I don't view it like that. I am giving my life to God. By serving in the Catholic Church, I will help others get through life's difficulties, and that will be my legacy. The lives of other people will be better because of me. The people I help will have children. They will carry on my memory."

"That is admirable. And if it makes you feel better, I guess that's another way of looking at it.

"Nino, I hope you aren't offended. I just view the world differently. By heritage, I am a Jew. I even believe in God sometimes. Nobody has proven there isn't a God, but nobody has proven there is. Life is short. We need to live it to its fullest and have fun."

"Do you mind if we talk about something else?" Nino asked.

"You're right. Politics and religion are taboo subjects at dinner, aren't they?"

"May I ask you a few questions, Hannah? I find the lives of other people interesting."

"What do you want to know?"

"How did your husband die?"

Hannah took a deep breath and looked to the ceiling.

"Camillo died in Palermo four years ago when he was visiting his family's cameo store in Sicily. He'd used one of his father's boats to travel there from Torre del Greco. When he started the engine to return home, it exploded. The police said there was an electrical malfunction. Camillo's brother, Manuel, believes differently. He's mentioned someone by the name of Omar who Camillo had a run-in with shortly before the explosion. He thinks this Omar person somehow set a charge in the boat."

"Do you agree with Manuel?"

"I'm uncertain. However, shortly after Camillo's death, I received a letter from Manuel. The letter simply said that Camillo's death had been avenged and that Omar was dead. We haven't discussed it since. I just miss Camillo. The past four years have been extraordinarily lonely. I have no other family; I was an only child and my parents are deceased."

"How did you meet Camillo?"

"He had moved to Chicago to expand the family's cameo business to America. I had been performing in a play that he'd gone to see, and I guess I caught his eye. We spent a little time together, fell in love, and were married shortly after—in Italy."

"What happened to the Chicago cameo store?"

"Camillo's brother and father came to America to close it. I had no experience running a business. There was nothing I could do to keep it open."

"What was he like? Camillo, I mean."

"In many ways, you remind me of a younger version of him. You share features. Like you, he had a kind, handsome face, and dark wavy hair. Although he didn't have your dimples," Hannah said with a smile.

"Thank you. Nobody has ever told me I was handsome. Other than my Mama, that is."

"I don't believe that, Nino. With those gorgeous eyes, you mean no pretty girl has ever looked into them and paid you a compliment?"

"I haven't been around too many girls. I grew up with my brother, I went to a boy's prep school in New York, then I lived at an all-boys home in Syracuse. However, I rode the train recently and sat next to a pretty girl. Her name was Katie. She giggled and laughed at me a lot, kind of like you have been doing this evening."

Hannah covered her mouth with her hand to hide her amusement, "Nino, you are so very charming."

Feeling uncomfortable, Nino changed the subject, "Do you have any children?"

Hannah looked down and wrapped her hand around Mr. Kruger's scotch. "No, I could never provide Camillo with a child. I have been pregnant twice. Neither made it full term. I lost the second after Camillo's death. The doctor believes it was the stress of the ordeal."

"I'm sorry I asked. I guess that was an inappropriate question."

Hannah reached over and laid her hand on top of Nino's. "No, it wasn't. There is no need to apologize."

The waiter arrived to take their order. "What may I serve you, signora?"

"I'll have the chicken," Hannah said.

"And for you, signore?"

"I would like the fish."

"By all means. Your glass is almost empty, signora. Would you like me to bring you another scotch?"

"Yes. And he would like another glass of wine."

"That won't be necessary. I'm feeling a little light-headed from the first one."

"Bring it anyway. He may change his mind."

"Si, signora," the waiter said before turning to the next table.

"Nino, after dinner, let's go up to the main deck and get some air."

Nino's heart raced. "I would like that very much."

Hannah slid her whisky glass across the table to Nino. "Here. Finish Mr. Kruger's scotch."

Nino reached for the glass and took a sip. His eyes squinted and his lips puckered before expelling a series of choking coughs.

Hannah laughed loud enough that the surrounding tables glanced in their direction.

"Can I assume that was your first sip of whisky, Nino?"

"Yes," he said with his hand over his mouth, afraid he may get ill.

With a grin, Hannah inhaled the smoke from her cigarette, then leaned her head back and blew it out.

"So tell me, is there anything else that the future Father Nino Servidei hasn't experienced that I can introduce you to?"

*

As he and Hannah stood at the railing, Nino gazed at the moon's reflection on the ocean.

"Was the woman you were saying goodbye to on the dock your mother?" Hannah asked.

"You noticed us?"

"I did. She's beautiful. And the other person—who was that?"

"My older brother, Angelo. He almost made her late. But it wasn't his fault. It was my papa's. I think he wanted them to miss saying goodbye to me."

"Why would he want that?"

"It's a long story. I'll explain it sometime."

"Your brother is rather fetching. He's almost as handsome as his little brother."

Nino smiled and watched as waves crashed against the hull of the massive vessel. The sound was a peaceful backdrop on an otherwise still evening.

"You like to embarrass me, don't you?" Nino said.

Hannah reached for Nino's hand. "Yes, I do. But that has nothing to do with the compliments I pay you. There is something about your innocence that I find irresistible."

Nino, not letting go of Hannah's hand, asked, "Would you like to walk?"

"That would be delightful," Hannah said, turning to stroll along the wooden deck.

Nino asked, "What will you do when you arrive in Italy? Will Camillo's family be waiting for you in Naples?"

"I'm not even certain I will be welcome."

"Why wouldn't you be welcome?"

"Because they barely know me. Our wedding was in Italy—Torre del Greco, where they own the cameo factory—and we spent a month there, but that was seven years ago. Other than when his brother and his father came to America to close the store, and a couple of letters here and there, I have had little contact with his family. I don't speak Italian. Camillo's brother Manuel and his wife Olivia speak English, but they live in Sicily. Camillo's parents only speak Italian. How will I communicate with them when I arrive?"

"Forgive me but I'm uncertain why you are going to be with them."

Hannah stopped and placed both hands on the railing.

"Because I'm financially destitute and have no place else to go."

"I would have never guessed that."

"Oh, I'm good at keeping up appearances, Nino. I'm just not that good with money. Camillo always handled that."

"When he died, his family was kind enough to leave me his inheritance. To me, it had seemed like an endless amount of money. I guess for most people, it would have been. I'd become used to a certain lifestyle when I was married to Camillo. I just assumed I could continue buying nice things even after he was gone and the money would always be there. I still spend too much. You would think I would learn. There are several department stores in Chicago that let me buy on credit. They will never find me in Italy. Everything I own is in my steamer trunk. I sold everything else just to buy the one-way ticket for this voyage."

"So, what you said to the Krugers at dinner about the family business being better than ever and Jews being safe in Italy was all made up?"

"I have no idea how their business is doing or what it's like to be a Jew in Italy."

"What happens if things don't work out with Camillo's family?"

"Let's not talk about such things anymore, Nino. Life is too grand, and here we are together."

Nino stepped back. "Hannah, I'm flattered you have spent this evening with me. You are the most beautiful woman I have ever seen, and I'm experiencing feelings today that I have never felt before. But it doesn't change the fact that in two weeks we will arrive in Naples and you will travel to Torre del Greco and I will go to Rome to study to be a priest. Then anything we experience here will be meaningless."

Hannah approached Nino, squeezed both of his hands and looked into his eyes. "Will it, Nino? Will it really be meaningless? Can't we just live our lives and enjoy the next several days together? Why spend them alone?"

Without speaking, Nino stared back at her. He felt her breath on his face as she got closer.

"Pardon us. Is that behavior appropriate in public?" an older gentleman in a top hat and dinner jacket sneered as he led his wife passed them.

Nino and Hannah watched them go on their way then grinned at each other.

"Come with me," Hannah said as she grabbed Nino's hand and escorted him to a stairway that led to the deck below.

*

"Your cabin is colossal compared to mine," Nino said as he entered Hannah's stateroom.

"Just more evidence that I am bad with money."

"You even have your own lavatory. Mine is down the passageway from my cabin."

Hannah removed her gloves, entered her bathroom, and said, "You are welcome to make yourself at home. I will only be a moment."

Nino sat in a high-back chair in the corner. The leather aroma reminded him of his papa's den.

What am I doing here? I should leave.

Nino scanned her stateroom. Much of the decor was dark wood with brass trim around the portholes. There was a single bed in the center of the room.

The trunk Hannah had sat upon at the dock was adjacent to the opposite bulkhead. It was open and filled with dresses, gowns, hats, and jewelry that sparkled in the dim room's light. It reminded him of his mother's things.

Hannah exited the lavatory, sat on the bed, and said, "Would you like me to order tea?"

"No, thank you."

Nino stared at the floor, unaware of what to say.

"Tell me about your father, Nino. Why would he want to make your mother and brother miss saying goodbye to you? Why wouldn't he want to be there himself?"

Returning his eyes to Hannah, he explained, "There are many reasons, I guess. Most of all, something happened several years ago when I was just fourteen. There was a crime involving my papa, and I told the police. I didn't mean to, but they tricked me. I haven't spoken to him since. The last time I saw him was when I left our apartment for the final time."

"Is that when you left for the boy's home?"

"Yes."

"Tell me about your father's crime, did he go to prison?"

"His lawyers got him off. But they executed Fredo Romano. He got the electric chair. He worked for my father."

"Executed? What did he do, kill someone?"

"A druggist—Mr. Giovanni. I was in the back room when Fredo killed him. When the police found out I was there, they picked me up and questioned me. The police pretended they would blame me if I didn't tell them who did it. I got scared, and I told them it was Fredo."

"All this is sad, Nino. No father should reject his son forever simply because he told the truth. You were just a boy when that happened."

"What you don't understand is that my father is a Sicilian through and through. He made my mother teach Angelo and me Italian before he would let her teach us English. To Sicilians, family loyalty is everything. It is never to be betrayed."

"So, your father believes you betrayed him? That must be awful to live with."

"Msgr. Nunzio, who was my priest growing up, says that sometimes God challenges you with difficult events and tough decisions just to see how you respond."

"I'm sorry to question your faith, but if there is a God, I don't believe he would allow that. I just think your father is an angry, bitter man."

"I wish you would stop doubting the existence of God, Hannah."

"You're right. There will be no more discussions of God tonight."

She stood from the bed, then knelt next to her steamer trunk. "I want to show you something."

She reached into a handbag and removed a series of cameos, handing one to Nino. "Camillo made these for me. Aren't they beautiful?"

"He was a true craftsman."

"He learned from his father, Solomon."

Nino caressed the image of the shell before returning it to her. "I think I should go now."

Hannah returned the cameos to the bag and laid it in the trunk. She then stood and embraced Nino, resting her head on his shoulder. The sweet smell of her perfume made his heart race.

She whispered in his ear, "Please stay, Nino," before placing a kiss on the side of his neck.

Her allure aroused him, and he returned her embrace. Lifting her head from his shoulder, she smoothed her thumbs over his cheekbones while holding his face in her hands. Her soft skin felt comforting to him. As Nino stared into Hannah's eyes, unfamiliar emotions overcame him. She was perfect, and at that moment, the rest of the world ceased to exist. When she kissed his lips, he pressed his mouth to hers and held her tight, their tongues touching. Blood rushed through his body and he felt her pull him to the bed. Their lips never parted as Nino gently lowered her as she undid his tie. He removed his jacket and leaned over her, hypnotized by her magnificence. Hannah slid his suspenders down and caressed his chest, before unbuttoning his shirt.

*

The couple sitting at the adjoining breakfast table rose and exited the dining room, leaving Hannah and Nino by themselves.

Nino glanced around, looking at Hannah before dipping a cloth napkin into his water. He then wiped the stain from his pants created after he dropped his pastry in his lap.

Hannah smiled and said, "That's why you are supposed to lay your napkin in your lap. Your mother looked like an elegant lady. I'm sure she taught you that."

"She did, but I forgot."

"Would you like me to clean your trousers for you?"

"Here?"

"No, silly. Back in my cabin."

"I think I have it. It won't show too bad."

Hannah took a sip of her breakfast tea, then lit a cigarette. The smoke rose as she exhaled, "Last night was magnificent, Nino. Thank you for allowing me to be your first. I'm honored."

"Was it that obvious?"

"Only the first time. The second time you were much better, and this morning, you were masterful."

Nino stared at his empty plate.

Hannah grinned. "Your face is turning red. Have I embarrassed you again?"

"You know you have. That was intentional."

"Yes, Nino, it was intentional. But embarrassing you is so much fun, and you are such a good sport about it."

"Do you view me as a boy, Hannah?"

"No, Nino, you most certainly are not a boy. You are a man. A man who I'm growing rather fond of."

"I shouldn't be with you."

"Why? Because you want to be a priest? You aren't a priest yet."

"That's part of it."

"What's the other part?"

"You make me feel things I shouldn't."

"And what do you feel?"

"I don't want to discuss it."

"That's not fair. You just told me that I cause you to have certain feelings, but you won't tell me what they are."

"I feel like I don't want this voyage to Italy to ever end."

"Nino, I'm sorry. We spent one night together. It was nothing more than that."

"I know you're right, Hannah. Once we exit the ship, we will go our separate ways and never see each other again."

"You'll forget all about me once you start school."

Nino said, "Che finché vivrò, i miei ricordi di te non mi sfuggiranno mai."

"And what did you just say to me, Nino?"

"That's my secret."

"Oh, I see. So, you are toying with *me*, now."

"Yes, Hannah. Yes, I am, but it is so much fun, and you are such a good sport about it."

"I know, I deserve that. But I still want to know what you said."

"I said, 'For as long as I live, my memories of you will never escape me.'"

*

118

Hannah stood in her nightgown and grabbed the washbasin as the SS *Vulcania* rolled over the ocean swell. Recovering her balance, she washed her ashen face, hoping she wouldn't be ill again. Her hair was disheveled, her eyes dark and sunken. The ship had hit a storm during the sixth nightfall of their voyage. Nino had brought meals to her, yet she couldn't hold anything down.

Exiting the lavatory, Hannah bent her knees and grabbed the bulkhead as the ship continued to rock. She watched Nino turn down the covers of her bed.

"Come here and lie down, Hannah. Sleep will do you good."

"Nino, please leave. I look awful. You can return once the storm subsides and I feel better."

He crossed the room and wrapped his arm around her, guiding her to the bed and tucking her in. "Rest," she heard him say.

She lay on her stomach and clutched the mattress hoping the spinning in her head would stabilize.

She felt Nino's presence as he sat on the bed next to her.

"Please go, Nino. I don't want you seeing me like this."

"Shh …. Be still, Hannah." He placed his hand on the center of her back. "This is what my mama did when I was sick."

His palm moving in a circular motion, his touch comforted her. He then slid his hands to her shoulders and squeezed them gently.

Although Hannah was ill, there was a strength in Nino's gentle touch that was soothing. This young man, who just a few days earlier was nothing more than her play toy, now comforted her, even as her stomach turned with sickness.

As her eyes closed, and sleep approached, she felt Nino's warm breath near her ear. He kissed the side of her head and whispered, "Sleep peacefully."

CHAPTER 9

THE ISLAND OF SICILY
PALERMO, ITALY
ROSEMAN CAMEO SHOP

Manuel slipped a handgun into his belt as he watched Alfonso DiVincenzo and his two bodyguards approach the entrance of the shop. Dressed in a white suit and hat, he stopped directly in front of the canopy above the door and looked up. He lit a cigar then glanced up again. First to the left, then to the right. He turned and whispered something to his two men before entering the shop, leaving them outside.

"You have a lot of balls coming here, DiVincenzo," Manuel said.

Alfonso said, "It has been a long time since we have chatted, *amico*. I bet you thought you'd seen the last of me."

"I was hopeful."

Alfonso chuckled as he removed the cigar from his mouth.

"You see, Roseman, I am a patient man. I want what I want, but I am also willing to wait for the right opportunity if I know it is coming. And soon, it will be coming."

Manuel said nothing as he watched Alfonso pace the floor of the shop.

"I know things, Roseman. Things you don't know yet, but soon will. I have friends in high places in Rome. They share things with me."

"You are speaking nonsense. Leave my shop now."

"I will leave in a few moments. I'm just trying to figure out how I will organize things when this becomes my company. And I mean the entire Roseman Cameo Company, not just this little shop."

"We have discussed this before. This will never be your company," Manuel said, as he pulled the Berretta from his belt.

"Don't be so quick to say never, Roseman. One day soon, you and your papà will be begging me to make you a decent offer. And if I feel kind, I may pay half of what the company is worth. But I don't feel kind very often, so you need to start treating me with a little more respect."

"What are you talking about?"

"I see I have piqued your interest."

"Not really. I'm just hoping you will get tired of talking and leave."

"Even though I have been sworn to secrecy, Roseman, I will tell you this. There are people gaining power in Mussolini's government who don't like Jews. Some might say they despise them. With each passing day, they gain more influence over *Il Duce*. They are not happy with the flood of European Jews pouring into Italy. Now that Germany and Italy are allies, many things will soon change for our country. Hitler is very unhappy that Italy has become a sanctuary for the Jews."

Alfonso returned to his inspection of the shop yet continued to speak.

"Roseman, did you know that Hitler himself is planning on visiting Rome in just a few weeks? Mussolini will welcome him with open arms."

"What does all of this have to do with my family's business?"

Alfonso turned and stepped behind the counter. He removed the cigar from his mouth and blew smoke in Manuel's face, then grinned.

"Laws will soon be passed, *amico*. Laws that will limit the freedoms of stinking Jews like you. One of those laws will remove your right to own a business. You and your family will be forced to sell to an Aryan. An Italian Aryan. That's when your papà will be contacting me, begging me to make him an offer."

"You don't know what you are talking about, DiVincenzo."

Alfonso said nothing before turning toward the door. He placed his hand on the doorknob, tipped his hat, and said, "I believe your papà knows how to contact me."

SS VULCANIA
BAY OF NAPLES

As they exited her stateroom, Hannah asked, "Why is the ship coming to a stop, Nino?"

"I don't know. It's too soon to have arrived in Naples. We still have time. And it is dark. Ships don't arrive in port at nighttime."

A steward strolling through the passageway said, "Signore, I apologize for listening to your conversation, but we are in the

Bay of Naples. We have arrived a day and a half early. We will drop anchor here until the morning sun comes up. Then we will pull dockside and disembark."

Hannah frowned. "We are in Naples?"

"It appears so," Nino said.

Hannah said, "But I'm not ready to ..."

"Nor am I. Let's go up to the main deck. I want to see Naples. My mother's parents left for America from here."

Nino and Hannah arrived to a deck crowded with many passengers lining the starboard railing, all wanting a view of the ancient Italian city.

"I didn't know Naples sat on a hillside," Nino said.

"Isn't it breathtaking? I remember it from when I was here for my wedding."

Nino grabbed her hand and led her through the crowd, elbowing his way closer to the railing.

"*La casa dei miei antenati.* The home of my ancestors," Nino said.

Hannah looked at Nino. He was exuberant. She squeezed his hand, he in turn released her grip, allowing her hand to fall. He nudged his way until he could rest a hand on the rail. The other passengers no longer blocked the evening breeze, and he could smell the sea as the wind swept across his face.

"You seem excited, Nino."

Nino turned to Hannah. "Aren't you?"

"No, I'm not. Those beautiful lights on that hill only remind me that our voyage together is about to end."

Nino grabbed Hannah's arm and led her away from the crowd, toward the center of the ship where there were fewer people.

Nino said, "Remember what you have told me for two weeks. You have said we need to enjoy our time together. We have done that. I'm confused. Our first morning together you dismissed me when I began to express my feelings for you. Now—"

Hannah interrupted, "That was before, Nino. That was when I thought you were nothing more than a handsome boy I could pass the time with. Now that I have spent two weeks with you, I realize you are so much more than that. You are a wonderful man with a kind heart. You fill me with joy I never thought I would know again."

She pulled away and held a lace handkerchief to her face. "After tomorrow, I will never see you again."

Nino grabbed Hannah and held her while whispering in her ear, "We still have this evening."

*

Nino laid with his arm around Hannah as she slept. Feeling her silky bare skin next to his was something he had grown to cherish. The aroma of her soft floral perfume enhanced her allure.

I hope I never forget your fragrance, my darling.

A tear rolled down his cheek and onto the pillow.

My dear God, what have I done? I have betrayed you, and my punishment will be a lifetime of longing for her, knowing I can never have her.

Thump—the ship shuddered as a tugboat pushed the vessel against the pier.

A knock sounded at the door, a steward announcing, "Breakfast will be served before we disembark." Another knock sounded on a neighboring door before the steward repeated the announcement to the adjacent stateroom.

Disembark? I haven't slept in my cabin since the day we boarded the ship. My Bible is still on the desk where I left it. I never opened it.

He soaked in Hannah's beauty one last time. Her hair was disheveled as it had been every morning, yet her glamour was always present.

Nino caressed Hannah's arm. "It is time to wake up, my lovely."

She rolled gently toward him and looked into his eyes before they embraced.

"I want to stay with you forever, Nino."

He held her close yet remained silent, kissing her forehead instead.

"We must get up, Hannah."

"No, Nino, we must stay here."

She pushed him on his back and rolled on top of him. Kissing his lips, then his neck, she slowly slid herself down and kissed his chest.

*

"It's a pretty day," Hannah said as they walked down the gangway.

Nino said, "Under different circumstances it would be perfect."

Hannah reached back and touched Nino's hand. "Don't be sad, my darling."

Nino watched Hannah step down the gangway and onto the dock. Soon, their lives would veer in opposite directions, and they may never see each other again. He wanted to be strong for her.

"Where do I go to get my steamer trunk? Do you know?" Hannah asked.

"The purser said we have to pass through the Office of Immigration first. They will direct us to another area where your steamer trunk will be."

"I envy you, Nino, all you have is your lone suitcase and the clothes on your back."

"That is true, but I don't look as ravishing as you."

Hannah pulled Nino aside to get away from the throngs of passengers exiting the ship. She wrapped her arms around his neck and kissed him as the crowd scurried passed them.

"Hannah, what are we doing? Soon we will be at the train station together, and you will go south to Torre del Greco and I will go north to Rome. We are about to start two different lives."

"Nino, one day when you are old and gray, a young man will step into your confessional. He will tell you of his indiscretions with an enchanting older woman. You will think of me, smile, and tell him his sins are forgiven and to go in peace."

Nino grinned. "You left out beautiful. He will add that she was the most beautiful woman he had ever seen."

Hannah's lip began to quiver. She looked down.

Nino placed his hand on her chin, raising it so he could look into her eyes. "Please don't be sad, Hannah."

"I'm going to tell you something, Nino. Don't take it lightly, because the only other man I have ever said this to is Camillo, but I can't let us part until you know. I love you. I love you, Nino Servidei, more than I should."

Nino held her face in his hands and kissed her forehead. "Hannah, I fell in love with you when I was worshipping you on the dock in New York. I fall deeper in love with you with every moment we spend together. I have never loved you more than at this very moment. You own my heart, Hannah Roseman."

PORT OF NAPLES
OFFICE OF IMMIGRATION

"Devo vedere I tuoi documenti."

"What did he say, Nino?" Hannah asked as she stood at the window of the waterside Office of Immigration.

"He needs to see our papers."

Nino was the first to hand his passport to the *carabinieri*, who looked at it, glanced up at Nino, then pressed a rubber stamp on the document.

Hannah presented hers.

The officer turned and showed her passport to his superior. He peered at Hannah and whispered something to the first man who opened a door next to the window and addressed Hannah, *"Devi venire con me."*

"What is he saying, Nino?"

"He wants you to follow him, but don't worry, I'll go with you."

As Hannah stepped through the door, the officer raised his hand, blocking Nino from entering.

Nino said, "She is with me. She doesn't speak Italian. I need to translate."

Stone-faced, the officer stared at Nino.

Hannah stopped and turned to Nino. "What is happening?"

Fear flashed in Hannah's eyes before the door slammed between them.

*

She was escorted to an open steel door of a vacant room. It only contained a single wooden chair. Hannah felt the officer's hand as he placed it on the center of her back. He shoved her in. The door closed as she stumbled forward, struggling to keep her balance. A set of keys rattled briefly before scraping against the metal door as the officer turned the lock.

*

Nino watched as the other passengers from the SS *Vulcania* stepped forward to the row of windows. Four windows down he saw Mr. and Mrs. Kruger, as well as Howard. Like most of the passengers, after a swift rubber stamp, they were on their way. The exception were the Jews. He heard their names— Dreyfuss, Shapiro, Goldberg; they were all detained and escorted through the same door Hannah had disappeared through.

Nino paced.

Dozens entered, yet none returned.

He found a nearby bench where he rested. An elderly couple approached, and he offered them his seat. The gentleman pulled a newspaper from under his arm and Nino glanced at the headline. What he read sent a chill down his spine.

"*Mi scusi, signore*, may I read your newspaper?" Nino asked the man. "I will return it momentarily."

The man nodded and handed him his copy of *La voce di Napoli.*

Scientific Evidence of Aryan Superiority

After years of research and extensive studies, a group of scientists led by biologist Edoardo Zavarttari have concluded what some have suspected for years.

Aryans are superior both physically and intellectually to the Jewish and African races. The scientific team conducting the study has recommended the implementation of restrictions on Jews and Africans. These restrictions should include, but not be limited to, federal employment, business ownership, cultural activities, and most important, immigration. Marriage between races should be strictly prohibited.

Nino returned the newspaper to the man on the bench, took a step away, and bowed his head.

My dear God, give me wisdom. Show me what to do.

"Are you ill?" the man asked.

As Nino turned to answer, he felt a bulge against his chest.

The money Mama gave me.

"I'm fine," Nino said before striding toward the carabinieri who had detained Hannah.

Nino cut in line, excused himself, and pulled the envelope from his inside breast pocket and approached the window.

"What do you want?" the officer said.

Nino laid several large bills of Italian lire in front of him. "I want you to let the girl I was with free."

The officer chuckled. "That amount is nothing. In a month it will be worth even less."

After looking in both directions, the officer leaned forward and lowered his voice. "You are an American. Why are you giving me lire? I want American dollars. It holds its value, not like this Italian shit Mussolini prints."

Nino said, "I converted all of my American money on the ship. All I have are lire."

The officer leaned back and shook his head. "You are a fool. Get out of my face."

Nino stepped away then stopped. He remembered the bills Angelo slipped him to buy a whore. After reaching in his coat pocket, he once again cut in line, apologizing to the agitated couple.

Without counting it, Nino placed the money in front of the carabinieri. The man slipped it into his shirt pocket while standing and grabbing a ring of keys hanging on the wall. He then exited a back door of the office.

Nino resumed his pacing in front of the door Hannah had entered. Those in the front of the line eyed Nino with disdain. Those in the back dispersed to other windows, realizing he had caused a delay.

The door opened, and out stepped Hannah. Her eyes were red, and Nino could see remnants of dried tears on her cheeks. He kissed her forehead. "You are safe now. But we need to get your passport."

Hannah held it up. "I have it here. He already stamped it. I can go."

Nino said, "Let's get out of here before he changes his mind. We need to find your steamer trunk."

*

"*Scusami*, where may we find our steamer trunk?" Nino asked. "We disembarked the SS *Vulcania*."

Without verbally responding, the dock worker pointed to a warehouse.

Upon entering, Nino and Hannah joined other passengers claiming their possessions. In the center of the warehouse, dozens of trunks were organized neatly in rows. In the corner sat two dozen more. Unlike those in the center, nobody was near the far trunks. Those lay open and in disarray, much of the contents scattered on the concrete floor.

Hannah said, "There's mine. I see it in the back."

When they arrived, Hannah's, as well as all the other trunks in the corner, had been rummaged through.

"Has anything been taken?" Nino asked.

Hannah sifted through the few clothes that remained at the bottom of her steamer. Picking up a large tweed purse, she said, "My jewelry is gone. I had stowed it in this bag. The cameos Camillo made me were in there. My gowns and shoes are gone, too. The only things left are this bag and a few of my undergarments. We need to find a policeman."

Nino looked at the name tags attached to the disheveled steamer trunks.

"I don't know if that would be a good idea, Hannah. We aren't in America anymore. There is a reason we are the only people standing here. Look at the names. The owners of these trunks are all Jews. The owners of these trunks are still being detained, as you were."

"Because we are Jews, people think they can steal our possessions?"

"You need to return to America, Hannah. Italy isn't safe for you. We have only been here a few hours, and look what you have been subjected to."

"Go back to what, Nino? Loneliness and sadness? Besides, the only thing I had of any value was my jewelry. Now it is gone. I have nothing but the dress I am wearing, the few things that weren't stolen, and a little money. How would I pay for a trip back to America? What would I do when I arrived with no way to support myself? My only hope is Camillo's family. I must have faith that they will take me in."

"I'll get the money for you to return to America. This lire in my pocket must be worth something."

"I can't take your money. You will need it. And money isn't the only reason I can't go back to America."

"What is the other reason?"

"I can't go back because you are here, Nino. I know I can't have you, but I can't leave Italy because you are here."

NAPLES, ITALY
NAPOLI CENTRALE RAILWAY STATION

Nino extended his arm to Hannah and guided her down the steps of the bus.

"Where do we get our train tickets?" Hannah inquired as she scanned the façade of the station.

"It's this way," Nino said.

While they crossed the street, Nino noticed a sign nailed to a tree with a Jew waving the Russian flag that read, *Gili ebrei sosno Comunisti.* Jews are Communist.

Another sign hung next to the entrance of the train station depicting a rabbi as a rat.

Inside the enclosed train station, steam whistles, bustling people, and announcements of departure times muffled the words of the other travelers.

Nino led Hannah to the platform where four rows of tracks currently held three trains, steam spewing from their underbellies. Two of the trains pointed north, the third, south.

Nino leaned toward Hannah's ear, "Stay here. Don't move. I'll be right back."

"Where are you going? We need to buy tickets."

"We will. Just trust me. I'll be right back."

*

Several paces away Nino was swallowed up in the crowd. He stopped and looked back at Hannah. She stared in his direction but appeared to have lost sight of him. A train whistle caused her to flinch. She turned around, then looked back for any sign of him.

*

When he returned, Hannah said, "Where have you been? I was worried. Will you help me buy my ticket to Torre del Greco? I don't have much money left, and I don't want to get swindled because I don't speak Italian. I can't trust any of these people."

Nino reached into his breast pocket. "Here you are, Hannah. Our tickets to Torre del Greco."

"'Our' tickets? You're coming with me? But what about your school?"

"Let me worry about my school. I still have time. I'm not leaving your side until I know you are safe."

CHAPTER 10

T he front of the building comprised the showroom where the cameos were on display for the public. The factory, which housed the craftsmen at work, was located behind the showroom and could be entered through a short hallway. A stairway leading to the second-floor living quarters was located in the hallway.

Beulah, who managed the showroom, locked the front door and climbed the stairs to their four-bedroom apartment. She laid a letter and newspaper on the kitchen table for Solomon to read when he finished his work. She filled a pot with water, set it on the stove, and began to weep.

Solomon broke from carving a cameo, wiped the sweat from his hands, and went upstairs to join his wife for dinner.

Upon entering the kitchen, he rolled up his sleeves, sat at the head of the table, and said, "I sent the craftsmen home for the remainder of the week. I can finish up the few orders we have. I'm thinking of letting Emilio go. I can't afford to pay an apprentice in these trying times."

His wife said nothing while sitting at the other end of the

table slicing carrots.

Solomon said, "What is it Beulah? You look troubled."

She nodded at the letter sitting in front of him.

"Read the letter. It's from Manuel. He says that Alfonso DiVincenzo paid him a visit. He claims that his connections in Rome are telling him laws will soon be passed making it illegal for Jews to own businesses."

Solomon opened the letter.

"This is nonsense, Beulah. This will never happen. We are well-respected. The people of Italy would never stand for this."

Beulah said, "You also told me that our business would thrive under Mussolini. Now we are barely hanging on because customers who have traded with us for years have stopped doing business with Jews. Italy is not the same country you fought for in the Great War, Solomon."

"I understand that things haven't been the same the past few years, but I don't believe that anybody will force us to shut down the cameo business. Not even Mussolini."

Beulah stood and flipped the newspaper over so Solomon could read the headline.

"German Führer Adolf Hitler to join Mussolini in Rome"

"He is coming to visit—Hitler himself," Beulah said. "German Jews have flooded into Italy for the past six years attempting to flee his wrath. Now he is coming here to call attention to his brotherhood with Mussolini. The two fascist dictators are one and the same. They are becoming like old chums."

Solomon said, "That doesn't mean anything. A few anti-Jewish posters scattered here and there is one thing. But there are hundreds of Jewish businesses in Italy. They employ thousands of Italians. Mussolini can't just shut them down."

Beulah raised her voice. "Have you not been paying attention, Solomon? Do you not listen to the radio or read the newspapers? Officials in the Italian government have sanctioned ridiculous studies which report that Jews are intellectually and morally inferior to Aryans. They have referred to us as Communists and disease-infested rats. Schools are beginning to teach these beliefs in the classroom. Jewish children have been beaten and spit on by their classmates. Solomon, you are fooling yourself if you think somehow Italy is just going to one day wake up and protect its precious Jews from the evil that is spreading through Europe."

Solomon stood, approached his wife, and kissed her cheek.

"We will survive this, Beulah. Italy will survive this."

They held each other in silence before banging on the front door of the shop below disrupted the quiet.

"Who could that be?" Solomon said before descending the stairs, followed by Beulah.

When they arrived at the double glass doors, Solomon pulled back the curtains.

Beulah gasped and covered her mouth with her hand. "Oh my, Solomon. Is that Hannah?"

*

Beulah embraced Hannah. *"Ciao, Hannah, è così bello vederti. Ma perché sei qui in Italia?"*

Hannah, with her arms around Beulah, glanced toward Nino.

"She said it is good to see you. But wants to know why you are in Italy. What should I tell her?"

Hannah remained silent as she released her arms from Beulah and wrapped them around Solomon's wide frame.

Solomon said, "*La sposa di Camillo è tornata a casa da noi.*"

Nino translated, "He is excited that Camillo's bride has returned home to them."

"Tell them I am happy to see them."

"Hannah is happy to see you both. My name is Nino Servidei. I have escorted her here from Naples to ensure her safety."

Solomon said, "Thank you, Nino, for bringing her to us. Italy is not safe these days. Please come upstairs, both of you. We will be having dinner soon. You must be hungry after your journey."

Hannah helped Beulah prepare dinner. They occasionally glanced at each other yet, said nothing due to the language barrier.

Nino sat at the table with Solomon and noticed the headline featuring Hitler's impending arrival.

Solomon said, "You have an interesting accent, Nino. You are clearly an American, yet I hear a touch of Sicilian."

"My father is from Sicily. He moved to America many years ago."

"I, too, grew up in Sicily. What part of Sicily was your papà from? I'm not familiar with the last name of Servidei being prominent on the island. The Servidei name is more prominent near Sorrento. But, of course, I can't possibly know every family in Sicily."

Before Nino could explain his name change, Beulah said to Solomon, "Go downstairs and get two bottles of wine. No. Make it three. We must celebrate Hannah's arrival."

"Yes, of course. I will be right back."

Hannah stirred the stew while watching Nino.

Beulah said, "Nino, were you and Hannah on the same ship? Is that where you met?"

"We met at the dinner table. When we arrived in Naples, I knew it would be difficult for her to find you since she didn't speak Italian."

"That was kind of you. Are you here to visit family?"

"I'm traveling to Rome to study to be a priest."

"So, you will be in Italy for several years then."

"Si."

"Did Hannah tell you how long she will be visiting with us? It can't be long. She has no luggage. Where are her things?"

Nino translated Beulah's questions and asked Hannah how he should respond.

Hannah stared at the floor and took a deep breath. Beulah looked to Nino hoping for an explanation. The uneasiness in the room was broken when Solomon returned with the wine.

"What did I miss?"

Hannah stopped stirring the stew and sat at the table.

"Nino, you might as well explain everything to them. Including my mismanagement of Camillo's inheritance. Let them know I have no place else to go."

Nino communicated everything in detail, including her detainment and the rummaging of her trunk in Naples.

Solomon poured four glasses of wine, sliding the first across the table to Hannah.

Beulah rested her hand on Hannah's and said to Nino, "Tell her she is safe now. She may stay as long as she wishes."

*

Beulah filled each bowl with stew before placing them on the table.

"They want to know about your life in America with Camillo," Nino said to Hannah. "They said not to leave anything out."

The discussion eventually turned grim as Nino informed them of how the Jews on their ship were mistreated when they disembarked. Solomon and Beulah mentioned that their cameo sales had been reduced by half since Mussolini began his anti-Semitic propaganda campaign.

"There are rumors that laws may soon pass forcing us to sell our business to an Aryan," Beulah said. "We have owned this business and employed dozens of Italian citizens for forty years. Solomon fought for Italy in the Great War. And this is how they treat us. We may be forced to sell to a brutal thug in Sicily simply because we are Jewish."

Solomon pounded his fist on the table. Nino saw Hannah flinch.

"No! I will never sell to that pig DiVincenzo. I will close the business completely before that happens."

Nino swallowed hard.

DiVincenzo? Grandpapa?

Beulah said to Hannah, *"Perdona Salomone. È un uomo stupido."*

"What is happening?" Hannah asked Nino.

"New laws may soon force them to sell their business to a non-Jew."

"Why? That isn't fair."

"I told you, Hannah. We aren't in America any longer."

Nino asked Solomon, "Who is this DiVincenzo?"

"He's the head of the Cosa Nostra in Sicily. He has always

been a murdering thug. The *polizia* and government officials in Sicily are on his payroll. He's been harassing my son, Manuel, and other business and landowners for years. He extorts them for payment or strong-arms them until they sell over ownership to him. Now that the political climate in Italy is changing, he is using his influence to try and intimidate me, too. He wants my entire company. He's told Manuel that once the laws are passed, he'll pay me a visit and force me to sell him everything at a fraction of what the company is worth."

Beulah said, "Don't speak of such things, Solomon. Now is not the time."

Solomon said, "Please excuse me," before leaving the room and descending the stairs to the factory.

Beulah said, "When do you need to be in Rome, Nino? We hope you can stay with us for a few days."

"I still have a little time before my studies begin, but I will need to find lodging. The school has dormitories, but I must check in and become familiar with my surroundings."

"Can you stay through Saturday? Our daughter-in-law, Olivia, will be arriving from Palermo then. She and Manuel manage our shop there. She too speaks English and hasn't seen Hannah since the wedding. She will be happy to fill in as Hannah's translator in your absence."

"Si, I will leave Saturday after she arrives."

"You can stay in Manuel's old room. Hannah will stay in Camillo's room, of course."

"What are you discussing, Nino?" Hannah asked.

"I will be here a few more days until Olivia arrives from Sicily."

Hannah smiled.

*

As they walked along the beach, Nino skipped rocks from the shoreline into the Tyrrhenian Sea. He watched them bounce across the surface as a light sprinkle of rain fell from the evening sky.

When he bent to pick up another, Hannah said, "Since our arrival, I have missed waking up next to you."

Nino said, "Beulah and Solomon suspect we were more than just dinner companions on a voyage."

"You are paranoid. We have the perfect cover for the lustful adventures we had. I am a Jew, and you are on a journey to become a Catholic priest. Anyone who suspects the truth will naturally laugh it off as folly."

"Is that what we had, Hannah? A lustful adventure, that in the end was just folly?"

"That remains to be seen."

"What do you mean?"

"Tomorrow you will board a train for Rome and start a life that has nothing to do with me. If you are able to do so with no hesitation, as I suspect you will, then yes, what we had was folly."

"You know that isn't true, Hannah. Our voyage together will always remain the most wonderful experience of my life. Do you think when I board that train tomorrow my heart won't be broken?"

The cool drizzle intensified to a downpour. Their hair and clothes clung to them.

"I'm a mess," Hannah said.

"You have never looked more beautiful."

They ran to a series of overturned, multicolored rowboats.

When they arrived at the first, Nino lifted the side.

"It's dry under here."

Hannah crawled under. Nino followed and eased the boat down over them. He lay on top of her and pushed her damp hair from her face and kissed her cheek.

"I love you, Hannah. I will always love you. Just as I have since the day I met you. I'll spend my life praying for your protection, as well as your happiness."

"It's not your prayers I want."

"That's all I can give you."

Nino kissed her lips. She slid his suspenders down over his shoulders, then unbuttoned his shirt.

As the pounding rain landed on their shelter, they shared their love, each realizing it would be their last time together.

CHAPTER 11

N ino watched Olivia step off the train. She, too, was beautiful. Not Hannah beautiful, but beautiful.

The Roseman boys really know how to marry.

"Hannah, it is so good to see you," Olivia said. "Beulah wired us and said that you had arrived from America. Manuel and I are pleased to have you in Italy. He wished he could come up, but of course, we have the shop to run."

"It is good to see you, too, Olivia," Hannah said as they embraced.

"Where is Solomon? He usually picks me up when I come to Torre del Greco."

Hannah said, "He said he had work to do. He is working alone now and has several pieces he must complete by next week. We came here by taxi."

"Olivia, this is my friend, Nino."

"*Ciao,* Nino. Beulah mentioned you in her wire. She said you'll be living in Rome to study for the priesthood."

"I will soon begin my studies at the University of Rome."

"When do you leave?"

143

"My train for Rome departs in less than an hour."

"I'm sorry you can't stay a little longer. Perhaps next time."

"Perhaps."

"Have you ever been to Rome, Nino?"

"This is my first visit to Italy."

"Rome is a beautiful city," Olivia said. "I'm sure you are anxious to start your new life there."

Nino glanced at Hannah. "I hope it is as enchanting as my voyage to Italy."

Hannah reached for his hand.

There was silence as they stared at each other.

"I must go now," Nino said.

"Write to me," Hannah said before she wrapped her arms around his neck and kissed him passionately. She whispered in his ear, "I will always love you, Nino Servidei. I will never forget you."

Nino glanced at Olivia who raised her eyebrows then stepped away to give them privacy.

"Are you not concerned what Olivia thinks?"

"I'm a grown woman, and the man I love is about to leave me forever. There's no way I'll let you board that train without letting you know how I feel. Olivia's opinion is of no concern to me right now."

"I'm going to miss your fiery spunk, Hannah."

"It's fake, Nino. It's all fake. You forget that I was once an actress. My heart is breaking right now. I considered asking you to stay, but I won't because that wouldn't be fair to you. You came to Italy to be a priest. You didn't come to Italy to play knight in shining armor to a Jewish girl who can't manage her money."

"I think I would like being your knight in shining armor."

"You are my knight in shining armor, Nino. You always will be."

Nino stared into Hannah's eyes. A tear slipped down her cheek as he kissed her lips then whispered in her ear, "I will always love you, Hannah."

*

Hannah stood at the entrance of Beulah's kitchen and watched Olivia embrace her in-laws while they spoke Italian. The conversation began jovial, yet the mood quickly turned somber.

Olivia picked up her bag and asked Hannah to follow her to the bedroom that once belonged to Manuel.

As they entered, Hannah said, "Nino told me that it may become unlawful for Jews to own businesses. Is that what Beulah and Solomon were upset about?"

"Right now, that is just a rumor. But the way things have been changing in Italy, I doubt that it will stay just a rumor. In Palermo, we have Jewish friends who have government positions. They may lose their jobs soon to make room for unemployed Aryans."

"What is Solomon going to do with the company?"

"Solomon is a proud and stubborn man. Manuel is afraid he'll hold off selling until the end, and his bargaining power with whomever buys the Roseman Cameo Company will be gone. But let's not worry about what hasn't happened yet."

Hannah watched as Olivia unpacked the few things she'd brought for her short visit, then walked over to the nightstand. She picked up a photograph of Camillo and kissed it.

"I miss my Camillo," Hannah said. "Life has been lonely without him. Sometimes I feel like my life ended with his."

"Camillo worshiped you, Hannah. You were his everything."

"And he was mine."

"Nino looks so much like him," Olivia said. "When Beulah wired me about you and Nino being here, she said that when they pulled the curtain back at the door, they were astonished. Not just because your arrival was so unexpected, but because Nino's resemblance to Camillo is striking. They suspected you were lovers until they found out he was in Italy to become a priest. They still find him to be a curiosity. He appears to be just a boy."

Hannah laughed, "Nino is no boy."

"How old is he?"

"Eighteen."

"And how old are you, Hannah?"

"I turned thirty last month."

"Does Nino know that?"

Hannah set Camillo's photograph down and sat on the bed.

"Why are you asking me these questions, Olivia?"

"Because that goodbye at the train station was more than just two acquaintances who met on an ocean liner."

"My plan was to hide my feelings for Nino. But I wanted him to know how I felt before we parted. I may never see him again."

"Was he your lover?"

"Will you think less of me if I told you yes?"

"No, I would not. You're a woman with needs. Camillo has been dead many years. I'm sure Nino filled a void."

"Nino didn't just fill a void. I'm in love with him. Yes, as odd as it sounds, I am a Jew who is passionately in love with a man twelve years her junior, who—as we speak—is on a train to Rome to become a priest."

They both laughed at the words Hannah just spoke.

"Could you have picked a more inappropriate man to fall in love with?"

"No, Olivia. If I had purposely set out to get my heart broken, I couldn't have done a better job. But I can't help it. Nino is so easy to love. I adore him."

CHAPTER 12

His room was in the basement. The cold, damp hallway felt refreshing on a warm day.

"The last room on the right—room six," the dormitory manager had said.

Before he put the key in the warped wooden door of his new home, something caught Nino's attention. There was a small gap in the brick wall at the end of the hallway. He felt the cool breeze first. It had a unique smell that made him nauseous.

The room was much like the hallway, damp and enclosed with crooked bricks, laid centuries earlier. There was a small stove heater in the corner with a pipe protruding through the wooden floor of the room above. A stack of wood lay next to it.

Two desks sat adjacent to bunks on opposite sides of the room. He had hoped for a window but accepted that wasn't the case.

Nino opened his suitcase and laid his Bible on the desk.

My neglected friend.

My Dear God, I am sorry I have forsaken you. Please forgive my indiscretions.

Nino removed a piece of paper, pencil, and envelope and sat down at his desk to write to his mother.

The door flung open.

"Ciao, mio amico. My name is Vito Bianchi. It looks like we will be roommates. Where are you from? I always want to know where my roommates are from. Where they are from tells much about them, you see. I am from Milan. My father is a doctor. And you?"

Nino stood. "I'm Nino Servidei, from America. New York City."

"New York City? Do you know any gangsters? American gangsters from Italy are always in our papers. They are famous, like actors."

Nino remained silent.

"Being an American in Rome is good, amico. The signorinas love Americans. Especially Americans who look like handsome Italians. I bet you'll bed more *ragazze* than even me, and that is quite an accomplishment. What are you here to study? "

"Here? Philosophy first. Then I hope to get into the *Pontificio Collegio Etiopico."*

"The Vatican? You want to be a priest?"

"Si. My desire is to be a priest."

"Oh my, Nino. I hope you take no offense, but I need to request a different room. It is nothing personal, but this room is small, and I have been known to bring my evening companions back to my dormitory. Last year, my roommate just put his pillow over his head to drown out the sound of my squeaky bed springs. But having a priest in the room is no good. It will cause me to lose my concentration."

"I take no offense. But I don't think you will have any luck finding another room. I overheard the dorm manager tell someone there were no more vacancies. Why do you think we are in this dungeon? There is nothing else."

Vito put his hands over his face and fell back on his bed.

"Oh, no. It is because of Mussolini's war in Ethiopia. Cowards are attending university to avoid the army. What are we going to do, Nino? I can't room with a priest."

"I don't know what you are going to do, Vito, but I am going to get an education."

ROME ITALY
'CAFE ALL' ANGOLO'

"Here, Nino, have some more wine," Vito said as he filled Nino's glass for the fourth time.

Vito snapped his fingers. "*Cameriera*, another bottle of wine. Nino, our cameriera is so beautiful, isn't she? When she walks toward our table, I can't take my eyes off her. Do you see the way her hair catches the breeze? I think I'm in love with her."

"Vito, I have only known you for six hours, and our *cameriera* is the third woman you have fallen in love with. That is two heartbreaks per hour. Why do you torture yourself so?"

"Because I love women. They are God's gift to man, and I cherish them all. I cherish the old ones for their wisdom, and I cherish the young ones for how they stir my soul. How about you, Nino? Have you ever loved a woman other than your mother and the Madonna?"

"Si, I have loved deeply. Recently, even."

"What happened?"

"God is what happened. I want to be a priest. I guess you could say I love God more."

The cameriera brought their wine, opened the bottle, and began to pour.

"*Bella donna*, my name is Vito Bianchi. I was just telling my friend Nino here how I can't take my eyes off you. You are one of God's greatest creations. Is there anyone in your life to adore you as you deserve?"

She smiled. "No."

"Do you think you could find it in your heart to have dinner with me soon so that I may spend an evening worshiping you?"

She laughed, turned to leave, then hesitated.

"I haven't eaten this evening. This café closes at eleven, but the restaurant down the street is open until two." She pointed. "It's there. The one on the left, *L' Amore Della Madre*. I'll meet you there at eleven thirty."

She looked at Nino. "My roommate works there. She has nobody who adores her, either, if you would like to join us?"

Nino smiled and looked down at his wine glass. "I'm afraid I will have to—"

"He would be delighted to join us," Vito interrupted.

"Good. We'll see you then. My name is Claudia. My friend is Elena."

*

Nino's head was spinning as they climbed the stairway to the third-floor apartment. Nino and Vito each held a bottle of wine in their hand. Claudia led the way, followed by Vito then Elena. Nino, the last of the group, focused on the image of Elena ascending the stairs in front of him. She wore a tight black skirt and white blouse. He found her curves to be glorious. Vito stumbled twice, both times almost falling backwards, causing the group to erupt in laughter.

Claudia unlocked the apartment door and turned on the light. "Open the windows, Elena. I'll get the wine glasses."

Nino and Vito sat down on a sofa in a small foyer. Vito leaned toward Nino and whispered, "Are you having a good time, Fr. Servidei?"

"I shouldn't be here."

"But you are. Why is that? Nobody dragged you up those stairs."

"I'm here because I am a flawed man who lusts for things he shouldn't."

"You aren't flawed, Nino. God has given us a gift, you and me. Our gift is that we bring joy to beautiful women. That is not a sin. If it were, God would have never given us such a gift."

Nino shook his head. "I think you own the same version of the gospels as my brother."

"Nino, don't screw this up by telling Elena you want to be a priest. You may as well tell her you have syphilis."

"Here are our glasses," Claudia said as she and Elena entered the room.

The sofa was large enough to seat four, but it was snug.

After she poured the wine, Claudia said, "Vito and I will take our bottle to my room, and you two can stay here and talk into the wee hours of the morning if you wish." Claudia led Vito by the hand, their laughter fading as they made their way down the hall.

Elena said, "So, Nino. Tell me all about America. It seems so exciting. Have you ever met any movie stars?"

"I hate to disappoint you, but I've led a rather boring life."

Elena gave Nino a sharp peck on his lips. "How can that be? You are from New York City. Nothing is boring in New York City."

Nino laughed, "I didn't live in the city my entire life. Before I came to Italy, I'd been living in a boy's—"

Abruptly, Elena threw her leg over his lap, straddling him and they kissed. Wrapping her arms around his neck, she penetrated his mouth with her tongue and pulled him closer.

Reaching out blindly, Nino located the table next to the sofa and placed his wine glass on its surface. He then wrapped his arms around Elena and returned her affection with equal passion.

Releasing him, she unbuttoned her blouse. Nino became aroused as she squirmed on his lap. Behind her, a painting caught his attention. It was the Madonna cradling the Christ child. Guilt overcame him. He was betraying God, and in his heart, he was betraying Hannah.

As Elena reached to unhook her bra, Nino grabbed her wrists.

"I'm sorry, Elena. You are beautiful, and there is nothing that would please me more than to stay here for hours making love to you. But I can't. My heart belongs to someone else."

CHAPTER 13

From the passenger window, Hannah watched shoppers pick through produce as Olivia parked Solomon's pickup truck near the outdoor market.

"I don't think Beulah likes me," Hannah said.

After shutting off the engine, Olivia said, "That's not true, Hannah. She just—"

"She just what?"

"She's disappointed that you became Nino's lover on your voyage to Italy."

"I told you that in confidence. Why did you tell her?"

"I didn't have to tell her. Nino was here for two days. She saw how you looked at each other."

"Nino told me he suspected Beulah knew. I told him he was paranoid."

"That's not the only reason she is upset. She's discouraged that she can't have a conversation with you."

"I'm trying to learn Italian, but it's going to take time."

"She thinks you are miserable. You haven't smiled in days. She wishes she could talk to you about it, like a mother and a daughter. She wishes she could comfort you."

"I'm sorry, Olivia. Will you apologize to Solomon and Beulah for me? I can't seem to allow myself to be happy."

"Is it because of Nino?"

Hannah remained silent.

Olivia said, "Nino is just a boy compared to you, yet he has moved on and you must, too. Why did you come to Italy? To fall in love?"

"I came here to be part of Camillo's family."

"And we have accepted you. You need to accept us. You need to accept your new life with us. We own a cameo company. You need to learn our business and learn our language as quickly as you can. That's all we ask."

"You're right, Olivia. My sadness should not be everyone else's sadness."

"I've been thinking about something. Why don't you come back to Sicily with me? Our apartment isn't large, but we have an extra bedroom. You are welcome to use it. Manuel and I both speak English and can easily teach you Italian. I have a friend who is a language teacher. She will have books that may help you. Within a few weeks, you will have the basics, and within a few months, you will be able to have a conversation with anyone. Once you learn Italian, you can return to Torre del Greco if you wish. Or you can stay in Sicily. It would be up to you. Learning Italian will give you freedom."

"Are you sure Manuel won't mind?"

"Manuel gets along with everyone. He won't mind."

"That sounds lovely, Olivia. I'll go with you to Sicily."

THE ISLAND OF SICILY
PALERMO, ITALY

Unable to sleep, Hannah rose early. She had been living with Olivia and Manuel for several weeks, having arrived in southern Italy with Olivia by train. They'd then taken the ferry to Messina before riding the bus to Palermo. Not lost on Hannah was the fact that the very dock where Camillo had been murdered rested only a few blocks from the cameo shop. Several times, she had considered going there. She realized it would be too painful, so she always removed the idea from her mind.

She'd sent a telegram to Beulah asking if Nino had written to her in Torre del Greco. He would have no way of knowing she'd moved to Sicily. Beulah replied that she had received nothing from Nino.

As Olivia and Manuel entered the kitchen, Hannah looked up from the newspaper.

"You're up early," Olivia said. "What's in the paper today?"

"I'm not certain. I only recognize a few words. Hitler, Mussolini, *parata, unita, and asse*. I believe it is discussing Hitler's upcoming visit and how Germany and Italy have become united."

Manuel said, "Are you sure that paper isn't a day old, because that was yesterday's headline."

"It will be tomorrow's headline, too," Olivia said.

Hannah said, "And there is another story with the word *criminalità* in the same sentence as the word *ebraica*. So, I guess that means we Jews are responsible for the rise in crime."

Olivia said, "Your Italian has come a long way in the short

time you have been here. I heard you negotiating with a customer in Italian yesterday. He was only partially confused."

Hannah said, "You laugh, but I sold him the cameo, didn't I?"

"That is only because he was a man and you are a beautiful woman," Manuel said. "Why do you think I have Olivia wait on the male customers?"

"And why do you think I have Manuel wait on the female customers?"

"Do you really do that?" Hannah asked.

"Yes, Hannah, we do," Olivia said. "Men like to flash money in front of pretty women, and when ladies pin a cameo to their dress, they want to be complemented by a handsome man. Products have been sold this way for centuries."

"So, you prostitute each other for sales. Now you are prostituting me."

"You groan, but you will be receiving a nice commission for that sale," Manuel said, before kissing Olivia and leaving for work.

"Addio," Olivia and Hannah said in unison.

"A commission? But you and Manuel are letting me stay in your home for free. And you are feeding me. I can't take your money."

"You don't eat much. And once you master Italian, and are comfortable enough to travel on your own, you will need money when you visit Nino in Rome."

"What makes you think—"

"You fell asleep with your light on the other night. When I entered your room to turn it off, there was a train schedule lying next to you. You had all of the Rome arrival times circled."

ROME, ITALY
NINO'S DORMITORY

Nino laid in bed studying Latin, but his mind wandered to Hannah. In recent weeks, he had written her multiple letters yet received nothing in return.

Vito swung open the door with his usual glut of energy.

"Let's go, Nino. The motorcade is getting ready to start. You must see this. There are thousands of people in the streets."

"I have no interest in seeing Hitler's motorcade."

"We mustn't miss this. Italy and Germany are becoming allies. It's history, taking place right in front of our eyes. Plus, there will be women everywhere."

"I appreciate you thinking of me, Vito, but you go. Soak up the majesty of it all if you wish. I will stay here. I have work to do."

Vito crossed the room to Nino's bed and grabbed his arm, yanking him to his feet.

"Oh no, my dear *amico*. I am tired of seeing you mope around. Life is sweet. You must get out and enjoy it. You are bringing even me down, and I wake up every morning determined to soak up the glory of the world."

"Okay, okay, I'll come. I need a break anyway."

They exited their dormitory and Vito kick-started his motorcycle. Nino climbed on back as he had done a dozen times before.

"Where are we going?"

"We are going to the *Colosseo*. That will allow us the best view."

*

Vito slowed to a crawl as he guided the bike through the crowd. Nino followed Vito's lead and touched his feet to the asphalt to keep the motorcycle from tipping over.

After parking in an alley, they sprinted to the *Piazza del Colosseo*, elbowing their way through the crowd until they stood at the edge of the curb.

People lined both sides of the street. Nino stood and stared up at the nearly two-thousand-year-old Colosseum. His mind drifted to the barbarism that once took place inside in the name of entertainment for the Roman people. In addition to gladiators fighting to the death, he had recently read of the *Damnatio ad bestias*, a form of criminal execution at the jaws of wild animals.

Occasionally, Nino glanced at Vito, who spent more time studying the women around him than watching for the motorcade.

With an abrupt roar, the crowd began to cheer as a series of polizia motorcycles approached. They were followed by a convoy of open-top Mercedes-Benz automobiles. The first vehicle held a group of German officers, none of which were known to Nino. The second vehicle was the same.

Then, among an increased outburst of cheering, Nino watched as Adolf Hitler's car passed by.

Nino's eyes followed the vehicle as it drove on. He was unimpressed by the figure passing before him and wondered why the Italian people had such admiration for a man reported to be a tyrant, even to his own people.

When the commotion ceased, Nino turned to find Vito standing behind him.

"Nino, I want to introduce you to Rosa and Priscilla. We are taking them to dinner this evening."

1939

CHAPTER 14

As the taxi turned onto *Via al Mare*, his heart pounded in his chest.

Nino paid the cab driver and took a deep breath before entering the front showroom. Above his head, a bell rang as he opened the door.

Beulah was showing a customer a silver chain to match a cameo, glancing at Nino, she said nothing. Nino stepped gingerly around the showroom, pretending to browse while looking for any sign of Hannah. He walked toward the entrance to the back room seeking something hopeful to cling to. Hearing the cash register ring, he turned to see Beulah wrapping a small box containing her latest sale.

As the customer exited the shop, Beulah said, "Nino, it is so good to see you. How is Rome? How are your studies coming along?"

"Rome is beautiful. I'm never bored. There is always so much to do, although my studies occupy much of my time."

"I'm sure they do. Are you here to shop for a cameo for someone special, or are you looking for Hannah?"

"I don't have the money to purchase a cameo. I was hoping to see Hannah. I just want to know she is safe and happy."

"She is happy, Nino. Her letters from America are joyous. She has returned there."

"America?"

"We discussed it as a family and believed that was the safest place for her. We provided her with money to pay for a voyage and to settle in."

A lump formed in Nino's throat; he felt ill.

"How long has she been gone?"

"She left shortly after you went to Rome. I'm sorry you missed her."

"Do you have her address? I would like to write her."

"I don't think that would be a good idea. She has found someone. A Jewish man. He is a little older than her and has a good job and is making her happy. They are engaged to be married. I think it would be best if you let her be."

Nino's legs were weak. He wanted to sit down but pulled himself together.

"How are you and Solomon doing? How about Olivia and Manuel?"

"Things are difficult, Nino. But of course, many in Italy are suffering, not just the Rosemans."

"I know. I see it every day."

"I'll tell Solomon you came. Be well, Nino. I'm glad you came by."

"You too, Beulah. Thank you for telling me about Hannah. At least I know she's happy. That's what is important."

Nino exited the shop and walked the few blocks to the shoreline. He retraced the steps he and Hannah had made the night before he'd left for Rome. When he arrived, just as when he was with Hannah, a series of overturned, multicolored rowboats rested on the shoreline. He made his way to the first one, caressed it, then sat down and wept.

THE ISLAND OF SICILY
PALERMO, ITALY
THE ROSEMAN CAMEO SHOP

Hannah enjoyed polishing the cameos in the display cases every morning before opening the shop. She found the alone time to be therapeutic, her mind often wandering to her voyage with Nino and their final night together.

Proud of the advances she had made in learning their native language, Hannah had persuaded Manuel and Olivia to let her open the shop by herself every morning. It forced her to interact with the few customers they had at that early hour, which accelerated her progress with the Italian language. Manuel was pleased with the results, for she had increased their sales during a time that normally saw few transactions.

After she returned the last piece to the display case, she walked to the front to flip the sign to Open. She noticed a commotion in the street. A crowd was gathering around a newspaper boy.

Hannah opened the door to hear him yelling, *"Edizione speciale!* New racial laws to be enacted in three months."

She waited her turn in line and bought a copy of the special edition paper before returning to the shop. She laid it on a display case and began to read.

"Parliament Enacts New Racial Laws"

Parliament has agreed to enact laws based on the *Manifesto on Race* which was proposed by the Italian scientific community and endorsed by Prime Minister Mussolini and King Victor Emmanuel. The laws will be introduced in increments over the next several months. A general outline of the legislation is as follows:

Foreign Jews will be forbidden to settle in Italy, Libya, or in the colonial possessions of the Aegean.

The Italian citizenship granted to Jewish foreigners after January 1, 1919 will be revoked and those Jews will be required to leave Italy by April 1, 1939.

Jews will be prohibited from working in jobs in the government, banking, insurance, education, entertainment industry, and the practice of law.

Jews will be banned from enrolling in educational institutions.

Marriage will be prohibited between Jews and non-Jews.

Jewish property ownership will be significantly reduced, and in many cases, property will be confiscated if the current Jewish owner is unable to find a buyer by April 1, 1939.

Jewish businesses will be Aryanized. All Jewish businesses that have not been sold to an Aryan by April 1, 1939 will be confiscated and redistributed

to a qualified Aryan of the highest bidding.
All foreign Jews must leave Italy by April 1, 1939
or they will be arrested and incarcerated.
Jews will be forbidden to employ non-Jewish
Italian domestics.
Jews will be forbidden to serve in the military.
A special Jewish census will be conducted at
once. Any Jewish household who is not registered
or refuses to cooperate fully will be arrested,
incarcerated, or deported.

Hannah was unfamiliar with many of the individual words she had read, but she was versed enough in Italian to understand the evil that would soon engulf Italy.

Manuel and Olivia entered the front of the shop with their own copy of the newspaper. Manuel reached for the Open sign that Hannah had just flipped and turned it around.

"We are closed indefinitely," Manuel said. "I'm going to wire Papà to let him know we will leave tomorrow morning for Torre del Greco. Soon, we must find a buyer for the Roseman Cameo Company. A buyer we can trust. And Hannah, consider yourself fortunate that you have someplace you can go to escape the madness that is coming. You will be returning to America at once. Otherwise, you will be arrested."

Torre del Greco, Italy
The Roseman Cameo Factory

Hannah sat next to Olivia and clung to every word. Although much of the conversation was in rapid-fire Italian, she was pleased that she knew what they were discussing, even if she didn't know the details.

Solomon looked around the kitchen table at his family. "I received a telegram today from Alfonso DiVincenzo. He has made me an offer for the company."

"No, Papà. We still have a few months to find a buyer. We just need to keep trying," Manuel said.

"We are in the worst possible position to negotiate," Solomon said. "Hundreds of Jewish businesses will soon be for sale, and wealthy Aryans are sitting and waiting for the clock to tick down. If we have no buyer by April, our business will be confiscated, and we will have nothing. Time is not on our side."

"I say we just let them take it. Let the government have it, because this business is useless without you, Papà," Manuel said.

"DiVincenzo has offered to keep me on to manage. He will pay me a salary. A salary that will keep food on the table."

Beulah, who sat at the opposite end of the table began to weep.

"No, Papà!" Manuel said, "What has happened to you? You said you would never sell to DiVincenzo. He was involved in Camillo's death."

Beulah, in a rare outburst shouted, "Our home is above the business we spent our lives building. If he owns the business, he owns our home, too. He will charge us rent to live in our own home, Solomon. I will live out in the cold before I pay rent to Alfonso DiVincenzo."

Solomon stood, expressing rage in his own way. "This is my business. I built it. My sweat saturates the floor of that factory below us. I don't need either of you telling me how painful this is because you have no idea. But as the head of this household, I'm not just responsible for the business. I also have an obligation to support my family any way I can. And I have craftsmen who have been loyal to me for decades. Abraham has been with me for over twenty years and Levi has been with me for thirty—they have families to feed. DiVincenzo has promised to keep them on at their current salaries."

"Any new owner would have no choice but to keep them on, Papà," Manuel said. "Without you, and without them, there is no business."

Solomon sat back down and looked down at the coffee cup before him.

"They have already informed me they will not work for anyone else. If I'm forced out, they will go, too. What would they do?"

"They are skilled craftsman, Papà. The finest in the world. We are the only Jewish cameo company in Italy, so the others won't be threatened by the new laws. Abraham and Levi would simply go work for them."

"It doesn't matter how skilled they are, Manuel. They are Jews, just like us. There are no guarantees for them."

Olivia slammed her palm on the table. "This isn't fair. Why is our own country doing this to us?"

Beulah shouted, "Because your Papà's precious Mussolini admires Hitler. He would do anything to please him."

"Enough!" Solomon shouted. "None of that matters. Manuel, tomorrow you and I are going to Sicily to sell the business. If the weather is clear, we will take one of the boats. If not, we will take the train. Olivia, tell Hannah we are sending her back to America. Let her know we will send her off with enough money for her voyage and to support herself for a few months once she arrives. Tell her not to squander it this time."

"I won't tell her the last part, Papà," Olivia said. "That would be rude."

In broken Italian, Hannah said, "You don't have to tell me any of it, Olivia. I know what he said."

She turned to Solomon, "I won't squander your money. And once I get back to America, I will find a way to pay you back."

CHAPTER 15

Solomon watched Manuel shift from third gear to second, guiding the Fiat sedan down the steep hill.

"It has been many years since I drove through these mountains, Manuel. I believe the last time I was here was for my mamma's funeral. These hills look no different than when I grew up here as a boy."

"You haven't missed anything, Papà. These mountain passes are dangerous, not only because of the roads, but because DiVincenzo believes he owns them. The few farmers and landowners who have held out from selling to him must pass through cautiously. When they are home, they must sleep with one eye open. Unknowing travelers get detained and robbed by his thugs. Many a young woman has made the mistake of passing through here unaccompanied."

"One day, he will get his, Manuel. He will push the wrong person over the edge."

"It won't be a simple task, Papà. He never travels without his bodyguards. It would be a suicide mission unless it's someone who earns his trust and has penetrated his inner circle. Perhaps someone he does business with. Or a visiting family member."

"You sound like you have given DiVincenzo's assassination some thought."

"His death has become an obsession to me."

"Don't let another man's evil consume you, Manuel. It does no harm to him. It only eats into your soul. A man's soul is too precious to waste on piles of dung like DiVincenzo."

"He sanctioned Camillo's death, Papà. It was Omar's doing, but DiVincenzo knew about it ahead of time and gave his blessing. He told me the day he busted up our shop. He told me—with joy—that he was behind my brother's death. He referred to 'baking' Camillo. Now he is taking advantage of the new laws to try and force us to sell to him. I want to go to his compound and kill him."

After a brief silence, Solomon asked, "Was it you who killed Omar?"

Manuel glared out of the windshield yet remained silent.

"Be careful what you do. You don't want to leave Olivia a widow."

They drove the remainder of the journey in silence. Their voyage crossing the Tyrrhenian Sea had been rough, the air chilly. The warm Sicilian sun was comfortable.

When they reached the peak of the hill, they stopped and looked down to the valley below.

"Bellissima Valle is as beautiful as I remember," Solomon said. "It will be good to see my old friend Bruno again."

Manuel said, "I just hope the Leones will agree to buy us out."

*

Lorenzo heard Isabella screaming from the courtyard, "Papà, someone is coming."

He stepped onto the front porch to see Eduardo running from the bunkhouse, machine gun in hand. Aldo rolled out from under the truck he was repairing. He fastened his holster around his waist and grabbed a rifle.

Bruno exited one of the barns and pulled his revolver.

The four men went to the center of the courtyard, all armed with weapons loaded and ready.

"That is Manuel's car," Aldo said.

"Manuel Roseman?" Bruno asked. "I haven't seen that boy in years."

The Fiat entered the courtyard and stopped. Manuel and Solomon exited.

"Solomon? Solomon Roseman, is that you?" Bruno said.

"Yes, Bruno my friend, it is. I am now old, fat and gray, but yes, it is me in the flesh."

Bruno approached Solomon and they embraced. Both men were thick around the chest and waist, and Lorenzo laughed, thinking they looked like large grizzly bears wrestling in the woods.

"What brings you to Bellissima Valle?" Bruno asked.

Solomon said, "Business, old friend. I have a business proposition for you and Lorenzo. It is a proposition that cannot possibly work out well for me, but if I'm going to get screwed in a business deal, I would prefer to get screwed by an old friend."

"What the hell are you talking about?" Bruno said.

"I will tell you. But first, it has been a long journey up the mountain from Palermo, and I could use a cool limoncello."

"Come inside," Lorenzo shouted. "Limoncello it is."

*

The kitchen table sat fourteen yet held only four. Solomon, Manuel, Bruno, and Lorenzo were seated while Isabella put away the dishes from lunch.

As Lorenzo poured limoncello, he pointed to Solomon. "Isabella, Mr. Roseman is the man who made the cameo of your mamma."

Isabella pulled the chain from under her blouse and displayed it.

"*Grazie*, Mr. Roseman. It is beautiful. I kiss it good night before I go to bed."

"Isabella, you are growing up to be a beautiful young woman," Manuel said. "How come you never come to Palermo with your Papà anymore? Olivia misses seeing you. She enjoyed her talks with you."

"I miss seeing her, too."

"How old are you now?" Manuel said.

"She's fifteen," Lorenzo answered.

"She looks so much like Eva."

"She does, and I'm proud of her." Lorenzo turned to Isabella. "Run upstairs, honey. You can finish your chores later. We have business to discuss."

"Si, Papà," she said before heading up the stairs.

Addressing the elephant in the room, Lorenzo said, "So, how may we help you?"

"Gentlemen, as I'm sure you are aware, the laws of Italy have not been turning in favor of the Jews."

Lorenzo acknowleged by stating, "We are aware, Solomon. Papà and I have been concerned for you and your family."

"Are you concerned enough to purchase the Roseman Cameo Company?"

Lorenzo looked at Bruno before saying, "Please explain."

"Soon, Jews will no longer be allowed to own businesses. We must sell to an Aryan."

Lorenzo and Bruno remained silent momentarily until Bruno spoke up. "We understand the predicament you are in, Solomon, but we know nothing about running a cameo company."

Lorenzo added, "Nor are we in a position to pay you what it's worth."

Solomon said, "We will never receive what it is worth. There are hundreds of Jewish business owners currently rushing to find buyers. There are more businesses for sale than there are buyers. Right now, the only person who has expressed interest is Alfonso DiVincenzo. He murdered my son. The Roseman Cameo Company will collapse around me before he gets his hands on it. That's why I am asking you to buy it. You can pay me what you wish. The amount is not important. Myself, my family, and my craftsmen will stay on under your employ. All we ask is that you pay us all a fair wage. In return, we'll work just as hard for you as we did when we built the business. You may keep all of the profits."

"No!" Bruno said. "That's not how this will work. I have faith that one day Mussolini will die or get thrown out of office. Then Italy will return to its senses. In the meantime, we will in fact purchase your business. We'll pay you one lira. But the profits will go into an account that the Leone family will never touch. You have our word. Your salaries, an amount determined by you, will be paid out of that account. When the time comes for

Italy to overturn these ridiculous laws, we will sell the business back to you for one lira, and all profits that have been earned will be received by you."

Lorenzo said, "I agree with that, Papà. That's the only way to do this. The Roseman Cameo Company is yours. It must always be yours."

Solomon got a lump in his throat. "I humbly came to Bellissima Valle with no other options. My only purpose was to save the company I spent my life building. All I can say is grazie, old friends. There's only one family in all of Italy I trust to keep their word with such a transaction, and I'm sitting at their kitchen table."

ITALY

NORTHBOUND TRAIN TO NAPLES

As Hannah's train pulled away from the Torre del Greco station, she waved at Olivia and Beulah.

The wooden seat upon which she sat made an uncomfortable companion as the train rumbled down the track. Hannah planned to purchase her ticket for the SS *Conti di Savoia* upon arriving in Naples. She would stay in a hotel overnight before her voyage to America departed the following morning.

She watched the countryside through the window as she reminisced about her time in Italy—an experience that was coming to an end. She worried about Camillo's family and the challenges that lay ahead for them. She thought of Nino and smiled.

Oh, my Nino. To you, I'm just a faded memory.

She eavesdropped on the couple sitting behind her. They

spoke in English, but the male had an Italian accent.

"I'm worried about my mamma," he said. "I wish she would come to America with us."

"She's an Italian. She will never leave."

"She's an Italian Jew, which is not the same as being an Italian anymore."

"She isn't a Jewish immigrant. That's who needs to worry. Like your uncle Ira. The one from Poland."

"He can't go back. Poland is worse for Jews than Italy."

"What will he do?"

"I spoke to him. He said he'll stay in Italy and take his chances with the immigration laws. He said something about hiding in plain sight, hoping they never ask for his papers."

The conductor slid open the door to their compartment. Hannah watched as he made his way down the passageway. He checked each ticket before stamping it.

Two seats in front of her, an old man in a dusty dark suit said to the conductor, "I purchased a ticket for Naples, but my plans have changed. I wish to go all the way to Rome. Do I need to get off at Naples to buy another ticket, or can I purchase one from you?"

"You may purchase your ticket from me," the conductor said. "That will be six hundred and fifty lire."

After taking the man's money, the conductor approached Hannah.

"Your ticket, signora."

As Hannah handed him her ticket, she also handed him six hundred and fifty lire. "My plans, too, have changed. I will be getting off in Rome."

CHAPTER 16

*N*ino lives down here? How does he stand it? It is so cold and damp.

Hannah walked the basement hallway looking for the room that had taken her hours to find. The dorm manager had been rude but eventually told her, "He's in room six, located at the furthest end of the building, then down the stairs. Take them all the way to the bottom."

Room four, room five, room … six.

Hannah paused. Her stomach tightened.

What if he rejects me?

She considered walking away, but she had come this far.

Stepping forward to knock, the breeze of foul odor caressed her face and nose. It only distracted her for a moment, then she heard squeaking bed springs mixed with panting and voices.

A male …

Is that Nino?

And a female. They were giggling like children.

She turned to leave, but after several steps she stopped.

No. I must at least say goodbye. We owe each other that.

She returned to the door, took a deep breath, and knocked. The voices stopped. The bed squeaked again, then ceased abruptly.

Her heart pounded.

The door opened.

The woman in the room wore only a bed sheet, and the man she hid behind stood wrapped in nothing but a towel.

"May I help you?" Vito asked.

"I'm sorry," Hannah said. "Maybe I have the wrong room. I am looking for Nino Servidei."

Vito said nothing for a moment as he stared at her. "You are Hannah."

"How did you know?"

"I know all about you. Nino never shuts up about you. He worships your very existence."

Vito grabbed the top of his towel with his left hand and reached out with his right. "My name is Vito Bianchi. I am Nino's roommate and best friend in the whole world." He turned to the girl behind him. "This is Rosa Zerilli. We were just studying. Please wait here. Pardon us while I close the door. We will make ourselves more presentable, then you may come in and wait for Nino. He will be home in an hour, perhaps longer. Maybe sooner. When he sees you, his heart will burst with joy. One moment please," Vito said before closing the door.

Hannah leaned against the wall. She looked up at the arched brick ceiling, then closed her eyes.

He hasn't forgotten me.

Tears streamed down her face. She wiped them away instantly so Vito and Rosa would not know she had been crying.

The door reopened, and Vito invited Hannah in and directed

her to Nino's chair. As she sat, she glanced at the items on his desk: his Bible, books written in both Italian and Latin, notes—most of which she didn't understand. Tucked under his desk lamp was a small piece of paper with only the corner exposed. It read, *Ti amo, Hannah.* I love you, Hannah.

A lump filled her throat.

Vito, who sat on his bed with Rosa, said, "I didn't think you were real. I thought Nino must have created you in his imagination because no woman could be as perfect as he described you. But now that you are here, I see what he—"

Rosa punched his arm. "I'm here, too, Vito."

Vito leaned toward her and kissed her forehead. "Yes you are, my darling. And you, too, are perfect. You are an incredible creation."

Hannah was amused at Vito's exaggerated charm. But more so at how Rosa fell for it.

"Nino said you were in America. He said you were engaged to another man."

"He said what? Where did he get that idea?"

"I'll let him tell you. All I know is that he wrote you several letters and you never replied. Then he went to wherever you were living, Torre del something or other, and someone said you had moved to America and were engaged to someone else—a wealthy Jewish man."

Beulah?

She looked back at the note under his lamp.

Oh my, Nino.

"Are you sure you don't mind if I wait? I can return later when Nino is here."

"No, stay. Nino won't be long. Today is Sunday. Nino goes

to Mass on Sunday. He also goes on Wednesdays. I say to him, 'Why do you go to Mass on Wednesday? Do you forget what you learned on Sunday?'"

"I didn't think about him being in Mass today," Hannah said.

"Why should you? You are a Jew. I am Catholic and I don't even think about Mass."

Hannah grinned. Vito was growing on her.

"Rosa and I are going to eat. Tell Nino we will be at *il bar del quartiere* at 8:00 p.m. We hope you both will join us for a bottle of wine."

"I will let him know," Hannah said as she stood and closed the door behind them.

*

After unlocking his door, Nino's key slipped from his hand. As he pushed the door open, he bent down to pick it up then stopped. Something in his room caught his attention. He looked up to see Hannah standing before him.

Hannah said, "*Ciao, Nino. È bello da vedere. Mi sei mancata.*"

Though Nino was amused at her broken Italian, he was impressed. In English he said, "I can't believe you are here. I thought I would never see you again."

Hannah said, "I didn't think you wanted to see me. When I never heard from you, I thought you had discarded me."

"You thought I discarded you? Hannah, I would never ... I went to Torre del Greco to see you, and I wrote but—"

Her lip quivered as tears flowed down her cheeks before she stepped forward, wrapped her arms around him, and kissed his face twice. He returned her embrace.

"Nino, I'm sorry. I never knew you came to see me, and I

never knew you wrote me. I was living in Sicily with Olivia and Manuel when you came to find me. Beulah lied to you. She kept your letters from me. I never went to America, and I'm not engaged to anyone. I've never stopped thinking of you, and I've never stopped loving you."

Nino squeezed her tight, not wanting to release her. His body shivered when he grabbed Hannah's hand and led her to the bed. They sat, neither releasing their grip on the other. They kissed, then stared at each other, uncertain what to say.

"You have learned a little Italian," Nino said.

Switching to Italian, Hannah said, "Si, I have learned much Italian. I may sound funny to you, and I don't always understand every word that is said, but I found you by asking everyone I saw if they knew where I could find Nino Servidei. Every conversation that led me here was in Italian. They understood me, and I understood them. When I was in Sicily, I studied and studied, immersing myself in the Italian language. I lived with Olivia and Manuel for a year. I refused to let them speak to me in English. Eventually, I was able to wait on customers in their shop."

"I'm proud of you, Hannah."

"I did it because of you, Nino. You are what drove me to learn Italian. My initial plan was that if you were in Italy, then I must be in Italy, and if I must be in Italy, I must know Italian."

Nino leaned forward and kissed her lips. Embracing, they laid back on the bed.

Hannah laughed. "Your bed squeaks. So does Vito's. When I arrived, he was in here with Rosa. His bed was squeaking until I knocked on the door, then it stopped. When Vito opened the door, he was only wearing a towel and Rosa was wrapped in a sheet."

"You are wrong, Hannah. You forget we are in Rome. Vito was wearing a battle skirt and Rosa was wearing a toga."

"I think my timing was bad because Vito still had his sword on display under his battle skirt when he opened the door."

They erupted in laughter as Nino rolled on top of Hannah. Her long hair flowed on the bed as he gazed down into her sparkling eyes.

"What now, Nino? Even though I am here, nothing has changed. I am still a Jew and you still want to be a priest. Solomon and Beulah gave me money to return to America. There is a ship scheduled to leave from Naples for America in the morning. My plan was to be on it. I came here to say goodbye."

Nino rolled off her, sat on the edge of the bed, and placed his face in his hands.

Hannah sat next to him. "I can't stop being a Jew, Nino. It is my heritage. But as for my religion, I would convert to Catholicism today if it meant I could spend the rest of my life with you. But what good would that do me if you choose to be a priest?"

Nino stood and walked across the room.

"I am tormented, Hannah. For a year I have longed for you. My heart has ached for you. Now that you are here, the thought of you leaving so soon ..."

With choked words, he paused to regain his composure.

"Your arrival brings me immense joy. But up until twenty minutes ago, I had accepted that you were gone forever. My mind has been set on becoming a priest. As much as I love you, I can't just turn that off now that you are here. There is a lot of pain in the world, and the Catholic Church is needed more than ever. The Catholic Church needs priests more than ever. That isn't something I can just abandon."

Hannah stood and crossed the room. They embraced and she looked into his eyes.

"Nino, one of the reasons I love you is because the kindness that emanates from your heart is like nothing I have ever seen. That same kindness has drawn you to the priesthood. I can't compete with what you perceive to be God's plan for your life. My head tells me I should be on that ship tomorrow. But there will be other ships to America. I've always wanted to see Rome. Do you mind if I stay awhile?"

"Nothing would please me more."

*

Nino and Hannah approached the sidewalk table.

Vito stood, cigarette in hand. "Ah ... *Benvenuto.* There is my amico, Nino, and his bellissima, Hannah. Sit, sit. Share wine and break bread with us. I want to learn more about the magnificent Hannah now that I know she is actually a real person."

Hannah said, "I think I am going to be embarrassed this evening. Let's not talk about me. I want to know what it is like to live in Rome."

Vito offered Hannah a cigarette and she accepted. "Rome is the ancient city. The ancient city of love. It is magnificent."

Rosa said, "How long are you going to be in Rome, Hannah?"

Hannah looked at Nino. "I don't know. I was supposed to travel to Naples to board a ship to America in the morning. But I don't plan on waking up in Naples tomorrow."

"Oh ... I like this one, Nino," Vito said. "She is a woman who knows what she wants, and she wants you. Love is life's greatest gift, and that gift is sitting right next to you. Promise me you won't mess this one up."

"This one?" Hannah asked.

"Just ignore him," Nino said.

Vito said, "Let me tell you, Hannah, my darling. I have spent many nights out on the town with my amico, Nino, here. He has had the chance to bed some of the most beautiful women in all of Rome, yet he has refused. He claims that it is because of his devotion to God, but I know better. It is because of his devotion to you, and the proof will be tonight. Tonight, you and he will make passionate love, and he will not let his devotion to God get in his way."

Nino said, "Vito, please be quiet, or I will need to find a new best friend."

"Nino, there is no better friend than Vito Bianchi. You should know that by now."

Vito looked at Hannah, and pointed toward Nino, "I have never met a finer man than Nino Servidei. He is like gold. You must fight for him. Fight for him with everything you have, and do not let him go. You and I are now a team. We must talk him out of becoming a priest. His destiny is to be with you forever."

Vito stood up and leaned over the table to get near Nino's face. "Nino, if God wanted you to be a priest, he would have never blessed you by placing this beautiful creature in your life. Don't be a fool."

Nino stood. "If you'll excuse me, I need to find the water closet."

As he walked into the restaurant, Vito shouted, "You can't run from fate, Nino."

"Vito, you are too hard on Nino," Rosa said.

"No, I am not hard enough. He is a brilliant man, yet a complete buffoon when it comes to love. It annoys me to watch."

"Hannah," Vito said. "I will be staying at Rosa's apartment tonight so you and Nino may have privacy and get reacquainted."

"Thank you, Vito. And thank you, Rosa."

"I don't mind," Rosa said. "I wish Vito would spend every night with me. But that isn't possible. I live with my mamma. She isn't very fond of Vito. She thinks he loves too many women and that he will one day break my heart. But I understand how Vito is. I don't like it, but I accept it."

"Why are we having this discussion right now?" Vito said.

Rosa asked, "Do you need a place to stay, Hannah? I mean, after tonight. You can't stay in that little room Nino shares with Vito. It's too small and smells like mold and man stink."

"What are you talking about?" Vito said. "I'll have you know that any man stink in that room is caused by Nino, not me."

Hannah and Rosa were laughing when Nino returned to the table.

"What's so funny?" Nino asked.

Hannah said, "Vito was blaming you for all of the odors in your room."

Nino looked at Vito, "You are one to talk. What about that time you ate two large plates of cabbage casserole and I had to leave the room for two days? I lived on the street until it was safe to return."

Vito said, "I always smell good, Nino. You are just jealous."

When their laughter subsided, Hannah reached for Rosa's hand, "Thank you, Rosa. Yes, I would be grateful if I could stay with you and your mother. I promise to be quiet as a mouse."

When their cameriera approached their table with more wine and bread, Rosa looked toward another table at the end of the sidewalk, "Mi scusi, signora. That cameriera waiting on that other table, is her name Ester Dreyfuss?"

"Yes, she just started working here."

"She used to be my schoolteacher," Rosa said.

"She can no longer teach school because of the new racial laws. She is a Jew."

CHAPTER 17

"I'm here to see Solomon Roseman."

Beulah said, "He is busy working in the back. Who may I say is asking for him?"

"Alfonso DiVincenzo."

Blood rushed through Beulah's body. She was ill. Standing before her was the man who'd ordered Camillo's murder. She both despised and feared him. Behind him were two large men, each with revolvers holstered to their belts.

"I'll let him know you are here," she said, as she made her way to the factory.

*

"Go upstairs, Beulah."

"What are you going to do, Solomon?"

"Go upstairs. Now! I won't tell you again."

Solomon advanced toward the showroom.

"Don't do anything stupid," Beulah said.

Solomon's heart raced with rage the moment he saw Alfonso.

"Get out of my shop you swine, or I will kill you."

Alfonso said, "Why do I always bring out the worst in the

Roseman men? I come in peace. I come to help you. You only have two weeks before the Roseman Cameo Company will be confiscated by the government and sold off. I'm here to make certain you get something for it."

"You have balls, I'll give you that, DiVincenzo."

"It's *Mr.* DiVincenzo. After all, you'll soon be working for me."

Solomon leaned back and laughed.

"You are a fool, DiVincenzo. Your strong-arm tactics may work with some, but not for all of us. I sold the Roseman Cameo Company a few weeks ago. I got top dollar for it. I'll tell you again, DiVincenzo, get out of my shop." Solomon reached under the counter and pulled out a sawed-off shotgun.

DiVincenzo's men stormed Solomon and aimed their revolvers at his head. Solomon kept the shotgun aimed at Alfonso. Everyone was still.

"You and whoever stole this deal out from under me have made a big mistake, Roseman. A big mistake."

CHAPTER 18

Nino caressed Hannah's back as they lay nude under the covers. She had awoken once, just long enough to roll on top of him. Her leg extended across his body; her face nuzzled his chest.

He hadn't woken next to her since the last morning of their voyage. It was something he had yearned for, and it felt natural. He wrestled with how something so beautiful could be wrong in the eyes of God.

He thought of Vito's words, "Nino, if God wanted you to be a priest, he would have never blessed you by placing this beautiful creature in your life."

Nino lifted the covers, peeked at Hannah's naked form, and became aroused.

She is magnificent.

He wanted to wake her. During the voyage, their morning playtime had been his favorite.

He kissed her forehead.

Rest, my darling.

He stared up at the ceiling, soaking up the joy he felt,

wondering how it all would end.

Can I really let her go again?

My dear God, I feel unsettled. I do not want to betray you, but I love my precious Hannah deep into my soul. As I hold her, I feel her heart beating in rhythm with mine; as though you, God, have made us into one. Please guide me and give me courage to do what is right. Fiat mihi semper fidelis.

There was a knock on the door.

Hannah awoke and whispered, "Who is that? Is it Vito?"

"I don't know."

Hannah rolled over, allowing Nino to stand and approach the door, his bare feet frigid on the brick floor.

"Who is it?" Nino asked.

"My name is Msgr. Vasquez. I am looking for Nino Servidei."

Looking back at Hannah, Nino whispered, "He runs the scholarship program."

"What is he doing here?" Hannah whispered.

"I don't know."

"Hello, hello," he said as he knocked on the door again.

"Si, Monsignor. I'm sorry. I just woke up. Please give me a moment to get dressed."

"Take your time, my son."

With the bed springs singing, Hannah leaped to her feet and grabbed her clothes. Nino was dressed by the time she fastened her bra.

He stood at the door and watched her throw her dress over her head, frantically buttoning the front. She then slipped her feet into her shoes and sat down at Vito's desk chair.

"I'm ready," she said.

Nino wanted to warn her that her hair was a mess and she

had missed one of her buttons, but instead he opened the door.

"Ciao, Msgr. Vasquez. It is good to see you again."

Nino watched the monsignor enter the room, assessing the unmade bed before looking toward the disheveled Hannah.

"I see you have a guest."

Nino's stomach tightened.

"Yes, Monsignor, this is Hannah. She was helping me study."

"I thought you said you just woke up."

"Ah … well, we were studying well into the night and fell asleep."

"What were you studying? Your scriptures, I hope."

"We were studying Latin."

"Latin is an important subject for a future priest."

The monsignor turned to Hannah, his back to Nino.

"So, tell me, Hannah. How many letters are in the Latin alphabet?"

Nino got Hannah's attention and held up two fingers followed by three.

"Twenty-three," Hannah said.

Grinning, the monsignor said, "You are clearly an expert in the Latin language, Hannah. Nino is lucky to have your tutelage."

"Thank you, signore."

The monsignor said to Nino, "Do you have class tomorrow morning?"

"No, Monsignor."

"I will expect you at my office at 8:00 a.m. You are long overdue for your annual scholarship review. Then I will assign you a job. In their second year, all of our scholarship students are expected to work at one of our community projects. You will work as a driver once per week delivering food to an orphanage near San Marino. You do know how to drive, don't you?"

"I have driven a vehicle before, yes, Monsignor."

"Can you drive a truck?"

"I will figure it out, Monsignor."

"Have you been attending Mass since you arrived, Nino?"

"Si, I attend *Cappella del Pamphili.*"

"Ah, Fr. Stefani. He is a fine mentor."

The monsignor turned and glanced back at Hannah.

"You are welcome to join Nino in Mass on Sundays."

Hannah said, "We were just discussing my possible involvement in the Church yesterday, signore."

The monsignor grabbed the doorknob to exit, then turned back to Nino.

"Mr. Servidei, when Msgr. Nunzio wrote and asked me to make room for you in the scholarship program, he spoke highly of you. He is my dear friend, and I trust his judgement. But let me remind you, every year, hundreds of young men apply and are rejected for the program you are in. Please don't take this opportunity lightly."

"No, Monsignor. I won't."

As the monsignor stepped out of the room he stopped and turned around.

"Nino, I have one last question. Why is it that only one of the beds is unmade?"

Hannah spoke up, "I slept on top of the covers, signore."

"Si, of course," the monsignor said. "I'm sure that's exactly what you did. Good day to both of you."

ROME, ITALY
THE ZERILLI APARTMENT

Hannah set her suitcase down in the entranceway and looked around the tiny, second-floor apartment.

"Mamma, I'm home," Rosa said. "Hannah is with me."

"I'll be out in a minute," Cecilia Zerilli said.

The drapes had been drawn, cloaking the apartment in darkness. A small foyer sat off to the right which showcased faded fabric on a sofa and two chairs with patterns that appeared to have been vibrant during a different time.

The entranceway was at one end of a short hallway and two bedrooms were at the other. A table and two chairs were in the kitchen to the left.

Hannah greeted Cecilia as she approached.

"Mrs. Zerilli, thank you for allowing me to stay here. I am grateful."

"Hannah, please call me Cecilia. It is wonderful to have you in our home, but I must warn you, there is no luxury here. We barely have enough room for Rosa and me, and you passed the only water closet down the main hallway at the top of the stairs."

"Your home is lovely, Cecilia."

"Rosa says you will be staying with us for a while. At least until you go home to America."

"Right now, I'm uncertain as to when I will return to America."

"Rosa says you are Jewish. Are you unaware of the new racial laws?"

"My heritage seems to be important to a lot of people these days."

"Please, don't take offense. But I'm curious why you would rather be in Italy than America. You would be much safer in America. You know that, don't you?"

"America would be safer, yes I agree. But I have my reasons for being here."

"I see how Jews are being treated," Cecilia said. "I read the papers and listen to the radio. It appalls me. This isn't the Italy I grew up in. I once dated a Jewish boy. He was a wonderful lover."

"Mamma, I don't want to hear that."

Cecilia laughed. "Oh, don't be so stuffy, Rosa. Look who you spread your legs for every time he knocks on the door."

"Mamma, I'm not having this discussion about Vito right now."

Hannah looked on, amused at the exchange.

"Cecilia, I plan on getting a job so I can pay you rent and so I won't spend what little money I have," Hannah said.

"You will never find a job," Cecilia said. "Your Italian isn't good enough. But most of all, you are a Jew."

"Hannah, follow me," Rosa said. "You will be sharing my room. I think my bed is large enough for both of us, but if not, I'll sleep on the floor."

ROME, ITALY
THE PARISH OF SAINTE BERNADETTE

Nino had spent the previous day with Msgr. Vasquez completing his annual scholarship review. The rules Nino had learned during his initial orientation were reiterated. Although not an official vow, Msgr. Vasquez put extra emphasis on the promise of celibacy Nino had made when he first arrived. A promise Nino knew would be impossible with Hannah in his life.

*

Nino had taken the bus to the parish of Sainte Bernadette in order to receive his work assignment.

A nun at the main entrance directed him to a warehouse in the back where he addressed a young man wearing dark pants and a dirty white shirt.

"I'm here to report to someone by the name of Gaetano Perrone about a job delivering food to an orphanage. My name is Nino Servidei."

The young man set his clipboard on the desk and placed his pencil behind his ear. "I'm Perrone. I hope you can drive a truck through rolling hills because to get to the Basilica of San Marino you must drive through the mountains."

"I'll figure it out."

"What days do you have class?"

"Monday through Thursday."

"You will be here every Friday at 7:00 a.m. The Basilica of San Marino is six hours away. You will return well after dark. I won't be here, so insert the clipboard and the paperwork in the mail slot there in the door."

"Who loads the supplies in the truck?" Nino asked.

"I do. You don't need to worry about that most of the time, but if for some reason you ever need to load a truck, the supplies are in the back. Mainly fresh vegetables, canned goods and a few donated clothes. The list of what gets loaded is hanging on the wall near the door. Do you understand, Servidei?"

"I understand."

"Be here Friday."

1940

CHAPTER 19

N ino stood next to Vito as they watched Hannah and Rosa approach the fountain.

Rosa yelled to Vito, "I'm throwing all three coins this time, Vito."

"You'd better not, Rosa my darling. Two coins only please," Vito shouted back.

"What does she mean by 'all three coins'?" Nino asked.

"Nino, we must get over there and stop them. Tradition says that if you throw one coin into the Trevi Fountain, you will one day return to Rome. If you throw two coins in, you will find love in Rome. However, the third coin is the dangerous one. The third coin means that you will one day marry in Rome."

"Do you really believe that, Vito?"

"No, of course not, but why take any chances."

"Hannah," Rosa said. "This is how you do it. You stand with your back to the fountain. You put the coin in your right hand, and then you throw it over your left shoulder into the water."

As Nino and Vito approached the fountain, Hannah asked, "Nino, how many coins should I throw in?"

"Are you asking me how many you *should* throw in or how many do I *want* you to throw in?"

"Both."

Nino remained silent as he stared at the water falling from the front of Oceanus. The sound was refreshing as it flowed into the pool.

"You should only throw in two. But if you happen to throw in the third, I would not be unhappy. I will only smile and dream of what can't possibly be."

"Then I will only throw two."

"No, Hannah," Rosa said. "You must throw three, like me."

Hannah stood with her back to the fountain and threw the first coin into the water.

"There's one, Nino."

She repeated the process.

"There's two, Nino."

As she held the third coin in her hand, she asked Nino once again, "What should I do with this third coin, Nino?"

Nino stood silent as vehicles thundered down the narrow *Via della Murratte*. Pedestrians cleared the streets as a convoy of two dozen German staff cars and military vehicles zipped past at speeds much too fast for the narrow passages of Rome. The lead cars were open-top Mercedes like the one he'd seen Hitler in when he visited in 1938. The vehicles bringing up the rear were *Kübelwagens* with armed soldiers.

"What the hell is this all about?" Vito said.

A stranger standing next to them replied, "Get used to it, my friend. Now that Italy and Germany are allies, we won't be able to escape them. Germans will be all throughout Italy, from Milan to Sicily."

Rome, Italy
The Zerilli Apartment

"Hannah, you must promise me that you will never leave this apartment on your own," Nino said. "It was bad enough when we only had the Italian polizia to worry about, but now the Germans are here. It is only a matter of time before Italian Jews get taken away just like it's happening in other parts of Europe."

Cecilia said, "Mrs. Epstein on the first floor has told me nightmares from Austria. In Vienna, the Germans beat her sixty-seven-year-old brother to death because he refused an order to lick the sidewalk. They have sent other members of her family to work camps and nobody has heard from them. Now those same Germans are here."

"Hannah, I would be happy to get you anything you may need. Just ask me," Rosa said.

"If you must leave the apartment, be certain one of us is with you," Nino reiterated.

"I understand," Hannah said. "I won't leave the apartment by myself."

1941

CHAPTER 20

A s Nino approached his dorm room, he saw Vito on his knees at the end of the hallway, the sound of bricks scraping across the floor echoed throughout the narrow corridor. The source of the breeze and pungent smell that had permeated the passageway since he'd moved in was revealed. Vito had removed several bricks from the wall and laying on the floor next to him was a series of weapons. They consisted of knives, handguns, a machine gun, and several boxes of ammunition. Vito was inserting them into the opening of the wall.

"What are you doing, Vito?"

Vito turned around, "Nino, my friend, I was hoping to keep my secret from you—to protect you."

"Protect me from what?"

"Go into the room. I'll be in momentarily to explain."

"What is behind that wall? It looks like a tunnel. Are those catacombs?"

"Indeed, they are."

You mean all this time we have been living here, the bones

of the dead have been behind that wall? How long have you known this?"

"I found out when I was searching for a place to hide these weapons."

"Why do you have them?"

"I got them after the Germans arrived. We have a plan."

"Who's 'we'?"

Vito didn't answer.

"If the polizia catch you with those guns, Vito, you'll be arrested. They would never let you out."

After Vito replaced the final brick, he stood, wiped his hands on his pants, and pulled Nino into their room, closing the door behind them.

"Listen to me, my friend. There is a group of us. I won't tell you who the others are—for your protection and for theirs—but we are making ourselves prepared."

"Prepared for what?"

"Prepared for the day when Mussolini and his German friends must go."

"So, you're involved in a resistance movement. You're crazy."

Vito chuckled, "That shouldn't be news to you by now."

"What can I say to talk you out of this?"

Vito stepped toward the door while looking Nino in the eye, "Say nothing."

As Vito exited, he nodded toward Nino's desk. "You have a letter. It arrived today. I placed it there on your desk."

Nino sat at his desk. The letter was from Msgr. Nunzio.

Dear Nino,

It is always wonderful to hear from you. I found your most recent letter to be intriguing yet troubling.

You are not the first young man who has started a journey into the priesthood then found himself questioning God's plan for his life. And yes, those questions are often initiated by the allure of the opposite sex. I, too, was tempted to stray in my youth. But in the end, my heart knew what God had in store for me, and I didn't waver. I have devoted my life to serving God through ministering his people. It has been my highest honor, and I have no regrets. To the contrary, had I chosen a different path, I believe my heart would have suffered a permanent void, for I would have shunned the purpose God had intended for me.

Nino, as I have always told you, you are an exceptional young man. Your kind heart is rare in this evil world. But I also must remind you that you are no longer a boy. You are a man who has made commitments. I know God has special plans for you. I believe those plans are to serve your fellow man as a Catholic priest. I pray God will continue to direct your path toward your intended destiny.

Your friend,
Monsignor Nunzio

ITALY
The Road to the Basilica of San Marino

"It feels wonderful to get out of that apartment," Hannah said. "Thank you for allowing me to come with you on your delivery."

"I enjoy our time together," Nino said.

"There has been less of it in recent weeks. Why is that, Nino?"

Nino glanced toward Hannah as he shifted the gears of the delivery truck. "Do you ever regret not returning to America when you had the chance?"

"Why would you ask me that? Do you wish I would have gone home to America?"

"You would be safer."

"And you would be rid of me."

"Hannah, please. That's not what I meant."

"Things haven't been the same between us, Nino. You don't look at me the same. A year ago, when I first moved in with Rosa and Cecilia, you came to visit me every day. You brought me gifts. We would sneak out every night. Now, you only come by a few times per week. I never know when I'll see you. I spend my days looking out the balcony window and cleaning an apartment that isn't dirty. Vito comes by to see Rosa more than you come to see me."

"I've told you, I'm busy with my studies."

"You're busy with your studies unless we are alone in your room. Then I finally receive some affection."

"I have a lot on my mind."

"And I don't, Nino? I'm a Jew living in Italy illegally. I can't leave the apartment by myself."

*

Nino and Hannah spent much of the remainder of their trip in silence until they neared the Basilica of San Marino.

"You are going to love the children at the basilica. When I drive through the gate, they all run to me because I give them chocolate. There is a little girl—her name is Lilia, she's about four or five—she never wants any chocolate, she just wants to be near me. I wish I could adopt her."

"That makes sense. A priest with a Jewish mistress and an adopted daughter."

Nino ignored the comment and said, "When we get there, we must check in with Fr. De Carlo, then we will unload the supplies."

*

Hannah watched Nino as he drove through the gate, his smile radiant as he gazed at the children approaching the truck. After he stopped, he reached under the seat to grab a bag of chocolate, leaped from the cab of the vehicle, and found himself surrounded by screaming orphans.

"Nino, Nino, can I have two pieces today?" a young voice shouted.

"Only one. We want to be certain everyone gets a piece."

Hannah's heart felt warm. Seeing Nino's love flow toward these children of hardship reminded her why she adored him.

Exiting the delivery truck, she approached the swarm of children and stood with her arms crossed, soaking up the joy surrounding Nino.

At a tug on her dress, she looked down at a skinny little girl with dark hair and eyes.

"I'm Lilia," the little voice said.

Hannah bent down and picked her up, "Hello, Lilia. My name is Hannah."

"You are pretty," Lilia said.

"I'm not as pretty as you, my sweet."

Lilia wrapped her arms around Hannah and squeezed her tight. Hannah returned the embrace and kissed the side of her head.

Hannah's thoughts went to her miscarriages and the children she'd lost. She wept unexpectedly, never wanting to release Lilia from their embrace.

"Why are you sad?" Lilia said.

"These are happy tears, Lilia. I'm happy because I get to hold you so tight."

Lilia laid her head on Hannah's shoulder. "Will you take me home with you?"

"No, my darling, I can't. But oh, how I wish I could. Nothing would make me happier."

"Why can't you?"

Nino approached. He felt blissful at the sight of seeing them together. "I see you have met Lilia."

"Signor Nino, why can't I go with you and Hannah?"

Nino saw the tear tracks on Hannah's face.

"Maybe one day you can, Lilia. But not today."

*

After checking in with Fr. De Carlo and unloading the supplies, Nino and Hannah made the trek home.

"It will be dark before we arrive in Rome," Nino said.

There was no response.

Nino looked at Hannah. "Is everything all right?"

"No, Nino, everything isn't all right."

"What is wrong now?"

"You are what is wrong, Nino. You and your Catholic priest drivel. Why are you doing this to me? No, the question is, why am I allowing you to do this to me?"

"What are you talking about? What am I doing to you?"

"Nino, if at this very moment I could create my perfect life, you and I would go back and get Lilia and the three of us would find a way back to America. But no. Instead, I find myself living in fear that I'll be arrested for having the audacity of being born a Jew. I share a little bed every night with a twenty-year-old girl who falls asleep telling me how your best friend Vito cheats on her. And I do all of this for what? So that after devoting several more years of my life to you, I can watch proudly as you put on your little white collar and swear a vow of celibacy for the rest of your life. And in the meantime, what do *you* get out of it? You get to screw your little Jewish whore whenever you want until it's time to discard her. It isn't fair, Nino. It isn't fair at all."

Nino pulled the truck off the road and parked on top of a hill. As he applied the brake, he looked out over the horizon, observing what appeared to be a prison. He'd never noticed it during any of his previous trips to San Marino. Dismissing it, he turned toward Hannah.

"Hannah, do you think all of this is easy for me? When Beulah told me you were living in America and engaged, it was as if she had cut my heart out of my chest. I knew at that moment I'd let you get away. I stopped going to class, I couldn't eat, and I had a week of late-night drinking binges. Vito had to drag me back to our room every night. When you returned to me, and I opened the door to my room to see you standing there, my heart filled with joy as it never had before."

"So why is becoming a priest more important to you than I am?"

"You saw those children back there. I would love to go back and pick Lilia up and take her to America. The three of us would make a glorious family together. But what about the other children? Lilia isn't the only one. What if Fr. De Carlo and the nuns who run the orphanage would have chosen a different path for their lives—an easier path? Where would those children be then? When I look at you, I see the greatest blessing God has ever given me. I wouldn't change a single moment we have shared together. But deep in my heart, I know God has chosen a different path for me. He's directed me to find the thousands of children in the world like Lilia and care for each one of them as if they were my own. I know this is hard on you, Hannah, and I'm sorry. I am so deeply sorry."

Nino looked down. He sensed he was losing Hannah, and in his heart, he wondered why it had taken this long for her to break.

"What is that, Nino?"

Nino looked up at the prison he had seen earlier.

Hannah said, "Why are there children inside the fence? There are old people, too."

"Let's go see what we can find out."

After driving down the hill, they entered the town of Arezzo.

Nino parked the truck, saying, "Stay here, Hannah. You will be safer."

Nino leapt from the cab and approached a group of men playing cards at a cafe.

"*Mi scusi, signori,* I noticed a prison camp in the valley. It appeared to have children and old people in it. Do you know what it is for?"

"Jews," one of the men said. "Immigrants. They were warned to leave the country but failed to do so. Mussolini gave them plenty of time to leave. They chose to stay."

*

Hannah opened the window of the second-floor apartment. It was early morning and the building faced west; shade blanketed the street. She glanced down to see a mother walking with her daughter, holding hands as they made their leisurely journey. Her thoughts went to Lilia, reliving their embrace. She inhaled deeply, and the smell of fresh bread and pastries from the bakery down the street made her smile.

There were no Germans or polizia visible.

She left the window and said to Cecilia, who was sitting at the table, "I'm going to go to the bakery to get fresh bread."

"No, Hannah. It isn't safe."

"I will be careful. It is just down the street. I'll be right back."

"Let me go get your bread, Hannah. Please, stay here."

"I must get out. It's a beautiful day. I need to be in it, if only for a moment."

Hannah grabbed her handbag and made her way down the stairs. She turned left and again saw the mother and daughter sitting on a bench at the bus stop.

She entered the bakery and breathed in the aroma that was even more delicious than what flowed through the street. She looked into the display case and pointed, remaining silent to conceal her American accent.

As the baker reached in, the bell behind her rang and two German soldiers and a *poliziotto* entered. She glanced at them and quickly returned her gaze to the baker, anxious for him to hurry. She handed him her lira and the baker hesitated.

"This is too much. It is early in the morning, and I have no change."

Remaining silent, she pulled out a few coins. The baker took it and gave her the loaf of bread.

As she turned to leave, one of the German soldiers said, *"Hallo wunderschöne dame."*

She shook her head, letting him know she didn't understand German. As she made her way to the door, the poliziotto stepped in front of her. "Would you like me to escort you home to keep you safe?"

Again, she shook her head, saying nothing. As she tried to pass him, he grabbed her arm. "What is your name?"

Her heart pounded in her chest.

He gripped her tighter, causing a sharp pain. "I said what is your name?"

"Hannah."

"And your last name?"

"Servidei. I am Hannah Servidei. My husband is a student at the University of Rome."

"Where are you from?"

"I moved here from America many years ago to marry my Italian husband."

"Where is your wedding ring?"

"It was stolen. We don't have the money to replace it."

The moment the poliziotto released his grip, Hannah stepped forward and turned the doorknob.

"Let me see your papers," the poliziotto said.

Hannah took a deep breath and turned around to face him,

trying to stay calm. "I left them in my apartment. If you'll wait here, I will go retrieve them for you."

He yanked her handbag from her grip and rummaged through it, removing her passport.

"Hannah Roseman. You are a Jew. An American Jew."

He grasped her forcefully and led her out of the store as she stumbled. His grip kept her from falling. "You are under arrest."

"Please, believe me. I am who I say I am. I am married to an Italian."

*

As they entered the station, Hannah noticed several officers watching her as the arresting poliziotto led her into an office. He forced her to sit, then exited, leaving Hannah by herself without her handbag, passport, or money.

Blood rushed through her body as she sat quietly and closed her eyes, listening to the rhythm of her heart pounding in silence. She took several deep breaths trying to calm herself.

Why did I leave the apartment? Why did I not listen to Cecilia when she told me to stay?

After several minutes, the same officer returned with another. One sat behind the desk, and the one who'd arrested her stood in the corner.

The one behind the desk said, "Remove your clothes, we need to search you."

"I will not!"

"You will stand and remove your clothes or we will remove them for you."

"You will not touch me. If you do, I will go to the American Consulate."

The men looked at each other and laughed. The arresting officer stepped toward her as she stood and backed against the wall, fighting him off with punch after punch. The second officer stood and made his way toward her. A hand squeezed her throat. She felt another reach under her dress and grab her thigh.

The door flung open and a man in a brown suit said, "What is going on here?"

"We were just searching the prisoner for contraband."

"You will do no such thing. Unhand her. Get out of here before I suspend both of you."

The two officers left and the man in the suit held the chair for Hannah to sit down.

"Signora, I am Deputy Superintendent Lombardi. You have my deepest apologies. With the army taking my finest men from me, I have had to lower my hiring standards to keep my force at proper levels. What just happened is regrettable."

"Signore, I demand to be released. I have done nothing wrong. I purchased a loaf of bread. Since when is that a crime?"

"It is no crime. However, being a Jewish immigrant is in fact a crime. It is a crime punishable by imprisonment."

"But as I told the officer, my husband is an Italian. His name is Nino Servidei. He is studying at the University of Rome. If you go find him, he will confirm what I am saying."

"If your last name is Servidei, why does your passport say Roseman? It has a stamp saying you arrived from America two years ago."

"We were married in America shortly before arriving in Italy. I haven't received my new passport yet."

"How foolish do you think I am, Miss Roseman? Do you

know how many arrests we have made of Jews who have some ridiculous story to justify why they are still here? You are only the second American who has been reckless enough to stay here. Most of the others are Poles, Germans, or Austrians. I understand why they are here. But you? An American. You are unwise. It baffles me."

"What is going to happen to me?"

"This afternoon, you will be taken to a camp near Arezzo. What happens to you after that, is not up to me. You may stay there indefinitely, or you may be deported next week. But once you leave here, you will be someone else's problem."

"Will I get my passport and my money back?"

"They will do you no good, but yes I can arrange for you to have them returned to you."

The deputy inspector stood and approached Hannah from behind. He leaned down, squeezed her breast, and whispered in her ear, "You would be much safer in Italy if you were not so beautiful."

ROME, ITALY
THE CHAPEL OF CAPPELLA DEL PAMPHILI

Nino knelt by himself at the altar as he recited his daily litany of prayers. The invocations included everything from his own personal discipline to protection for those he loved. Hannah and his mother were always the first mentioned.

The chapel door creaked open, followed by approaching footsteps that stopped directly behind him. Nino remained undistracted and continued with his prayers.

Vito took a deep breath and said, "I'm sorry to interrupt,

Nino, but brace yourself. Hannah has been arrested."

Nino crossed himself before leaping to his feet. "When did this happen?"

"Sometime this morning. Rosa tracked me down at school and pulled me out of class. Hannah left the apartment to buy some bread. Cecilia was sweeping off the balcony and saw the polizia dragging her away. What should we do, Nino?"

"Did you walk here or bring your motorcycle?"

"I rode my motorcycle."

"Good, we are going to borrow a truck."

ROME, ITALY
THE PARISH OF SAINTE BERNADETTE

Nino ran into the office of the warehouse and found Gaetano Perrone.

"You aren't going to like this, Gaetano, but I need to load the truck with supplies and make a delivery."

"To where?"

"To a Jewish internment camp."

"A what?"

"I don't have time to explain. Take the expense of the supplies from my wages."

"You don't earn enough in a year to pay for a truck filled with supplies."

"Gaetano, I'm begging you, please don't argue with me."

"Okay, Nino. But only because it is you. I don't do this kind of shit for just anyone."

"Thank you, Gaetano. I will be eternally grateful."

"Your gratitude will do me no good when I lose my job."

Nino backed the truck up to the warehouse door.

"Vito, help me load. You grab those clothes, and I'll grab these canned goods."

"Where are we going?"

"I'll explain on the way."

*

Nino parked the truck on the hill he and Hannah had been at weeks earlier.

"How do you know she is in there?" Vito asked.

"I don't. It's only my best guess based on what the men in the village told me."

"I don't see too many guards, and the ones I see are Italians, not Germans, so that is in our favor."

"I noticed that when I was here with Hannah."

"What if she isn't there?"

"She has to be," Nino said. "Even if she isn't, we will find her."

Nino bowed his head.

My dear God, I know I have forsaken you time and time again. I am not worthy of your mercy, but I beg you to guide me. Let me save Hannah. After that, I will choose whatever path you want for me. Just let her be safe.

"Vito, we will wait here until morning. Then, we will try to enter the gate. You will be behind the steering wheel to answer their questions. I sound like an American, which is no good."

Vito opened his jacket to reveal a Berretta. "I would have brought one for you, but I know how you feel about guns."

"Are you stupid? You know they will search us."

"I'm not going in there without it. I'll hide it under my seat."

AREZZO, ITALY
THE INTERNMENT CAMP

Hannah woke on a straw mattress in a bottom bunk, shivering under the one wool blanket she'd been issued. The wooden bunks were stacked two high and around the barracks, she saw families with children and women and men of all ages. She stood, grabbed her handbag, and wrapped the blanket as tight as she could before making her way to the entrance of the barracks. It had been dark when she'd arrived the previous evening, and she wanted to get a lay of the land. The door was warped and didn't close completely, allowing the wind to penetrate the building.

She stepped out and felt a cool gust across her exposed legs as her once white dress flapped in the breeze.

Will they feed us? I feel sick.

There were several other white buildings identical to her own—two rows that ran parallel, with the last one adjacent to a warehouse.

She turned to see the mountains in the horizon. The hill where she and Nino had parked caught her attention.

Does he know I am missing?

Hannah felt the need to lie down, so she turned back toward the barracks. A feeling of nausea overcame her, and she began to vomit. She had consumed little water or food during the previous twenty-four hours, and her attempts to discharge the contents of her stomach were futile. Only a small amount of mucus came up as her muscles tightened around her abdomen, painfully forcing out air.

She leaned against the wooden structure, fear overcoming

her. She had experienced this sudden sickness before. Both times, she had been pregnant.

*

"We are from the Diocese of Rome," Vito said. "We have supplies to deliver."

The gate guard looked at his list.

"I see nothing about a delivery from any Diocese of Rome."

"It took us hours to get here," Vito said. "You are going to make me drive all the way back to Rome, and they are going to make me come back tomorrow. Tomorrow is my day off. I have a date with a *bella donna* tomorrow. Please don't make me miss my time with her because I must drive back here."

A supervisor overheard the conversation and said, "Let him go. There is not enough love in the world. We don't want to contribute. But first search them. Make certain they aren't smuggling anything in."

The gate guard said, "Get out and stand to the side."

Both Vito and Nino thought of the Berretta under the driver's seat. Vito left the motor running as they stepped out of the vehicle. The guard opened the back of the truck first and rummaged through the clothes, ignoring the canned goods. He then made his way to the passenger side where Nino had been sitting. First, he opened a small storage box on the floor, then looked under the seat.

As he made his way to the driver's side, Vito stepped toward him and displayed a pack of cigarettes. "Do you have a match?"

As the guard reached into his pocket he said, "You have Turkish cigarettes. I have never tried them. I hear they are the world's finest."

"Oh, they are, mio amico. But they are strong and not for everyone. Would you like one?"

"Si."

"Here, take two," Vito said while slipping one into the guard's breast pocket and handing him the other.

The guard lit his own first then struck another match and lit Vito's cigarette for him.

"Enjoy them, mio amico," Vito said as he climbed behind the steering wheel.

"Where should we take the supplies?" Vito asked.

The guard replied, "There's a warehouse toward the back, at the end of that row of white barracks. Ask for Sergio. He'll help you."

After closing his door and glancing at Nino, who was taking a deep breath, Vito put the truck in gear, rolled up his window, and entered the camp.

"You are clever," Nino said.

"I am Vito Bianchi. Being clever comes easy for me."

*

Her blanket was only large enough to cover her legs or her upper body if she lay prone, so she curled in the fetal position while her mind raced. She considered the possibility of a pregnancy. Would she tell Nino? Would he stop pursuing the priesthood? Would he resent her? How long would she be detained? Did they have a doctor?

Since Camillo's death, she had often been alone yet had never felt as lonely as she did in that moment. She wanted Nino. Despite everything, she knew he loved her and was always quick to protect her. Regretting her decision to leave the apartment, she began to weep.

What have I done?

She became nauseous and sat up. Taking a few deep breaths, she felt better and laid back down, only to feel another urge to vomit. She stood and made her way to the door. Once outside, she tried to empty her stomach, yet like before, was unable to.

As she rested against the side of the building she looked toward the warehouse.

She saw a truck and realized it looked like Nino's delivery vehicle. Once again, she thought of him.

Vito stepped into view.

Vito?

Then she saw Nino. He was with the warehouse manager. The man pointed inside the building, and Nino nodded his head. When the manager stepped away, Nino stood next to Vito and they scanned the compound. Hannah made certain no guards were in sight, dropped her blanket to the ground and waved her hands frantically.

Vito spotted her first. He grabbed Nino's arm.

*

"Hannah," Nino said softly. "Stay calm, Vito. We only have one chance to get her out of here. We are going to finish unloading the food from the truck but leave the clothes. Then, we are going to pull over near Hannah's barracks, and you will lift the hood as if you are having engine trouble. The doorway where she is at should be blocked from view. That will give her a chance to make it to the truck. I'll have her hide under the pile of clothes."

*

As they approached Hannah's barracks, she was no longer in sight. Nino noticed two guards approaching on foot and tapped Vito's arm.

"I see them," Vito said.

Vito stopped the truck, and made an attempt to start the ignition, halting before it turned over.

Vito exited the cab and shouted, *"Accidenti a te pezzo di merda!"* pretending to be irritated the engine wouldn't turn.

As the two guards approached, one said, "Fiat piece of shit. I would never own one again."

"I don't own it; it belongs to the Diocese of Rome."

"Maybe if you pray over it?" the other guard said as they continued their stroll, laughing as they went.

Nino watched them go around the corner then leaped from the truck and ran into Hannah's barracks. She was inside of the door, shivering in the blanket.

"Hannah," Nino said, embracing her intensely, holding her close in an attempt to warm her.

With Hannah's head resting on his shoulder, Nino noticed the other prisoners. They appeared cold and pitiful. The sadness in their eyes was difficult to bear. He wished he could rescue all of them, but he was there for Hannah.

"Nino, how did you find me?" Hannah asked.

"We did. That's all that matters." Nino peeked out of the door, and Vito signaled all clear. Swiftly, Nino placed Hannah in the back of the truck. "Hide under the clothes, Hannah. Don't move."

Vito closed the hood, and they drove toward the entrance.

"This will be the tricky part," Vito said. "You might want to squeeze in another prayer before we get to the gate."

"I've been praying since we got in here," Nino replied as Vito applied the squealing brakes. "We are almost free, Hannah. Just a little longer."

"All delivered?" the guard asked.

"All delivered. I appreciate you letting me through," Vito said as he began to accelerate.

Someone banged on the side of the truck. "Stop!"

For a moment, Vito considered stepping on the gas, but didn't.

Nino looked at him. "Don't you dare grab that gun."

Vito shook his head in agreement, while taking a deep breath.

A different guard approached Vito. "Do you have any more of those Turkish cigarettes?" he asked.

Reaching in his pocket, Vito removed what remained of the pack and handed it to him. "Enjoy them."

"Grazie," the man said before waving them on.

CHAPTER 21

Nino followed Hannah into the apartment. Vito was behind Nino.

"Hannah!" Cecilia shouted. "We were afraid we would never see you again."

Rosa embraced Hannah, weeping, "I have been so scared for you. How did you persuade them to let you go?"

"I didn't persuade anyone. These two rescued me."

"We were just lucky their security was so poor," Nino said.

Cecilia said, "I bet you are hungry, Hannah."

"I'm starving. I haven't eaten since breakfast yesterday."

"Open a bottle of wine, Rosa."

"I didn't make enough spaghetti for everyone," Cecilia said. "I'm sorry."

"You ladies eat, Vito and I are fine," Nino said.

"You eat, Hannah," Cecilia said as she set a plate of spaghetti on the table.

Hannah wasted no time grabbing a slice of bread and dipping it into the spaghetti sauce.

"I have never felt so hungry. May I have some water?"

Cecilia placed a glass in front of her.

Rosa poured a glass of wine for Hannah.

"Someone else can drink that," Hannah said. "It doesn't appeal to me. I just want water."

"I'll have it," Vito said, reaching for the wineglass.

After Hannah ate dinner, everyone made their way to the parlor.

Just as Nino sat down next to Hannah, Vito approached him and grabbed him by the lapel of his jacket before dragging him into Rosa's bedroom. Vito slammed the door, then pushed Nino backward until he fell on the bed. Nino's mouth fell open in disbelief as Vito pointed his finger at him.

"Now you listen to me, and you listen good, you self-righteous bastard. I've had enough of your I-want-to-save-the-world-as-a-priest shit. It's over. Do you hear me? You always speak of God. Well, anyone who is paying attention can see that God sent you an angel, and she's sitting in that parlor. She's risking her life to be here with you. Now I have risked my life to save her, and it's all because of you. Can't you see what God really wants for you? Now, you are going to take her back to America, you are going to marry her, and you are going to live a good life together. If you don't do that, we are no longer friends because I don't have stupid people as friends."

Nino stared up at Vito, who was still panting from his fiery outburst. "May I speak now?"

"Not if it's to tell me you still want to be a priest. If you tell me that, you will be a priest with a black eye."

"Actually, Vito, I was going to ask you if you could help me sneak Hannah out of Italy."

"Are you going with her?"

"Si, of course. Then when we get to America, we are going to get married. I would like for you to be there, but that might be difficult since all of the Italian ports are closed."

Nino watched Vito reach down, and once again grab his lapels before pulling him to his feet and kissing each cheek.

"Finally, you bull-headed padre. You've come to your senses. When did you figure this out?"

"When you and I were up on the hill looking down at the prison. I knew if I got her out of there, I would spend my life keeping her safe."

Vito pointed at Nino. "I will let you tell her. Wait here. I'll get Hannah."

As Nino watched Vito leave, a peace filled him. The internal struggle he'd battled so long was over. He knew what was right, and there was no looking back.

Nino was sitting on the edge of Rosa's bed when Hannah entered.

"What was all of that commotion about?" Hannah asked as she sat next to him.

"Vito was just getting some things off of his chest."

"He said you wanted to talk to me."

Nino sat silent, fearful he may say the wrong thing. He then turned to Hannah and said, "You sleep with Rosa in this little bed?"

"That's not what you wanted to discuss with me."

"No. It isn't."

"Spit it out, Fr. Servidei."

"You always call me that when you are mocking me."

Hannah said nothing. Like Vito, she looked annoyed with him.

"Don't I get a kiss or something for rescuing you?"

Hannah grinned, then leaned forward, and they kissed before lying back on the bed. Then she straddled him, her face hovering over his.

"I love you, Nino. You did save me. I once told you that you would always be my knight in shining armor, and today you proved it."

"I couldn't have done it without Vito."

"I know. But Vito just followed your lead."

"Don't be so hard on Vito. He keeps telling me I should marry you."

"And what do you say?"

"Usually, I say nothing. But today, I agreed with him."

"Excuse me?"

"I said today, I agreed with him." Nino kissed her forehead. "Will you marry me, Hannah Roseman?"

"I thought you would never ask me that question, Nino. I've been so afraid of the day this would all end."

"It will never end, Hannah. I will always love you."

She leaned down and kissed him again as he wrapped his arms around her. She kissed his face, then his neck, then returned to his lips, all the while pressing her warm body on top of his.

Hannah said, "I guess today is the day for big news."

"What do you mean? What other big news are you talking about?"

"I think I'm pregnant."

"You think you're what?"

"I think I'm pregnant. I wasn't going to tell you because I didn't want to ruin your career as a priest. And based on my history, I'm doubtful it will survive."

Nino guided Hannah off him, rolling her gently so her back flattened on the bed. He leaned over her and kissed her stomach.

"Hannah. You don't know how happy this makes me. To know that a part of me is growing inside of you overwhelms me with joy."

"Really?"

"Why do you doubt me?"

"I don't doubt you, Nino. I don't doubt anything about you."

Nino said, "I'm glad you have so much confidence in me, because now I have to figure out how to get us back to America."

"When are we leaving?"

"Soon."

"We need to go get Lilia," Hannah said.

"Hannah, do you know what we are up against trying to get out of the country? The borders are closed. You are still a Jewish immigrant here illegally. Now, we are supposed to drive back to the other side of Italy to get a child who doesn't belong to us. We can't just stroll into the Basilica of San Marino and ask Father De Carlo to let us leave with Lilia. She isn't a goat you buy at a livestock auction."

"We have to try, Nino."

Nino sat up, leaned forward and put his face in his hands.

"First, we must figure out how to get out of here."

"No, Nino. First, we go get Lilia. We can figure out how to get the three of us home later."

CHAPTER 22

"**A**re you sure it's okay to take the truck, Nino?"
"Gaetano isn't working today. He will never know."
"I will hold Lilia in my lap for the trip back," Hannah said.
"You are more confident than me that we will leave with her."
"You'll figure it out, Nino. You always do."

*

It took longer than the normal six hours to get to the Basilica of San Marino. Nino decided to take side roads in hopes of limiting their chances of being pulled over and questioned.

They arrived at the basilica in the early evening, and Nino parked in front of Fr. De Carlo's office before he and Hannah made their way in.

"Father, do you have a minute?"

"Nino, my son. What brings you here? It isn't Friday."

"That's not why I am here, Father. I would like to speak to you."

"Yes of course, have a seat. And young lady, I know you

were here with Nino during an earlier visit, but I'm sorry, I forget your name."

"My name is Hannah."

"Ah. Yes, Hannah. Please come in and have a seat. Both of you."

Hannah and Nino sat across the desk from Fr. De Carlo.

"How may I help you?"

"Father, much has changed since we last met. I hate to disappoint you, but I have decided that I no longer wish to be a priest. Hannah and I are going to return to America and be married."

"That is wonderful, Nino. There is no need to apologize to me. You are not the first young man to realize the priesthood wasn't for him, and you won't be the last. It often happens after meeting a pretty girl."

Nino grinned. "I've heard that."

"You have driven a long way to tell me this, Nino. Is there something else I can help you with?"

"Father, I know there are strict rules for adoption. And Hannah and I don't align with any of them. We aren't married yet, and Hannah ..." Nino paused while he looked at Hannah.

"I'm a Jew, Father. Nino is trying to tell you I'm a Jew."

"I'm sorry, but I'm confused by all of this. You came here to adopt a child. Is that correct?"

"Yes," Nino said. "We want to adopt Lilia. We will be leaving for America soon, and we want to take her with us."

"I see. Do you plan on getting married in the Catholic Church?"

Nino said, "Yes we—"

Hannah interrupted Nino. "Yes, Father, we do. I've already

committed to Nino that I will do whatever I have to do to be with him, including converting to Catholicism."

"The Lord works in mysterious ways, indeed."

"What do you mean, Father?" Nino asked.

"Last week, a German officer came by here and asked me if any of our orphaned Jews were immigrants. I lied and said no. The expression on his face indicated he didn't believe me. I don't know what his intentions were, but his line of questioning concerns me. My suspicion is that he wanted to turn them over to the Italian authorities. Technically, they could be sent to an internment camp based on the new laws. So far, the Germans themselves have not mistreated Italian Jews like they have the Jews in the rest of Europe because we are allies. However, they are pressuring Mussolini to crack down on them. We do in fact have immigrant Jewish children living with us. There are seven of them. Lilia herself is an Austrian Jew. I have been racking my brain trying to figure out how to conceal these seven children or get them someplace safe. If you can get Lilia safely to America, then I would only have to worry about six."

"So, you'll allow it?" Hannah asked. "You'll let us adopt Lilia?"

"Yes, of course. I only have one request."

"What is that?" Nino asked.

"Although it isn't legal under Italian law because you, Nino, are a Catholic, and you, Hannah, are a Jew. And it won't be officially recognized in the eyes of the Catholic Church until Hannah converts, but I would prefer to adopt Lilia to a married couple. Would you allow me to conduct a brief marriage ceremony for you this evening?"

Hannah looked at Nino. "Yes of course, Father."

"Hannah Servidei. That sounds beautiful," Nino said.

"It does," Hannah agreed as she squeezed his hand.

"After the ceremony, we will work on Lilia's adoption. I can't provide you with an official document, for that can only be issued by the government. However, I will write a letter for you to carry. It will state that I have given my blessing and we are just waiting on the official documents."

"When can we see Lilia?" Hannah asked.

"It is getting late. Why don't you spend the night here? That will give us time to conduct the wedding ceremony and finish all the documents. We can give Lilia the good news in the morning. Then, you can be on your way after breakfast."

*

The next morning, they waited in Fr. De Carlo's office. Nino couldn't take his eyes off Hannah. Although it wasn't official, in his heart, she was his wife. Hannah directed her eyes toward Fr. De Carlo's door.

"I hope she is happy to see us," Hannah said.

"You are going to be a wonderful mother to both Lilia and the one you are carrying," Nino said as he touched her stomach.

"All of this is happening so fast, Nino. Are you sure you're okay with the sudden changes in your life?"

"I've never been happier."

Fr. De Carlo's office door was open, and they could hear them coming down the hall.

"I have a surprise for you, Lilia."

Her little voice said, "What is it?" as she turned the corner and saw Nino and Hannah.

She ran to Hannah and crawled into her lap, "Did you and Nino come to see me?"

"Yes, we did come to see you, Lilia. Are you happy to see us?"

"I missed you," Lilia said as she hugged Hannah.

"We missed you, too, darling. That's why we are here. We want to take you with us. We want you to live with us forever and ever."

Lilia squeezed Hannah tighter and began to cry. "You are going to take me home with you?"

"Yes, my darling. We are going to take you home with us."

ROME, ITALY
THE ZERILLI APARTMENT

As Vito rolled out a map of Europe on the kitchen table, Nino watched Hannah and Rosa playing with Lilia on the foyer floor. His wife's smile was radiant, and it filled him with joy. However, it was matched by his fear. A daunting task lay ahead of him, and he had no idea how he was going to get his new family safely to America.

"Nino," Vito said. "While you were away getting Lilia, I spoke to a few friends of mine about getting to America from here. They said the only safe way is through Portugal or Gibraltar."

Nino placed his finger on the map. "They are a long way, Vito. We would have to go here—through France—then through the Pyrenees mountains. Those odds aren't in our favor."

"Through France is one way. Another way is through Palermo. Here in Sicily. I bet Sicilians are still selling fruit, olives, and wine to Portugal. There may be cargo ships going from Palermo to Lisbon. We must figure out how to get you on one of those ships. But first, we must get you to Palermo."

Hannah stood up after overhearing the conversation. "I think I can get us to Palermo."

"Solomon?" Nino asked.

"The only problem is, he and Beulah think I have been in America for the past two years. They gave me money to get there. I'm sure they are angry at me for never contacting them. Now, I'm going to show up with my new family, once again asking for their help."

"Solomon can get us to Palermo by boat," Nino said.

"Are you listening to me, Nino? Beulah lied to you to keep us apart. They paid for me to escape to America, now I will show up with you and Lilia begging for them to help me again."

"Hannah, my job is to get you and Lilia home to America. I can't worry about someone's anger or hurt feelings. Solomon is a man of great character. He will take us to Palermo, I'm sure of it."

"If he still owns his boats. When I left, he had gone to Sicily to sell his business."

"It's our best chance, Hannah. We just need to get to Torre del Greco without being questioned."

"I suggest you take the last train out of Rome," Vito said. "I believe it is the 10:00 p.m., but we will confirm that. Few people are on the last train, which means you are less likely to see any polizia or German soldiers."

"When should we go?" Nino asked.

"Not the weekend. Too many late-night drunks, which means polizia. Monday is better."

"We'll leave this Monday then."

Rome, Italy
Nino's Dormitory

Packing his suitcase, Nino glanced at Vito who was lying in his bed smoking a cigarette.

"You aren't just my amico, Nino. You are my *fratello*, my brother. You always will be."

Nino stopped folding and walked across the room. Vito stood and they embraced.

"I owe you everything, Vito. You helped me save Hannah, and for that I will always love you, my fratello."

"Love is a beautiful thing, Nino. It's what drives me every day."

Nino returned to his folding. "I know you have a craving for beautiful women, but you have one who loves you in Rosa. She loves you enough to tolerate your wandering escapades. I love Rosa, too, Vito. Please stop hurting her. Respect her. Be faithful to her."

"That is the priest coming out of you, Nino."

"I don't need to be a priest to ask someone I care about to be faithful to someone else I care about."

"I have been faithful recently. I haven't been with another woman since … since Wednesday."

Nino shook his head.

"One day, I want you and Rosa to come visit us in America."

"We will do that, Nino. Just as soon as the world returns to normal."

"I'm afraid it is going to get much worse before it gets better."

Nino placed his Bible on top of his clothes and closed his suitcase.

As Nino reached out to shake his friend's hand, Vito said, "There is one more thing."

Vito opened the door and looked down the corridor. After seeing nobody, he turned and detached the loose bricks concealing the catacombs. He removed a Berretta and attempted to hand it to Nino, who refused it.

"I'm not taking a gun, Vito."

"Stop being a priest for a moment. You said yourself that your job is to get Hannah and Lilia safely home to America."

"That's why I'm not taking any guns with me."

"Nino, Rosa told me something that Hannah shared with her. I'm sure she's never told you. But when she was arrested …"

"What is it, Vito? Tell me."

"When Hannah was arrested, she was assaulted. Two polizia were in the room alone with her. She tried to fight them off, but they were strong and very rough with her. Someone else came in. He initially stopped them and made them leave. But before he himself left, he touched her, too."

Nino's knees became weak.

Oh, Hannah.

"The world is shit, Nino. The people in charge are shit. They are dangerous and there aren't a lot of people out there to stop them."

Nino grabbed the gun from Vito's hand. "How does this work? You have to show me."

"It is loaded, so be careful. It has seven bullets. This is the safety. You must slide this over before you fire it. Other than that, it is just aim and shoot."

Nino reached behind his back and slid the gun under his jacket and into his pants at the belt.

"Thank you for everything, Vito. Now I must go get my family. We have a train to catch."

CHAPTER 23

V ito's assessment of the late-night train ride was correct. When they boarded the train, there were only three other passengers who sat in the car in front of them. There would have been four, but a young teenage boy detained by the polizia missed his departure. Their own car, the last one, held only them.

Lilia was asleep in Hannah's arms, and though Hannah was sleepy, her nerves kept her awake.

"Hannah, don't be mad at Rosa, but she told Vito what happened to you when you were arrested. Vito told me." Nino got a lump in his throat and eyes watered. "I'm sorry, Hannah. I should have been there for you. It is my job to protect you."

Hannah touched his face. "No, Nino. Don't you dare blame yourself. You warned me, and Cecilia warned me. Even Rosa and Vito told me not to leave the apartment by myself, but I did anyway. What happened to me was my fault, not yours. And as for you protecting me, you rescued me from the internment camp. And you know what, Nino? When I was in there, I had a feeling that you would find me and get me out. I don't know why, but I just knew you would. That's how much faith I have in you. You are my hero, Nino. You are Lilia's hero, too."

Nino heard what she was saying, but his mind was elsewhere. He looked down and clinched his teeth. Rage overcame him as the thought of Hannah's assault filled his head with images. He had never felt anger like that before, and it scared him.

Nino looked into Hannah's eyes, then glanced down at the sleeping Lilia, and his heart filled with joy. It calmed him.

"I love you, Hannah."

"I love you, too, Nino."

"We should be there soon," Nino said.

He closed his eyes and sat quietly, listening to the rhythm of the train gently bouncing on the track. Spaced evenly apart, the rail joints offered a predictability in the relaxing sound.

He opened his eyes to see a polizia officer making his way back to their car. He slid the first door open, then lit a cigarette. As he passed them, he looked at Nino, then Hannah and Lilia, but kept walking until he arrived at the back. Nino turned and watched him slide the door open and step out onto the rear deck to smoke.

Nino kept his back to the officer. He wanted to keep watching him, but that would increase suspicion, so he kept looking forward. Hannah had finally fallen asleep, still holding Lilia tightly, as only a mother could do.

Nino heard the door slide open then slam shut. The sound of boots fell heavy on the wooden floor as the officer approached.

"I need to see your papers," he said when he stopped next to Nino.

Nino removed his passport and his documents proving he was a student, authorized to be in Italy.

"I need to see theirs."

"They are sleeping, won't mine suffice?"

"I need to see their documents."

"I have them here," Nino said, as he reached behind his back and pulled out the Berretta.

The officer reached for his revolver.

"Leave it alone," Nino said. "Walk to the back where you just came from."

Nino followed him through the back door and onto the deck.

Other than the lights from the railcar reflecting on the track, the evening was an abyss of darkness.

"Jump," Nino said.

"I'm not going to jump. And it wouldn't do you any good. Once I was off the train, I would find a telephone and every stop between here and Villa San Giovanni would have swarms of Italian policemen and German soldiers looking for you. You wouldn't stand a chance. So just give me the gun, and I'll take it easy on you."

Nino took a deep breath. He thought about Hannah's assault. He wanted to pray for guidance, but he knew what answer would be revealed—*Thou shalt not kill*. That answer would put his family in danger and was unacceptable.

My dear God, I am sorry. Please forgive me.

Nino released the safety as Vito had instructed him, aimed at the officer's heart, and pulled the trigger. He watched him grab his chest. His mouth opened and his eyes rolled back in his head. As his life escaped him, he fell back and bounced down the stairs of the platform, disappearing into blackness.

Nino leaned against the glass of the sliding door. He was ill and leaned over the railing, retching uncontrollably. When he finished, he looked at the gun in his hand and dropped it. It bounced once on the tracks before the darkness swallowed it.

The door behind him slid open. He wiped the bile from his chin as he turned to see Hannah, still holding the sleeping Lilia.

"What happened? I heard a loud bang. It woke me up."

"I heard it, too," Nino said. "That's why I came out here. It must have been something we passed along the tracks. Let's go back inside. I feel cold."

TORRE DEL GRECO, ITALY

Nino's heart pounded. He couldn't get the vision of the officer's face out of his mind as the train slowed into Torre del Greco. There was a row of lights on the platform. Many were burned out or broken, presenting an eerie darkness. Though midnight gloom presented opportunity for evil mischief, it also presented cover they may not have otherwise.

The trained stopped. He saw movement in the distance but couldn't see who or what it was.

Why did I throw the gun away?

The willingness to kill, albeit to protect his family, surprised him.

Nino stood so Hannah and Lilia could pass. He grabbed their two suitcases from under the seat and followed them out onto the platform. The thought of not finding a taxi at this hour never occurred to him, but that was the reality.

Nino saw a hint of fear in Hannah's eyes.

"How are we going to get to Solomon and Beulah's?" she asked.

"There's no need to worry, Hannah. I'll figure it out."

He escorted them to the street, hoping to find any form of safe transportation.

The figure he spotted on the platform as the train came to a stop was approaching them.

"Just walk slowly, Hannah. Behave as though we are just an innocent family trying to get home."

"Mi scusi, signore," the man shouted. "I am looking for my son. He was supposed to be on that train. He is only fourteen. He was wearing a brown jacket. Did you see anyone who fit that description?"

Nino turned to see a man dressed in blood-splattered coveralls and smelling of fish.

"Si, signore. A young man of that description was detained on the platform in Rome."

"By the polizia or the Germans?"

"The polizia."

"I must go find him. He has problems. He is … dumb. My wife told me not to let him go by himself. Why didn't I listen? I must go home and get her. We will drive all night to Rome and find him. Thank you for the information, signore."

As the man turned, Nino said, "Signore, I am sorry, I know you are desperate to get home, but we too are desperate. You appear to be a fisherman. Are you heading toward the waterfront? We need to get to the shore. May we trouble you for a ride?"

"Si, come with me, but hurry please."

TORRE DEL GRECO, ITALY
THE ROSEMAN CAMEO FACTORY

As they approached the storefront, the shop and second-floor apartment were dark. There was a slight chill in the air.

"They are in bed, Nino. We can't just bang on the door," Hannah said.

"If I were alone, I would lay here at the doorstep and go to sleep until morning. But I'm not alone," Nino said as he pounded on the door of the cameo shop."

Hannah sat down on the step and cradled Lilia. "Nino, no. I won't do this. We can't wake them in the middle of the night."

Nino ignored Hannah and continued to beat on the door until the lights came on.

"They are going to hate me," Hannah said.

Lilia stirred from the pounding.

Nino saw the silhouette of Solomon. His girth created an eclipse of the light he had just turned on.

"Hold on, hold on," Solomon shouted, as he pulled the curtain back to reveal Nino.

Nino stared back at the agitated Solomon as he turned the latch and opened the door.

"Nino. What the hell are you doing here?" Solomon said, as Beulah walked up behind him.

Beulah's face expressed disbelief, as she glanced over Nino's shoulder to see Hannah behind him.

"Hannah! I thought you'd gone to America," Beulah said. "And who is that child you are holding?"

*

Nino and Hannah sat at the kitchen table. Beulah and Solomon remained standing. Solomon had always been a man of few words, and today, Nino was grateful. Beulah had no problem speaking for them both.

Nino watched Hannah. The grimace on her face made her discomfort evident. He wished he could mediate, but he sensed he should take Solomon's lead and keep his mouth shut.

"So, when we gave you money to go to America, you took advantage of our generosity and went to Rome to be with Nino," Beulah said. "You are approaching your second year away and never even considered writing to us to let us know you were safe. Why is that?"

Lilia began to fidget and fuss in Hannah's arms.

Hannah squirmed. "I have no defense for my actions. I have been unfair to you both, and I am sorry."

"Unfair?" Beulah said. "You lied to us."

"No, I didn't, Beulah. When I left here, my intention truly was to go to America. But instead of getting off at Naples to catch my ship, I stayed on the train and went to Rome. I wanted to say goodbye to Nino, then return to Naples for my voyage home. I just never made it. I still have some of the money you gave me. You are welcome to have it back."

Beulah said, "It's not about the money."

Exhaustion overcame Lilia, and she began to whimper.

Beulah approached Hannah and took Lilia from her, "Explain this one to us. The child is at least four, probably five. I know she didn't come from you."

"We adopted her," Nino said. "Her name is Lilia."

Lilia calmed as Beulah walked the kitchen with her, eventually resting her head on Beulah's shoulder and dozing off.

"I often wondered what it would have been like to have a little girl around the house," Beulah said. "She is precious."

Solomon said, "So let me see if I understand this. An unmarried Catholic and Jew walk into an orphanage and say, 'We would like to adopt a child,' and they agreed?"

Solomon pulled two chairs from the table. "Beulah, have a seat. I think we are going to be here for a while as these two explain what they have been doing."

*

After several cups of coffee, Nino and Hannah had shared their adventures in Rome. Solomon and Beulah, in turn, explained the sale of the cameo company to the Leones.

Solomon said, "Business has been poor. People are scraping their lire together to feed their families. There are shortages of everything. Even the rich don't spend money on cameos anymore."

Beulah added, "And now we must pay Alfonso DiVincenzo a fee to keep his thugs away. He was furious that we sold to the Leones."

Nino fidgeted in his chair. He realized his own papa in New York had incorporated these same tactics of extortion. However, most of his young life, he was too naive to recognize it.

A thought emerged in Nino's mind that disturbed him. When they arrived in New York, Hannah and his mother would meet. An otherwise joyous occasion would reveal his secret—that Alfonso DiVincenzo was his grandfather.

He glanced at Hannah who was still tense from her exchange with Beulah.

Beulah said, "Hannah come with me. Let's put Lilia to bed."

*

Nino stayed at the table with Solomon and said, "Solomon, I don't know you very well. It is difficult for me to ask what I am about to ask, but will you take us by boat to Palermo? I have heard that the best way to Portugal is through Sicily by way of cargo ship."

"Maritime travel is risky these days, Nino. There are many military patrol boats and naval vessels who fire first and ask questions later. Mainly the Germans and Italians, but also the British. We must travel at night, but I will gladly take you to Palermo. Once you arrive, getting on a cargo ship to Portugal will not be easy. There is little trade these days, and if you are lucky enough to bribe your way on board, if you are caught, you still must have the proper documents. Hannah is here illegally and can still be arrested. And Lilia is a child with adoption papers held by parents who by Italian law aren't married. So, what are your specific plans when you arrive in Palermo?"

"I have no plans, other than to get to Palermo. I was hoping that once I arrived, the solution for boarding a ship for Portugal would reveal itself."

CHAPTER 24

S olomon cut back on the throttle when they saw the lights of Palermo in the distance. The voyage had been uneventful. The seas had been calm and only twice had they seen a spotlight from a coastal patrol boat.

Nino knew the story of Camillo well. It had been many years since his murder, but as they approached the harbor of Palermo, he kept his eyes on the darkened silhouette of Hannah. She was busy entertaining Lilia, which gave him comfort knowing she had a distraction. But as the illuminated docks came into view, her mood changed. She picked Lilia up and looked toward the rows of fishing trawlers and small boats tied to the docks. The reflection of light revealed her quivering lip as she scanned the shore from side to side. He considered trying to comfort her but realized this was her time alone with her thoughts of Camillo, and he would only be an intruder.

She approached Solomon who was guiding the small motor yacht through the harbor.

"Where was Camillo's boat when it happened?" Hannah asked.

Solomon pointed to a dock two positions down from where he was guiding the *Cornelian*. "That dock, there. He was tied on the starboard side, four positions deep."

"When we tie off, I want to go there," Hannah said. "I want to stand where Camillo was when it happened."

"I've done it many times myself," Solomon said.

After they disembarked, Nino said, "I'll take Lilia, and you and Solomon can go by yourselves."

"No," Hannah said. "I want you and Lilia with me. You are my life now. Camillo would be fine with you coming with me. You make me happy, and that would make him happy. Please come with me."

Hannah led the way, followed by Solomon, and Nino, who held Lilia, was the last to make his way down the dock.

"Where are we going?" Lilia's little voice asked.

"Hannah is going to see something important to her. She just wants to visit for a moment."

"Is it that boat?"

"She'll explain it to you later, sweetheart. You and I must be still for a little bit, okay?"

Solomon stood in the spot where Camillo had been. Even in the dark of night, the charred tie-off pilings that resulted from the explosion remained evident.

Hannah approached Solomon, and wrapping her arms around the large man, she began to weep. He returned her embrace, kissed the top of her head, and whispered something to her that Nino could not make out.

"Why is Hannah sad?" Lilia asked Nino.

"Because many years ago, someone Hannah loved very much left from that spot and never returned."

"Where did they go?"

"They went to Heaven, sweetheart."

*

Olivia grinned as she looked at Nino and Lilia sleeping on the bed that was once Hannah's when she'd lived in Palermo.

She whispered to Hannah, "It looks like those two have had a long day. You should join them."

"I must get these clothes ready to be washed tomorrow. Then I'll sleep," Hannah said.

"Don't stay up too late. Good night, Hannah," Olivia said as she closed the door behind her.

Hannah removed the garments from the two suitcases. She looked to her left and smiled at the two loves of her life. Nino cradled Lilia, appearing to protect her even as he slept.

As Hannah removed Nino's dirty clothes, she noticed an envelope extending from the pocket of his suitcase. It was a letter from his mother. Nino had told Hannah his mother's name was Maria, but she had assumed her last name was Servidei. Yet the return address read Maria DiVincenzo.

DiVincenzo?

After glancing at Nino to confirm he was still sleeping, she began to read.

My Dearest Nino,

I miss you so. I wish you would write more. I hope you have been getting the money I have been sending.

Your father has been insufferable as usual, and Angelo

is just like him. He is clearly Salvador DiVincenzo's son.

I long for you and am concerned for what I am reading from Europe.

The German army has ravaged Poland and is now occupying France. Many believe America will soon be at war with Italy and Germany. You are no longer safe in Italy, and it is time for you to come home.

I have spoken to Msgr. Nunzio, and he agrees with me. He said he will arrange for you to continue your scholarship program here in New York if you return.

Please come home, Nino.

Love, Mama

Hannah inserted the letter into the envelope and slid it back into the suitcase pocket.

*

"Nino, you are welcome to stay here with Olivia and me as long as you wish," Manuel said. "Olivia loves having Hannah and Lilia here. They make her happy."

"Italy isn't safe for Hannah and Lilia," Nino said. "I will not allow them to be locked up because they are foreign Jews. I must get them home to America."

"That journey will be dangerous," Solomon said. "The Mediterranean Sea is patrolled by German U-boats and the *Luftwaffe*. They have frequent skirmishes with the British. It is not uncommon for innocent fishermen to get caught in the crossfire."

"And it will only get worse," Nino said. "That is why we must leave now. I don't trust the Germans. In the end, the alliance

Italy has with Germany won't protect Italy's Jews. Mussolini and Hitler have become the same person. The Italians forced you to sell the family business. Jews can't teach in schools or work for the government or even visit public beaches.

"Solomon, you and your fellow Italian Jews fought gallantly in the Great War. But now Jews can't even be in the military, why do you think that is?" Nino asked.

"They don't want us to have guns," Solomon said.

"We have all heard the nightmares coming from the rest of Europe—work camps and people disappearing in the middle of the night. The Jews who have fled to Italy have only bought themselves time. The restrictive laws they have forced on you are only the beginning. Do you think they will be satisfied with just mistreating you? I have already gotten Hannah out of one prison, I might not be so lucky next time. No, we will not stay. I will find a way to get my family safely to America."

"He's right, Papà," Manuel said. "I would never say this in the streets of Palermo, but the worst thing that could happen for us is for Hitler and Mussolini to win this war."

"So, how do we get them out?" Solomon said.

Nino said, "A friend of mine in Rome, Vito, told me the best way is on a cargo ship going to Portugal."

Manuel said, "I have seen others bribe their way on board only to be turned over to the polizia by the same people they paid to get on the ship. The dockworkers get paid twice. Once by the people they offer to stow away and again by the polizia who offer them reward money."

"What about by airplane?"

"The only planes leaving Sicily are Luftwaffe and the Italian Air Force," Manuel said.

The room fell silent as the three men pondered the options.

"Wait here," Manuel said before stepping into the back office and returning with a map of the Mediterranean Sea.

After laying it on the counter and sliding his finger from Tunisia to Tangier, he said, "You can go this way through North Africa."

Nino said, "There are German's there, too."

"There may be a few German agents," Manuel said. "But they will be on the lookout for spies. Not families trying to get to America."

"Even families of Jews?"

"This part of the African coast is under the protectorate of Vichy France. You should be safe. There is a train from Tunisia to Tangier. The journey is two days, three tops. Once you get to Tangier, you just need to figure out how to cross the Strait of Gibraltar. It is less than twenty kilometers. I'm sure for a price, someone will gladly take you to Gibraltar. Once in Gibraltar, the British will protect you. Then, it is just a short train ride to Lisbon, then off to America you go."

"How do we get to Tunisia?" Nino asked.

With a bellowing laugh, Solomon slapped Nino on the back and said, "That is easy, my boy. I will take you."

"When?" Nino asked.

Solomon said, "The next new moon. We want our voyage to be as dark as possible."

"When is that?" Nino asked.

Manuel studied a wall calendar, looking closely. "A week from tomorrow. Eight days from now."

*

Olivia sat on the bed and brushed Lilia's hair. "You are a special woman, Hannah. I know why both Camillo and Nino fell in love with you."

"What do you mean?" Hannah asked as she sat next to them, watching Lilia enjoy the attention.

"You are a beautiful, intelligent woman with great courage. You came to Italy without knowing the language; then a few months later you were fluent. Instead of going home to the safety of America, you searched for the man you love and pilfered him from God Himself. Then you find this little princess, Lilia, in an orphanage and decide that you were meant to be her mother. Now here I sit, brushing her hair. That's what I mean, Hannah. Are you not astonished at your own determination?"

Hannah said, "I don't think about it. I just see the way things should be, and I make them so."

"I wish I had your courage. I need it right now," Olivia said as she stopped brushing Lilia's hair and looked at Hannah.

"I'm scared. Italy has been changing, and now that the Germans are here, things will get worse. There is a mindset that we Jews must be punished for something. Not just punished but humiliated at the same time. After the laws forced us to sell the business, it changed Solomon and Beulah. It changed all of us. I'm glad the Leones agreed to help us or we would have had to sell to Alfonso DiVincenzo. That would have killed Solomon and Beulah."

"I'm curious about this DiVincenzo," Hannah said. "Tell me about him. How does he get away with mistreating people as he does?"

"He intimidates by murder and the threat of murder. Many of the polizia, and even a few judges, are on his payroll. It was much worse before Mussolini. He, too, is a scoundrel, but at

least he cleaned out much of the Mafioso—they were running
Sicily. Most went to prison. Some escaped to other countries,
America mostly. DiVincenzo survived. But his son fled to
America after murdering someone here."

"Do you remember his son's name?"

"I don't believe I ever heard it. Why?"

"I'm just interested, that's all. Do you know where he lives
in America?"

Olivia tilted her head as she stared at Hannah, pausing
before answering the question. "I think Manuel said New York.
But I don't remember, you'd have to ask him. The person who
would really know is Solomon. His run-ins with the DiVincenzo
family spans decades."

*

Nino, Hannah, Lilia, and Solomon sat at a café across the street
from the cameo shop. They drank tea and wine, waiting for
Manuel and Olivia to close the shop and join them for dinner.

Nino asked, "What will the weather be like for our voyage
tomorrow, Solomon?"

"Not good, but acceptable. The water may be rough. But at
least the moon will be dark."

"How long will it take to get to Tunisia?" Hannah asked.

"If the current is in our favor, we can make it in twelve
hours. If not, it could be fourteen or fifteen. I plan on bringing
extra cans of fuel."

"May I have some *gelato*, Hannah?" Lilia asked.

"Not now, sweetheart, we will have dinner soon."

*

A Fiat sedan zipped around the corner and came to a stop in
front of the café. Nino watched the driver get out. An older,

heavyset man wearing a white suit stepped out and approached a table four down from theirs. The driver soon joined him.

"That's him," Solomon said. "Alfonso DiVincenzo."

He was an older version of Nino's father; the resemblance was uncanny. Nino's chest tightened, and he took a few deep breaths to calm himself. It was difficult to grasp what he was in the midst of—Hannah sat next to him, and his grandfather, the man who'd sanctioned the murder of Camillo, sat four tables away.

He glanced at Hannah who was shaking.

"Are you okay, Hannah?" Nino said.

"I need to leave, Nino. I need to leave now," Hannah said, as she grabbed Lilia's hand and walked away without waiting for the others.

"I'll go check on Manuel and Olivia," Solomon said, before standing and leaving.

Nino sat at the table by himself, hypnotized—he couldn't take his eyes off his grandfather. But his instincts told him to follow Hannah and Lilia.

Alfonso noticed him staring.

After lighting his cigar, he yelled at Nino, "Do you have a problem, kid?"

Nino stood and approached his grandfather's table.

The bodyguard, who outweighed Nino by nearly one hundred pounds, stood and placed himself between Nino and his grandfather.

"I want to speak to Mr. DiVincenzo."

"Let the kid by," Alfonso said.

Now only a few feet from his grandfather, Nino remained silent.

Removing the cigar from his mouth, Alfonso looked to his bodyguard and laughed. "It looks like Roseman sent this kid to speak to me because he doesn't have the balls to do it himself." Returning his gaze to Nino, he said, "What the hell do you want kid?"

"My name is Nino DiVincenzo. My father is Salvador DiVincenzo. I am your grandson. You and my father both repulse me."

*

In disbelief at what he had just heard, Alfonso sat in silence as he watched Nino walk away.

CHAPTER 25

L ilia screamed as the *Cornelian* leaped into the air and came crashing down. The violent motion tossed her up before the bunk she shared with Hannah caught her.

"You're okay," Hannah said, as she grabbed and cradled her. "I'm here. You are safe."

"I'm scared," Lilia yelled.

"We won't let anything happen to you," Nino said. "Try and go back to sleep. We will be there soon." Nino said to Hannah, "Are you okay?"

"I'm fine."

Nino bent his wobbly knees and squatted low while gripping the railing of the ladder. "I'm going up top. Solomon may want me to take the wheel so he can come down and sleep."

They were in the eighth hour of their voyage to Tunisia. They had left Palermo shortly after sundown with the intention of arriving before sunup. Solomon had set his compass for 323 degrees southwest, but the current and intense winds made it difficult to stay on course.

Nino climbed up from below deck. Solomon had been

running nearly full throttle; between the noise from the diesel engine and crashing wake, having a conversation without yelling was difficult.

Nino said, "Do you want me to take over so you can sleep?"

"These waters are not the place for you to learn how to navigate. I will be fine."

Solomon had turned off the running lights above deck and had instructed Nino to darken the cabin below before opening the hatch to ascend.

As the boat skimmed the surface, occasionally lifting from the water, Nino grabbed hold of anything fastened down as he maneuvered around the vessel.

He looked out at the emptiness of the night. Except for a sliver of moonlight, the darkness was that of a cave. Yet the vibrating deck, the sound of the motor, and the smell of the cool sea spray splashing his face reminded him that they were in the vastness of the Mediterranean Sea.

He could just make out Solomon's silhouette. Although he barely knew him, his reverence for the weathered Jewish businessman was immense. With rugged determination, he risked his life to escort his former daughter-in-law, her Catholic husband, and their adopted daughter to safer lands. Nino recognized that it was a rare breed of man who would be that unselfish.

With wet hair in the biting, cold wind, he considered going back down, but he couldn't leave Solomon by himself.

"Nino," Solomon shouted as he pointed to a storage compartment under the windshield. "There is a pair of binoculars in there. Pull them out and scan the horizon. I know it's dark, but if you look closely, what little moonlight we have might reveal other vessels."

After retrieving the binoculars, Nino was deliberate as he scanned the horizon.

"I see a distant light on the starboard side."

"Let me see," Solomon said.

Nino handed him the binoculars. Solomon looked once, brought them down, adjusted the lenses, then looked again.

"It is a cargo ship. Probably Italian—maybe German. Keep watching it. If the light gets brighter, it's headed towards us and we will need to avoid it. We are in a main shipping lane between west and east. Where there is one, there are others. We just can't see them."

With the eyepieces glued to his face, Nino gradually turned around, focusing on the slightest image that caught his attention.

"Solomon, what is that?"

Nino pointed east and handed Solomon the binoculars.

"It's a patrol boat. They are scanning the water with a spotlight."

"Are they German?"

"I don't know. They might be British, but I doubt it considering our position. They could be Italian."

"What if they spot us?"

"We are no prize. But they'll take us someplace for interrogation if they catch us."

Nino turned to the starboard side.

"The cargo ship is getting closer and headed right toward us."

"We will use it to our advantage."

Solomon navigated toward the oncoming cargo ship. As

their distance narrowed, he turned hard to port, shielding the *Cornelian* from the patrol boat.

AL HUWARIYAH, TUNISIA

Nino looked toward the village. "I need to find the train station."

Solomon tied his lines to the dock. "I need to find fuel for my trip back. The sun will be up soon."

"Thank you for getting us here, Solomon."

"Thank me when you get back to America. You still have a long way and many challenges ahead of you."

Nino said, "I'll go below and check on Hannah and Lilia."

"You won't need to go below," Solomon said as he looked over Nino's shoulder.

"Hannah's sick," Lilia said, as Hannah leaned over the boat's portside, violently retching into the water.

After she finished, Hannah sat down on the deck and took several deep breaths.

"You made it longer than me," Nino said. "I vomited twice during our voyage."

"I'll be fine," Hannah said. "Just a little morning sickness."

"We are going to look for fuel. Do you want to come?" Nino said.

"I do," Lilia said

"Lilia and I will stay here," Hannah said.

"But I—"

"Don't argue with me, Lilia," Hannah stated as she reached for her hand.

Solomon said, "If anyone approaches the boat while we are gone, down below there is a sliding door under the bottom bunk. Behind it, you will find a revolver, a Berretta, and a shotgun. Did Camillo ever teach you how to fire a gun?"

"We had a revolver in our apartment in Chicago. He took me out into the country once and made me shoot it."

Solomon said, "Nino, go get me the Berretta. Leave the revolver for Hannah."

*

There was nobody in the dockyard at that early hour, and they found no source of fuel.

"There might be something on the other side of the yard, Nino. Will you go look? I'll see what's beyond this building."

*

There was an eeriness in the air as Nino roamed the yard. It was dark and still with a warm breeze that blew sand across his face. An occasional gust would force him to close his eyes then blink rapidly to clear his vision.

There were a few small yachts in various stages of overhaul, but he saw no sign of fuel so he made his way behind the building where Solomon had wandered. As he turned the corner, Solomon stood talking to a man slight in stature whom he towered over. The smaller man had his back to Nino, and Solomon glared down at the man, stone faced and agitated. The source of his agitation revealed itself to be a gun pointed at his chest. The man spoke softly, but Nino was close enough to hear what he presumed to be Arabic.

Nino hid behind the building but kept his sights on the two men. As the gunman spoke, he motioned with his weapon for Solomon to raise his hands. After Solomon did so reluctantly, the man reached into Solomon's pockets and pulled out his

J.D. KEENE

leather wallet and Berretta. The criminal inserted both into his own pockets.

Nino watched as they walked toward the water, the gun held at Solomon's back.

Stone and stucco made up the surface of the building that was Nino's cover, some of which had dropped off over the years.

Nino picked up a rock and threw it toward them before ducking back behind the structure.

Hearing a gunshot, he peeked out from his hiding spot to see Solomon holding the man in a bear hug. Solomon's next move was to slam the robber's head into the concrete dock.

Nino approached Solomon while he gazed down at the motionless figure at his feet. His head lay in a pool of blood.

*

Hannah sat on the dock playing with Lilia, her look was curious as Nino and Solomon approached the *Cornelian* with a hastened pace.

"Why are you in such a hurry?" Hannah said.

"Get on board, Hannah," Nino said as he untied one of the mooring lines while Solomon removed the other. "We are going to the next port."

*

Nino and Lilia were sleeping below deck. The wind from the open sea caught hold of Hannah's hair while she stood next to Solomon as he guided the *Cornelian* to Tunis. She sensed from Nino and Solomon's silence that something had happened in Al Huwariyah. She would get the truth from Nino eventually, but for now, she had other information to obtain. She stared into the blackness of the sea, hesitant to ask the question she feared the answer to. She turned and paced the rear of the *Cornelian*, grateful the surface of the water had calmed.

After turning back to her father-in-law, she said, "Solomon, what do you know about Alfonso DiVincenzo's son? The one who moved to America."

Solomon glanced toward Hannah, "That's on odd question, my dear. Why do you ask?"

"I would prefer to keep that a secret."

"Okay. A secret it shall remain. As for what I know about Alfonso DiVincenzo's son—he is ruthless, just like his father. He moved to America to escape a murder conviction in Sicily. And Sicily is better because of it."

Hannah took a deep breath. She felt ill as she asked, "Is his name Salvador?"

Solomon once again turned to Hannah. This time pausing, not taking his eyes off her.

"Yes, Hannah. His name is Salvador."

TUNIS, TUNISIA

"There's a French restaurant," Nino said as he held Lilia on his hip. "They will have omelets."

Hannah grabbed his arm, kissed his cheek, and whispered, "Why does Solomon have blood on his shoes?"

Nino looked at her then stared forward, caught off guard by her question. "It was dark in the dockyard. He stepped on a dead cat."

"Don't insult me, Nino. You two wanted to get out of Al Huwariyah like the town was on fire. Now I see blood splattered on Solomon's shoes and pant cuffs. You're going to tell me what happened."

"I'll tell you later."

Drenched with perspiration, their waiter wiped his brow with a towel as he guided them to an outdoor table.

"Comment est cette table vous convient, monsieur?" the waiter asked.

"Ça va aller," Solomon said

"You speak French, Solomon?" Hannah asked.

"I have sold my cameos all over Europe. When I was a younger man, I traveled to my customers. I was forced to learn many languages. My business depended on it."

Nino sat Lilia down in a chair then pulled Hannah's out for her before sitting himself.

Hannah said, "Solomon, could you ask him to bring us a cool pitcher of water, please?"

After receiving the request, the waiter turned toward the kitchen.

Sweat caused Lilia's hair to stick to her forehead and Hannah wiped her brow with a handkerchief. As she did, she said, "Solomon, why do you have blood on your shoes?"

Nino looked at Solomon as the large man glared back at him for guidance.

"Don't expect me to help you," Nino said. "The best I could come up with was you stepped on a dead cat."

Solomon shook his head, "Nino will tell you later. Preferably tomorrow after I leave for Palermo."

The waiter returned with a basket of bread and their water. After he filled their glasses, Hannah dipped her handkerchief in hers, and patted Lilia's forehead.

Solomon stood and said, "If you'll excuse me, I must find the lavatory."

Lilia stared across the street and said, "What is that lady doing?"

Nino and Hannah twisted in their seats to see a thin, elderly woman on the corner. She bent forward as though her back were injured. Her tattered floral dress may have fit her once but appeared two sizes too large on this day. No other personal belongings were evident.

"She is asking people for money," Hannah said.

"Why?" Lilia asked.

"Maybe she needs money to eat."

"I'll share my food with her," Lilia said in her little voice.

Hannah looked at Nino and grinned. "She is learning from you, Fr. Servidei."

Nino thought of the polizia officer he'd killed on the train and the robber they'd left for dead in Al Huwariyah. "I haven't behaved very priestly recently."

Nino studied Hannah's expression of curiosity as she stared back at him.

"What do you mean, Nino?"

Realizing he should have kept that thought to himself, Nino was grateful when Lilia interrupted. "Can I go give her my bread?"

Hannah said, "We will give her money before we leave, sweetheart."

Nino rose from his chair and crossed the street.

As he approached the woman, he noticed her eyes were dark and sunken, her hair brittle.

"Do you speak English or maybe Italian?" Nino asked.

Her tone was surprisingly perky as she said, "I speak Italian and German."

"Will you join us for breakfast?" Nino said.

Nino gripped her arm as they leisurely made their way to the table. As they arrived, Solomon was also returning to the table, so he offered her his chair, then retrieved another for himself.

After they were seated, Nino made introductions.

The woman said, "My name is Zita Stein. I am Austrian."

"How did you end up here?" Solomon said.

"My husband, Alfred, and I were merchants in Mauthausen. He had relatives in Germany. Early on, they warned him what was happening. When the Germans invaded Poland in 1939, he insisted that we escape from eastern Europe. Our plan was to settle in Spain or Portugal."

"Where is your husband?" Hannah asked.

Zita paused and looked down. "Three weeks after we arrived here, my Alfred died. We were staying in a hotel. I woke first, as I always had. When I tried to wake him, his body was cold. That was four months ago.

"Two days later, after leaving the undertakers office, a young boy grabbed my suitcase then ran. Our entire life savings was gone in an instant. I have been desperate. I have survived by begging, as you saw today. Most people have been kind. Some haven't."

"Do you plan on staying here?" Nino said.

"I don't know what I will do."

"Do you have children?" Hannah asked.

"We had a son; he was killed in a mining accident six years ago. I struggled carrying our other children, so Gunther was our only child."

Hannah reached across the table and touched Zita's hand.

When the waiter returned to take their order, Solomon said, "Zita, you order first."

*

After breakfast, they stepped away from the restaurant. Zita sat on a bench while Hannah, Lilia, and Nino said their goodbyes to Solomon.

"It appears we must part ways now," Solomon said. "I will sleep on the *Cornelian* today and depart at sundown."

Hannah embraced him. "I owe you everything. I arrived in Italy three years ago not knowing how Camillo's family would receive me. You, Beulah, Manuel, and Olivia didn't just welcome me, you saved me."

"The day you married Camillo, you became our daughter. You will always be our daughter. Camillo loved you, and we love you, too."

Lilia stepped forward and looked up at Solomon. "Are you leaving?"

Solomon grinned as he bent down to pick her up. "I must return home. But it has been wonderful to meet you, Lilia."

"When will we see you again?"

"One day, you will return," he said as he kissed her forehead.

He set her down and turned to Nino. "I know you don't need to hear this from me. But take care of them."

"I will, Solomon. You will always have my gratitude," Nino said as he shook his hand.

After Solomon turned to make his way back to the docks, Nino whispered to Hannah, "What should we do with Zita?"

"She is coming with us, of course."

CHAPTER 26

T he first train station they would come to would be Algiers. Nino shared his seat with Lilia. Hannah was with Zita in the seat behind them. The windows were down, and the sand would sometimes blow in and sting Nino's face. The motion of the train combined with the warm breeze passing through their compartment made him sleepy. He considered dozing off as Lilia had done after lying across his lap. In spite of the challenges, Nino realized he had never been happier. Lying across his lap was a precious angel God had blessed him with. He stroked her hair, realizing there was nothing he wouldn't do for her. Behind him sat another. He closed his eyes and smiled as he listened to Hannah's tender voice while she spoke with Zita. It was pleasing to him.

"You can lean on my shoulder if you would like to sleep, Zita," Hannah said.

Nino heard no response from Zita, only sniffles.

"Why are you upset, Zita?" Hannah asked.

"I have been scared and lonely. I didn't know what I was

going to do. I thought I would die in that town. I don't know why you have chosen to help me."

Nino turned around to see Hannah wrapping her arm around Zita.

"You are safe now. We will protect you," Hannah said.

Zita buried her face in Hannah's shoulder and wept.

ALGIERS

After exiting the train in Algiers, Nino said, "Tangier is an overnight train trip from here. We need to find a hotel with a bath. And I must exchange our Italian lire for French francs. We spent too much at breakfast because we had the wrong currency."

"You can move around the city faster by yourself," Hannah said. "There is a bench under those palm trees. We will enjoy the shade while you look for a hotel."

"I won't be long," he said before giving Hannah a quick peck on the lips.

"Be safe," she said.

*

As Nino made his way to the center of town, the streets bustled with merchants and prostitutes, hoping to separate him from his money, while most of the sidewalk conversations he overheard were in Arabic or French.

On the lookout for a suitable shelter for the night, he kept his eyes focused forward for a hotel which didn't have small assemblies of young women at the door conversing with patrons.

He turned a corner where a boy bumped into him. Sensing his intent, Nino felt the young man's hands pat his trousers.

Nino placed both hands on the pickpocket's chest and shoved him away. The boy stumbled backward but regained his balance before pumping his fist and muttering something in Arabic.

Four blocks further, he found The Hotel Bayram. It had a groomed courtyard and palm trees. There was a Mercedes parked in front, and two well-dressed couples conversed near a fountain.

Nino entered the lobby to find another small fountain attached to the wall. The splashing of the cool water attracted him, and impulsively, he slipped his hand in then wiped his face. As he turned to check in, the front desk clerk shook his head and muttered something under his breath. The clerk was older and appeared to be of mixed race. His complexion was dark, yet his facial features were slight, as though one of his parents were Western European, or American even.

In Italian, Nino said, "Forgive me for bathing in your fountain. It has been a long and sweltering day."

"Yes, of course," the clerk said in English.

Nino grinned and in English said, "You don't speak Italian?"

"But you are an American."

"Does that matter?"

"Not yet," he answered. Nino said nothing as he stared back at the man who turned the ledger around for him to sign. "That will be 125 francs."

"I only have Italian lire."

"Then it will be six thousand lire."

"One hundred and twenty-five francs is closer to four thousand lire."

"Not in Algiers."

"Will there be a bath in the room?"

"Didn't you just bathe?"

"Is there another hotel within walking distance? One that is more hospitable?"

Grinning, the clerk said, "You have my apologies, sir. You are indeed welcome to stay here. And each floor has a bath at the end of the hall." Turning, he grabbed a key and handed it to Nino. "You are in room thirteen down the hallway. Would you like me to help you with your bags?"

"I must meet my party, but thank you for your ... hospitality."

*

Nino took a different route back to the train station. He wanted to find a more reserved path to avoid exposing Lilia to the prostitutes he had passed earlier.

This section of Algiers was more exclusive with jewelry shops and fine restaurants. He stepped into a cafe to look at the prices on the menu and realized they wouldn't be eating on this street. As he exited, he passed a series of outdoor tables and noticed that two men in suits stood from their unfinished meals and stepped onto the sidewalk behind him.

Nino picked up his pace and crossed the street, yet they remained. Not too close, but present.

After darting into a garment shop, Nino made his way to the back and pretended to look at rugs. The salesman approached, and in English, attempted to negotiate.

"If you buy two rugs, I will give you a third. You can choose from anything on this table."

Nino never took his eyes off the front. The men had continued walking. Although relieved, he knew he hadn't imagined their sinister intent.

Nino thanked the agitated salesman for his time and stepped

toward the door. When he was about to exit, he felt a small rug hit him on the back of the head. He stopped when the salesman shouted, "For you, my friend, I make a remarkable offer on that rug and that rug only. Fifty francs or two American dollars."

Nino bent down picked up the rug and said, "I'll give you two hundred Italian lire—no more."

"Agh ..."—the man said as he approached Nino—"give me the lire and get out of my store."

*

The men who had trailed him went left, so Nino went right before turning a corner. The street was narrow and between two buildings that created shade on both sides of the street. A cool breeze blew through. It was refreshing yet eerie, for there was nobody else within sight, which caused Nino to consider turning around.

A few steps later, the two men leapt from an alley, grabbed Nino, and threw him to the ground. One wore a gray suit, the other was in white. Gray Suit was in his forties and a little pudgy. White Suit was thin and a few years older than Nino.

Nino leaped to his feet then threw the rug at them. As he stepped back, he crouched in a fighting stance and put his fists in front of him, "What do you want?"

"Relax," Gray Suit said in an American accent. "We mean you no harm, we just want your help."

"Help with what?'

"Where are you traveling to?"

"I'm not telling you."

"Look, buddy. We aren't going to hurt you. We need you to take something to Tangier for us—an envelope. We need it delivered to the US Consulate."

"Why don't you take it yourself?"

The two men looked at each other. Gray Suit continued, "Because we are being watched."

"By whom?"

"That doesn't matter."

"It does if you want my help."

"Mainly, French police. But there are also German agents roaming these streets, too. The Vichy police like to search us. If they catch us with the wrong documents, we could be arrested as ..."

"As spies?" Nino said. "So, you want me to be the sucker who gets arrested as a spy."

White Suit spoke up. "No, dummy. We want you to go to Tangier and deliver an envelope to the US Consulate."

"Who are you guys anyway?" Nino asked. "Is that not a fair question?"

White Suit shook his head. "Look, we understand your apprehension. You don't know us, and we can't tell you who we are. But you can judge by our accents that we are Americans. Would you agree with that?"

"I've known my share of American scoundrels. Just because you are American is no guarantee I won't end up dead."

Gray Suit said, "I'm going to tell you more than you should know, but here it is. We work for the American government. We are Americans ourselves. We are on an observation mission. Every movement we make is watched."

"Even this one, so now I'm a target?"

"We were careful."

Nino took a deep breath. "If I do this will you help me?"

Gray Suit said, "What do you want? Money?"

"That's not what I was thinking, but yes, a little money would be useful."

"What else?"

"I need to get my family to America. My plan was to get to Lisbon by way of Gibraltar. I have no real plan to do it, I was hoping to figure it out along the way. If you guys are who you say you are, maybe you could pull some strings for me."

"Do you have passports?" Gray Suit asked.

"My wife and I do. We also have an adopted daughter. All we have for her is a signed letter from the priest who approved the adoption, but no legal documents. She has no American passport."

Gray Suit looked at White Suit and said, "That shouldn't be a problem. We will get you a separate document with your official request. The consulate certainly has the authority to grant your petition."

"There is one other thing," Nino said. "We have a nanny. She is an Austrian Jew who doesn't speak English. She comes with us or the deal is off."

Gray Suit frowned. "For her, all I can do is put in a request. I can't make any promises. But we help those who help us, so I think the consulate will cooperate."

"What now?"

"First, the more your family knows, the more they are at risk. It is easier for them to act calm if they don't know what you are carrying. If they know, they'll be nervous and look suspicious. So, keep it to yourself."

"That makes sense," Nino said.

White Suit continued, "Not far from the train station, there is a brothel on Jazirat Street. You will arrive after dark and request Gabrielle. Once you are alone with her, you will say, 'Haven't we met in Paris on top of the Notre Dame Cathedral? I believe it was two years ago?' She will in turn provide you with an envelope. In the envelope will be the documents we need transferred to the consulate. There will also be a request to the consulate to aid you on your journey to Portugal. When you arrive at the consulate in Tangier, ask to speak to the consul general. Give the documents to nobody else. Only the consul general. Is that clear?"

"Only the consul general—got it."

"There is one more thing," Gray Suit said. "When you are with Gabrielle, be sure and spend the full thirty minutes with her. If you run in and out too quickly, they will get suspicious."

White Suit added, "Security listens at the door. It is their form of sick entertainment, so at least make noises like you are having the time of your life. Or if you prefer, Gabrielle will accommodate you as if you were a regular client. It's up to you. Just don't leave without the document."

*

Nino sat in a corner chair and watched Hannah and Lilia enter their hotel room. They had just finished their bath down the hall. Hannah's wet hair reminded him of the rainstorm in Torre del Greco when they'd made love under the rowboat.

Clothed in a blue sundress, she held Lilia who was wrapped in a towel. Zita snored a bit while she slept in the only bed in the room. Hannah sat Lilia on the edge of the bed to dry her, careful not to wake Zita.

Nino stood and said, "I must step out for a little bit, Hannah. I need to check on something."

"Check on what? You need to stay in. It's not safe to be roaming these streets at night."

"I'll explain later."

"Nino, do you have any idea how many things you have promised to explain to me later? I'm keeping track of them. One day you and I are going to discuss this list of things that must always wait for later."

"And I am looking forward to it," Nino said. "But for now, I'll see you in a couple of hours. Hopefully less."

*

Nino took a taxi to Jazirat Street. The driver zipped right to the brothel as though it were a frequent stop. That was confirmed by the number of customers congregating, many of whom were French soldiers. Unable to find a place to exchange his money, Nino absorbed the wrath of the taxi driver who was unhappy with the Italian currency he received.

Nino elbowed his way through the crowd, determined not be be overcome by the smell of alcohol, cheap perfume, and cigarettes that surrounded him.

Once at the door, Nino approached a large hulk of a man and said in Italian, "I'm here for Gabrielle."

Confused by Nino's request, the man motioned for someone else to deal with Nino.

In Italian, the other man said, "What do you want?"

"Gabrielle," Nino said. "I want to spend my time with Gabrielle."

"She is with someone now, and there are two others ahead of you."

"I'll wait."

My tardiness is going to be hard to explain to Hannah.

"Be in this same spot in an hour," the man said. "Otherwise, I will give your time to someone else."

*

Nino didn't roam far. Although the people around him wouldn't have been his first choice for companionship, he believed they were there for reasons other than to rob him.

After an hour, he returned to the original spot, and the Italian-speaking man waved him into the building.

"What do you want?"

"I told you. I want to see Gabrielle."

"I know that, but what do you want her to do to you?"

"Why do you need to know that?"

"You've never been here before, have you?"

"No."

"It's like a restaurant. Different things cost different amounts. I need to know what you want her to do to you or what you want to do to her. That's how I'll know how much to charge you."

"I just want the cheapest thing she does."

"Give me one hundred francs."

"All I have is Italian lire."

"Then give me five thousand lire and go upstairs. Gabrielle is going to be thrilled with you," the man said with a chuckle. "She's up the stairs, fourth door on the right."

*

At the top of the stairs, another watchman paced the hall, occasionally pressing his ear to one of the eight doors on the floor. When Nino arrived at the fourth room, the door was open. A thin, exotic woman with long brown hair sat on the bed smoking a cigarette. She was about Nino's age. Her feet were bare and tanned, as were her long legs. She wore a short silk nightgown that appeared to have nothing underneath it but her.

In Italian he said, "Are you Gabrielle?"

"*Fermez la porte derrière vous.*"

Nino said, "I'm sorry, but I don't speak French. Do you speak English?"

She repeated her statement in English. "Close the door behind you."

After doing as instructed, he said, "Haven't we met in Paris, on top of the Notre Dame Cathedral? I believe it was two years ago?"

Gabrielle said nothing as she stood and pressed her cigarette into an ashtray on the nightstand. It was stacked high with half-smoked butts. Next to the ashtray rested a bowl filled with different colored poker chips. She bent down and lifted the corner of the mattress, revealing a small envelope which she handed to Nino.

He folded it then inserted it into his sock.

"What now?" he said.

"Did he give you a poker chip?"

"Who?"

"The guy downstairs. He was supposed to give you a colored poker chip so I know what you paid for."

"He never gave me a poker chip."

She stepped toward the door. "He forgot again. Wait here."

Nino grabbed her arm as she passed. "That won't be necessary. I just came to get this document. But I was told to stay here for a half hour, so they don't get suspicious. Can we just talk?"

"It's your money."

Nino led her to the bed, and they sat.

With the whores who work for his father in mind, he said, "I don't mean to pry, but I've always been curious. Why do beautiful young women like you choose to do this?"

"You mean sell our bodies?"

"I don't understand it."

"I can't speak for anyone else, but for me, it just happened. I was fourteen when I did it the first time. I was living in Rouen, France. I was cold and hungry, and a man bought me some food and invited me to his warm apartment on a frigid winter night. He offered me a few francs to do things to him, and I did them. It didn't take long, and I left his apartment with money. I haven't been cold or hungry since."

"Where were your parents?"

"I've never met my father, and my mother did the same thing to support herself. I guess that's why it has always been easy."

Nino looked at the floor and said nothing. His thoughts were of Lilia. At that moment he wanted to hold and protect her, as someone should have done for Gabrielle many years earlier.

Gabrielle reached into the nightstand before removing another cigarette.

Nino heard the click of the lighter and glanced at her.

She stared back at him. "It's a shame you don't want to do anything. You are the only handsome one I have had tonight. Do you prefer men?"

Nino laughed. "No, of course not. Like you, my wife is beautiful. I could never be unfaithful to her."

Gabrielle leaned forward and kissed his cheek, leaving lipstick. "She is lucky. I hope she knows that."

"I'm lucky to have her."

He watched her inhale the smoke, then blow it in the air. He remembered how Hannah had smoked when they'd first met on the voyage to Italy. It dawned on him he hadn't seen her smoke much since.

"Gabrielle, I was told that the guy on the other side of the door listens in and that I'm supposed to sound like I'm having a good time. Do you mind if I bounce up and down on the bed and make some grunting sounds or something?"

She leaned back in the bed, smiled, and took another puff. "As I said, it's your money."

Nino lifted himself from the bed and dropped back down, repeating the process over and over to make the bed springs squeak.

"I had a roommate who could really make the bed springs sing," Nino said as he bounced up and down. "His name is Vito. He'd have a girl over and I was awake all night with my pillow over my head."

Gabrielle began to laugh uncontrollably. She placed her cigarette in the ashtray and buried her face in the pillow so the thug in the hallway couldn't hear her. Nino made grunting noises to add to the effect. He grinned, realizing how ridiculous he must look to Gabrielle. Then, with one loud moan, he stopped bouncing and laid next to her.

"Do you think I fooled him?"

Gabrielle removed her face from her pillow and said, "I wish you could stay longer."

*

Nino was sweating as he approached the hotel room. Not just because it was hot but because he arrived two hours later than he'd told Hannah he would. He stood in the hallway and took a deep breath. When he opened the door, Hannah and Lilia were asleep in the bed and Zita was in the chair reading an Italian newspaper. He relaxed when he saw Hannah was resting.

"How long has Hannah been asleep, Zita?"

"Not long. I'm afraid to tell you that you're going to hear it in the morning."

"You must believe me, Zita—I can't tell you where I was at or what I was doing—I promise you, it will help us get to America."

"Nino, I am just an old woman and what you do is none of my business. I admit, I have only known Hannah two days, but I am a good judge of character. I think I know her well enough to know that if you don't wipe that lipstick from your face, you will never make it to America."

MEDITERRANEAN SEA
THE CORNELIAN

Solomon shined his flashlight into the engine compartment. He had made multiple attempts to restart the motor, but the oil oozing from the gaskets left him with little hope that it would cooperate.

Who would find him first? He had left Tunisia seven hours earlier, which put him halfway between Africa and Sicily.

He'd brought the shotgun and Berretta above deck, not knowing who he may encounter in the blackness of the night. He had given the revolver to Nino and Hannah.

Grateful the seas had been calm for the voyage back to Palermo, he sat in the captain's chair and stared up at the stars of the clear night. He looked forward to returning to Beulah. It had been nearly three weeks since he had been home to Torre del Greco. He closed his eyes and fell asleep.

*

He awoke to a rumble in the darkened night, uncertain where it was coming from. He grabbed the binoculars from beneath the steering wheel and scanned the dark horizon. The sparse moonlight revealed no clues as to the direction of the increasing reverberation.

He looked starboard, then portside. He hadn't dropped anchor, so he could have drifted anywhere. He glanced at the compass and realized that due west, the most probable direction of sea traffic, was now at the stern of the *Cornelian*.

As the thundering noise increased, he turned to see an enormous white wake of water in front of the bow of a forty-meter-high cargo ship. Solomon grabbed his flashlight and waved it toward the massive vessel, realizing it was futile. The last thing Solomon ever heard was the disintegration of the *Cornelian* as the force of the current sucked it under the keel of the one-hundred-thousand-ton vessel.

CHAPTER 27

The train sped continuously from Algiers throughout the night and was scheduled to arrive in an hour. Nino woke early and sat at a table in the dining car waiting for Hannah, Lilia, and Zita to join him for breakfast. He faced the front of the car, the direction they would come from. There were eight small booths in the car. Other passengers occupied four of them. He exchanged glances with a man in a light suit sitting at the furthest table.

As the man continued to watch him, the envelope Gabrielle had given Nino made his leg itch. He wanted to reach into his sock and scratch it, but he would have to pull his pant leg up, exposing the document. He knew the itch was psychological. Had the mysterious man not been there, he would have no itch.

The man rose and approached Nino's table, then sat down. He pulled out a cigarette case and in a poor attempt at American English said, "Do you have a match?"

"I don't smoke," Nino said.

The man returned the cigarette to its case.

"Our agents in Algiers have been captured and interrogated.

When you exit in Tangier, your life and the lives of your family will be in danger."

"You have me mistaken for someone else."

"No, you are our courier. I have confirmed that with the two men who gave you the document. I have been instructed to retrieve it from you."

"Two men didn't give me a document. Please excuse yourself from my table."

The man said nothing as he stared at Nino.

"You have an interesting accent," Nino said, "Where are you from?"

The man hesitated before saying, "Texas."

Nino reached under his jacket and removed the revolver Solomon had given him. From under the table, Nino pointed it at the man's abdomen. "I wasn't aware there were a lot of Germans who lived in Texas."

When the man made a move to reach into his jacket, Nino pulled back the hammer of the revolver, and it clicked.

"Put your hands on the table," Nino said.

The man did as he was instructed.

"You have put me in a difficult predicament," Nino said.

"You won't shoot."

"You have threatened my family. I will do anything to protect them."

The man's face became red.

Nino scanned the dining car. Unlike the train ride from Rome to Torre del Greco when he'd killed the polizia, it was now daylight. And there were other passengers and possibly other German agents on the train.

"You are going to stand, and head to the rear of the train. I don't want to kill you, but I will if I must. You wouldn't be my first."

The man obeyed, standing as Nino kept the gun hidden in his jacket pocket. They passed through three additional cars before arriving at the last car that was used to transport cargo.

When they entered, Nino instructed the man to open the side door.

"Are you going to make me jump?"

"You are going to exit this train. How you choose to do it is up to you."

"We are moving at an incredible speed. We are out in the middle of nowhere. What if I get injured? How will I survive?"

"Open the door. Now! I won't ask again."

The man grabbed the handle and slid the door open. The sun was bright, and the warm desert air rushed in, causing the man's tie to flap in the wind as he moved his feet to the edge.

"Don't make me do this."

Nino felt compassion for him as he looked into the vastness of the desert.

The man looked at Nino as though he was considering alternatives.

Nino said, "Please don't make me shoot another man."

The man looked out, took a deep breath and leaped. Nino watched as he landed, then rolled and bounced away from the train.

CHAPTER 28

T he consulate was unimpressive. There was a small reception area in the center and held a series of wobbly benches reminiscent of church pews. The floor consisted of warped planks. The front and back doors were propped open to allow a breeze. Nino noticed three offices along the side, the first had a glass window.

Hannah said, "Nino I don't feel well. I need to sit down."

"What's wrong?"

"I don't know. I just don't feel right."

He guided her to a bench where she sat with Lilia and Zita.

Nino said, "I need to find water for you."

"I'll locate water," Zita offered. "You go find whoever you need to see."

"Zita is right," Hannah said. "Go on, Nino. We will be fine."

Nino removed their passports from his jacket pocket, then pulled up his pant leg and removed the envelope from his sock.

"What is in the envelope?" Hannah said.

"I'll tell you later," Nino said as he turned and walked away.

*

Upon entering the first office, Nino approached a woman at the first desk. "I am an American citizen. I need to see the consul general."

"Let me see if he is available," the woman said as she rose and entered an office behind her desk and closed the door.

Nino looked out into the reception area where he saw Hannah lying down on the bench, resting a hand on her stomach. Lilia sat next to her, but Zita was nowhere in sight.

When the woman returned, she said, "The consul general is preparing to leave for an important engagement. He has requested that you return tomorrow."

"Please tell him that I have important documents for him. They are from Algiers. I was instructed to hand them to the consul general and nobody else."

Again, the woman rose and entered the office. In an instant, she returned. "The consul general will see you now."

*

Nino emerged from the office and wiped his brow with his handkerchief. Hannah was sitting up and drank from a metal cup before sharing a sip with Lilia.

"Zita, will you take Lilia outside while I speak with Hannah?" Nino asked.

"Go with Zita," Hannah said. "We will be right out."

Zita grabbed Lilia's hand and they exited the building.

Nino said, "Are you feeling any better, Hannah?"

"I'm fine," Hannah said as she took a series of deep breaths, then handed the metal cup to Nino. "You must drink, too."

He handed it back to her. "You and the baby need it more than I do."

"So, are we stuck here, or can they help us?"

"The consul general says there is a flight leaving for Lisbon in two days. He will confirm it has room for us. When we arrive in Lisbon, I am to report to the consulate there and they will arrange for us to return to America by ship."

"That is wonderful."

Nino said, "They'll take us all to Lisbon. You and me and Lilia can get to Portugal then to America easily because of our passports and her adoption letter. However, …"

"However what, Nino?"

"The consul general will work with the Portuguese government to get Zita a visa into Lisbon, but once there …"

"Nino, stop stalling."

"Once there, she must go through the proper channels to enter America."

Hannah said, "Then we will stay with her until she gets an American visa."

"That will take years. Probably more years than she even has to live. I'm not going to hold you and Lilia in Portugal for a visa that may never be issued."

Hannah said, "That poor woman has been through hell. Now we are going to abandon her?"

"The consulate general said Portugal is a haven for migrant Jews. There are Jewish organizations from all over the world that have sprung up in Lisbon for the very purpose of helping people like Zita."

"But—"

"But nothing," Nino said. "I will not keep you and Lilia in Portugal any longer than I must. I won't hear of it. We won't leave until we know Zita is safe and comfortable. There are other Austrian Jews there. She will be much happier in Lisbon with them than she would be in America where she doesn't even speak our language."

THE ISLAND OF SICILY
PALERMO, ITALY

"I need to charter a boat," Manuel said to the dockhand.

"I'm sorry, Manuel, but I can't. I have been instructed not to."

"Not to what? Do business with Jews? You have known me for years, Juan. You are going to suddenly keep me from searching for my father because of the laws? They are laws, Juan, nothing more. When they went into effect, they didn't change me, they only changed you. I will find someone else to get a boat from."

"Wait, Manuel," Juan said as he motioned for Manuel to follow him down the dock.

They approached a barge at the end of a wooden pier. Manuel saw piles of debris stacked high in the center.

Juan said, "Giuseppe Cannelloni leases this section of the dock from me for his salvage business. He scours the seas looking for debris he can sell as scrap."

Juan pointed to the middle of the barge and said, "I met Giuseppe out here yesterday to collect the rent payment when I saw this."

Manuel looked to see several large pieces of a motor yacht. One of the busted planks read *Cornelian*.

ABOVE THE GULF OF CÁRDIZ

The 1938 single-engine Lockheed Electra sat sixteen passengers, yet the seats were narrow, and the knees of each traveler impaled the seat in front of them. They were in their second hour of an initially turbulent flight which had calmed in the final hour. Hannah, Lilia, and a few others had been ill. Parts of the aisle and floor of the plane remained slick with vomit, the smell unbearable.

Hannah was asleep in the window seat, and as they began to descend, Nino leaned toward her to get a better view of the lights illuminated along the Portuguese coast. They had left Tangier in early dawn, and the sun showed hints of an appearance over the horizon. Zita and Lilia also slept in their seats across the narrow aisle.

Nino grabbed Hannah's hand. It was cold and her face ashen.

"Hannah, my darling. Are you ill?"

She slowly opened her eyes, yet her head remained still. "I'm not well, Nino. Something is wrong with the baby."

CHAPTER 29

"Please help me," Nino shouted in Italian, as he entered the front door of the hospital. He cradled Hannah in his arms, Zita and Lilia trailing behind him.

Upon exiting the plane, Hannah was conscious but weak. Nino had cleverly guided them past customs and directly to a taxi in front of the small airport. On the journey to the hospital, Hannah fell asleep. When they arrived, Nino was unable to wake her.

Several nurses approached. One pushed a gurney toward him. They said something in Portuguese.

"Do you speak English?" Nino asked as he laid her on the gurney.

"Yes," one of them said.

"Please help her. She is pregnant. I can't wake her."

When Hannah was wheeled away, Nino attempted to follow, but the English-speaking nurse stopped him. "Please stay here. The doctor will speak to you when we know something."

Nino turned to see Zita holding Lilia's hand as the little girl wept.

"What's wrong with Hannah?"

Nino knelt next to her and held her hand. "She is sick, sweetheart. The doctors will make her better."

"Can I see her?"

"Not yet, Lilia. We must wait."

*

Nino knelt at the altar of the tiny chapel in Hospital de Christ clutching his mother's rosary and reciting prayers. As he looked up at the image of Christ before him, he was aware of Lilia and Zita sitting in the pew behind him. The irony didn't escape him. He'd left America three years earlier to become a priest. Now, he knelt humbly before his savior pleading for the health and protection of his Jewish family.

Nino crossed himself, stood, and approached Lilia before picking her up. "Do you know what I was doing, Lilia?"

"You were talking to God like Fr. De Carlo did where I used to live."

"That's right, sweetheart. I was talking to God."

"What did you say?"

"I asked him to help Hannah and the baby feel better so they wouldn't be sick anymore. And I asked him to keep you and Zita safe."

Nino watched Lilia as she glanced above the altar at the image of the crucified Jesus.

*

After they exited the chapel, Nino sat Lilia down and reached into his pocket. "Zita, here is some money. You and Lilia haven't eaten since our plane left Tangier. There is a cafe across the street. Go and get something, please. I will wait here for the doctor."

*

Nino sat in a chair that gave him a view of the same hallway they had taken Hannah down. Every time he saw movement in the corridor, he stood.

What is taking so long?

Nino leaned forward closed his eyes and put his face in his hands. The white noise of multilingual chatter surrounded him. There were smells he couldn't define—most were a mixture of hospital chemicals and body odor. He sniffed his clothes, wondering if the worst of it was his own filthy stench. He longed for his mother. Her presence would be comforting.

Will Hannah survive to meet her?

"Mr. Servidei?"

Nino looked up to see the English-speaking nurse before him.

"Your wife and baby will be fine. We are providing them with fluid. It appears she was just dehydrated."

*

Hannah cradled Lilia as they both slept together in the hospital bed while Nino and Zita sat in chairs adjacent to them.

"You have a beautiful family, Nino."

"I do, don't I, Zita."

"I know you will make it safely to America and have a long and wonderful life together."

"If we could take you with us, we would. But as we've discussed, it will take—"

Zita interrupted him, "Do not apologize for not taking me to America with you. America was never the intent for Alfred or me. Our plan was always to make it safely to Spain or Portugal. You have gotten me here, and for that I will always be grateful. I am an old Austrian woman who has no interest in learning English. I will find a community of Austrian Jews and live the rest of my life safely with my people. You are young. Go back home to America knowing you saved an old woman's life."

CHAPTER 30

I t was their fourth day aboard the Portuguese SS *Santuário*. Their delay in Portugal had lasted nineteen weeks, which was brief compared to the other passengers. Those who weren't Americans had waited a year or more.

Though they were on the last leg of their journey to the United States, they still were not safe. Ships crossing the Atlantic were vulnerable to German U-Boat attacks, although Nino was grateful that the SS *Santuário* flew under the Portuguese flag. The Germans purchased tungsten from Portugal to manufacture weapons, so for diplomatic reasons, Germany seldom fired on Portuguese ships. However, there were two recent instances where it had happened. Both times, Germany claimed it had been an accident.

Nino's family shared a small cabin with another. There was only one double bunk. Nino, Hannah, and Lilia slept on the top half, the other family, consisting of four, slept on the bottom. There were no portholes and the stuffy room was empty unless someone was sleeping. The crew apportioned two small daily meals to each passenger. Nino only ate half of his morning meal, allowing Lilia and Hannah—now approaching her sixth month of pregnancy—to share the remainder of his ration.

Hannah was unable to stand for prolonged periods of time. With limited seating, other passengers were quick to offer her their chairs as she strolled the upper decks. On occasion, she felt the need to accept their generosity. It was October of 1941, and though the first three days on board had been cool, the seas were now calm and the wind had turned temperate, with the exception of the gusts that could be chilly.

Nino, standing next to Hannah while she sat, looked past the mass of passengers on deck and watched the ocean pass by. Lilia sat in Hannah's lap playing with a doll Zita had sewn for her from an old scarf and stuffing she had removed from a ripped hotel mattress.

Lilia looked up at Hannah. "I'm cold, Mama."

Nino removed his jacket and wrapped it around Lilia, then positioned himself to block the wind passing over them.

"Grazie, Papa," Lilia said.

"How are you, Hannah? Do you want me to retrieve a blanket from our bunk?"

"No, darling, I'm fine. But thank you."

Nino returned his gaze to the passing ocean.

Hannah said, "Do you think your mother has received your letter yet, Nino?"

"I don't know."

"Did you write to her about Lilia and me?"

"Of course."

"Will she be happy you are coming home with a family?"

"I believe she will be."

"Did you tell her we are Jews?" Hannah asked as she gently caressed the top of Lilia's head.

"I did."

"Will it bother her?"

"It may."

"Are we going to stay with your parents when we arrive in New York?"

"That isn't possible. I will find a place for us."

"That could take days."

Nino said sharply, and in a tone of exasperation, "Let me worry about that, Hannah. We can afford a few days in a hotel until I find a vacant room. Why do you insist on asking me these questions?"

Hannah snapped back, "Why is it that when I ask about your family, you become irritated with me? Then you change the subject. Is there something you aren't telling me?"

"No, of course not. Why would you ask me that? We need to find something for Lilia to eat."

"She just ate. Dinner isn't for several hours."

Nino knew that once Hannah met his mother, his secret would be revealed. She would soon know about his grandfather's involvement in Camillo's death.

He looked down at his wife as she sat stoned-faced, her eyes stared through him.

Hannah reached for his hand. "What is it, Nino? You can tell me."

Nino looked away from her and closed his eyes. "My last name was once DiVincenzo. For reasons I won't get into now, I changed it to Servidei before leaving for Italy."

He opened his eyes, but kept them looking forward,

avoiding eye contact with her.

"Why did you keep that a secret?"

"Because the man who set the explosive charge on Camillo's boat worked for Alfonso DiVincenzo, my grandfather."

Hannah gripped his hand. "I already know this, Nino. I've known since we left Al Huwariyah."

Nino looked down at her. He cocked his head to the side. "How could you possibly know that?"

"I found a letter from your mother in your suitcase. She mentioned your father by name. I knew you said he had once lived in Sicily, so when I saw his last name was DiVincenzo I started asking questions. Olivia referred me to Solomon. He was aware of your father before Salvador moved to America."

"So, Solomon and Olivia knew all this while I was with them?"

"I didn't tell them why I was inquiring, and they were kind enough not to pry. So, no, they are unfamiliar with the link between you and Camillo's death."

Nino let go of her hand and looked away. "How come you don't hate me?"

Retrieving his hand and squeezing it firmly, she said, "Because you aren't your grandfather, and you aren't your father. I know exactly who you are. You prove it to me every day in the way you protect me and Lilia. You are my husband. You are my Nino, and I love you with my very soul."

*

Nino woke first. He couldn't remember the last time he had slept through the night. His senses had grown sharp since he'd rescued Hannah from the internment camp, and every thump and bump put him on edge.

Behind him, the sun peered over the horizon, creating a reflection on the surface of the ocean. In front of him, a faint silhouette of America's Eastern Seaboard was visible. Standing alone at the bow of the SS *Santuário*, he watched the ship cut through the ocean. The frigid air both stung his face and was refreshing after the night spent in their dingy cabin. The smell of the sea and the sound of the crashing water against the side of the hull energized him.

It occurred to him that it was already midday in Italy. Before he'd left, there had been discussions of America possibly entering the war. There were anti-fascist groups that wished for an escalation of the conflict, believing it would put an end to the tyranny thrust upon them. He thought of Vito and his cache of weapons.

Stay safe, my fratello, for one day our paths may cross again.

As the image of America's coast became sharper, his thoughts turned to his mama. Her little boy would not be returning to her. Instead, she would see a husband, a father, a protector. He hoped that she would see a good man and be proud.

There would be new challenges to face once they were home. The American economy still struggled, yet he must find work to support his growing family. Working for his papa was out of the question for many reasons.

Metal clanged loudly behind him, causing him to whip around quickly. A crew member with a large wrench adjusted a turnbuckle, and Nino took a deep breath, slowly exhaling to calm his nerves.

Other passengers had begun to rise with the sun, and they strolled the deck. It would be breakfast soon.

"Much has changed in three years, Nino," Hannah said as they made their way down the dock to retrieve their luggage.

Nino stopped and set Lilia down. "You were standing in this very spot, Hannah."

"You remembered."

"I will never forget. You were wearing a gray wool waistcoat and matching skirt that draped just above your ankle. You had on black lace stockings. I noticed them when you sat on the trunk."

"You really were paying close attention, weren't you?"

"Of course, I had never seen anyone so beautiful in all my life. I couldn't take my eyes off you."

"Do you still feel that way?"

"You have never looked more radiant."

"You are still charming, Nino."

"And I remember your hair was tucked under a big hat."

"I remember that hat," Hannah said. "Right now, the wife of the culprit who ransacked my steamer trunk in Naples is probably wearing it."

"I'm sure it looks good with your jewelry."

As they continued their stroll, Hannah laid one hand on the curvature of her stomach and grabbed Lilia's hand with her other. "That's okay. I hope she enjoys my things. I'm returning to America with far more than I left with."

Other Books In The 'Nino' Series

J.D. Keene

Nino's War (Book 2 of the Nino Series)

A Novel of Love and Suspense set in WW2 Italy

Available now, in paperback and on Kindle,
from Amazon.

ALSO BY J.D.KEENE

If you've enjoyed *Nino's Heart*, you can also experience the excitement of J.D. Keene's *The Heroes of Sainte-Mère-Église: A D-Day Novel*.

On May 10, 1940, SS Sturmbannführer Gunther Dettmer stands on the border of Germany and France. He waits with the German war machine for the order from Adolf Hitler to start the western Blitzkrieg—the "lightning war."

Six hundred kilometers away, WWI veteran René Legrand plows his fields. He is enjoying the life he has made with his wife and two sons in the peaceful village of Sainte-Mère-Église. Since the end of the last war, he has tried to forget the atrocities he'd witnessed. Most of all, he has tried to forget the horrors he inflicted on others as the deadliest assassin the French Army has ever known, unaware he will soon need the skills of war he once used to perfection.

His youngest son, Jean-Pierre, lives the life of a typical thirteen-year-old. He attends school, helps his father in the fields, and tries not to be nervous around the mesmerizing Angelique Lapierre. Events will soon force him to become a man, and along with his father, brother, and a small group of citizens, they harass their German occupiers and help the Allies prepare for the D-Day invasion.

Guilty of nothing other than being a Jew, Jean-Pierre's best friend, Alfred Shapiro, flees to Spain with his family. They hope to make it through the treacherous Pyrenees Mountains before the Nazis capture them.

Working with the French Resistance, Gabrielle Hall uses her beauty and cunning to obtain military intelligence from the Nazi officers who frequent her café.

In Fort Benning, Georgia, Captain James Gavin discusses a plan with Major William Lee to begin the U.S. Army's first parachute platoon. Four years later, General "Jumpin' Jim" Gavin will descend through the night sky and into Normandy, France, along with the greatest invasion force the world has ever seen.

These and others are the heroes of Sainte-Mère-Église.

The Heroes of Sainte-Mère-Église: A D-Day Novel is availble now, in paperback and on Kindle, from Amazon.

Acknowledgments

I would like to thank the following individuals who contributed significantly to this novel. Their assistance was in the form of researching, advanced reading, editing, cover design or simply encouraging. Their support is vital, and their suggestions are often brilliant: Andy Keene, Colin Fradd, David Booker, Dawn Gardner, Elizabeth Gassoway, Evan Keene, Genevieve Montcombroux, John Kruger, Katie Keene, Kim Morrison, Krista Dapkey, Mark Keene, Mary Alice Thomasson, Mary Durr, Phyliss Sawyer, Tara White, Terry Gassoway.

FUTURE READERS WANTED!

If you would like to contribute as an advanced reader for a future novel, please contact me at **jdkeene@ww2author.com**.

ABOUT THE AUTHOR

Nino's Heart is J. D. Keene's second novel.

His first—*The Heroes of Sainte-Mère-Église*—has been ranked in Amazon's top 100 in the categories of Military Historical Fiction, Historical World War II Fiction and War Fiction.

He is currently working on book two of the *Nino* series— *Nino's War*—which will be released in 2021.

J.D. lives in Virginia with his wife Katie.

To stay in contact with J.D. Keene, please visit his website: **www.jdkeene.com.**

Printed in Great Britain
by Amazon